Acknowled

Small-town stories are a particular favorite of mine. I grew up in a small town, and when that's the case, I think there tends to be a bit of a love/hate relationship. You want to get out as soon as possible and run off to the "Big City." Everybody knows everybody, which means everybody knows everybody's business, personal or otherwise. That can be frustrating, even a bit invasive. On the flip side, however, is the fact that small-town folks tend to help each other. They tend to come together when they need to. My dad spent most of his adult life in a very small town, and the number of townspeople who came forward to help my sister and me after he died was astounding. I'd say eighty percent of them were people we didn't know. But more than once, when we thanked them, their response would be something to the effect of, "That's what we do here. We take care of each other." So with that being said, welcome to Crimson Valley, New York, a small town in the Adirondacks. I hope you enjoy your stay.

My usual gratitude to Bold Strokes Books and everybody there for all they do. The landscape of publishing—especially that of sapphic romance—is changing so fast, it's hard to keep up. But BSB does, and I'm so thankful for that.

I have a small but very valued circle of support, both friends and family, both writers and non-writers. I couldn't do what I do without each and every one of them. They know who they are.

And finally, I've said it a hundred times, but I'll say it again: if you're holding my book in your hands or reading it on your e-reader or listening to the audiobook, I want to thank you. It's not dramatic to say I wouldn't be where I am today without you, so thank you from the bottom of my heart. You keep reading and I'll keep writing.

To anyone who feels like their life didn't go according to plan.
Hang in there.
Your journey isn't over yet.

CHAPTER ONE

Am I the world's biggest failure? This is a serious question. 'Cause I think I am—*holy fucking shit!*"

"What?" April shouted through the speakers in Liz's car. "Liz! What?"

"Oh my God oh my God oh my God." Liz Brennan swerved her car to the right as the spider, which was certainly as big as a grapefruit, if not bigger, lowered itself to the steering wheel and began crawling toward her right hand. She yanked her hand away and drove left-handed, trying to keep an eye on the road and the spider and failing miserably, as evidenced by the jolting of the car as it hit a curb and stopped with a jerk up against the bicycle stand cemented into the sidewalk.

Liz jammed the gearshift into park and tore the door open. She fell out of the driver's seat onto the cold asphalt parking lot, then scrambled backward like a crab. A loud car horn startled her as another car screeched to a halt just before running her ass over right there in the parking lot of— Where the hell was she, anyway? Pulling her gaze from the way-too-close front grille of the Honda Civic that had honked at her, she glanced past her own car to the sign on the building that, had she not hit the brakes when she had, she'd have run right through its front window.

Whimsy.

Well, isn't that cute, she thought as the cold of the pavement began to seep through the ass of her jeans.

"Liz! Liz, answer me!" came from inside the car, April sounding just this side of panicked.

"Hey, lady, you gonna sit there all day, or can I be on my way?" The guy in the Civic was hanging his head out his window and looked at her expectantly.

"Oh. Yeah. Sure." She pushed herself to her feet just as a very pretty woman came rushing out of the shop. Whimsy. The window display was only partially done, and Liz wondered if this pretty woman with the chestnut-brown hair in a simple ponytail had been working on it.

"Liz!"

"I'm fine, Ape," she shouted at the car, leaning toward it, but not wanting to get too close. "I'll call you back."

"You're sure? Swear to me."

"I swear. I'm fine. I'll call you back in ten minutes."

She heard the click of the line hanging up as the Civic drove on by, the driver shaking his head and probably muttering. The pretty woman took in Liz's car—the passenger side was up on the curb, tilting the vehicle at an angle, and the driver's side door was still hanging open—then turned to her.

"Are you sure you're okay?" she asked, her voice laced with what seemed like genuine concern.

"I think so," Liz said, brushing stones and dirt off her ass. Only then did she notice how cold it actually was. Yeah, welcome to the Adirondacks in November.

"What happened?" The woman put her hands on her hips and studied the car, then shifted her gaze to Liz, clearly trying to figure out if she was impaired in some way.

Liz pointed a shaky hand toward the car. "*Sp*—" She cleared her throat, swallowed, and tried again. "Spider."

"A spider? In your car?"

"Huge." Liz held her hands a good three feet apart. "Massive."

The woman nodded and, without another word, dipped her head and stuck it in the car, searching.

Liz gasped. Had the woman lost her mind? Was her ponytail too tight, thereby cutting off circulation to her brain, not allowing her to think straight? Had she not heard what Liz had said? There was a *monster* spider in the car. "I don't...you shouldn't...it could bite you..." She reached out a useless hand but couldn't make herself step any closer to the spider-infested vehicle. It was too bad she'd have to send it to the junkyard now, so they could burn it to a crisp, and get a whole new car because—

"This little guy?"

Liz gaped at the woman who held a small, brown spider in the palm of her hand. What in the creepy-crawly insect hell was she doing?

"He wouldn't bite you. He's just a tiny guy."

And then Liz watched in abject horror as Ponytail walked past the shop and the parking spaces to a little patch of grass and trees and set the spider loose on a branch. She stood there for a moment in her tall black boots, leggings, and gray hooded sweater and seemed to watch, then turned and walked back to Liz. Who hadn't moved an inch.

"Are you gonna be okay?" the woman asked, and Liz could've sworn she wore an amused smile.

"You're, um, you're sure that's the only one? 'Cause the one that attacked me was a hell of a lot bigger than that."

"Let me check again, just in case."

Okay. It was official. Liz was a fool. A jumpy, paranoid fool. And this really was the cherry on top of the past four hellish months she'd lived through. Goddamn it.

"I don't see any other spiders," Ponytail said as she stood up out of the car again. "Only a couple crumpled McDonald's bags, the lingering smell of french fries, and some questionable taste in Altoids."

"What's your beef with peppermint?"

"I prefer the cinnamon. The peppermint are too much for me."

"I mean, they *are* curiously strong. Says so right on the tin."

And then there was an undeniable moment. Yes, Liz was sure. They had a moment. They stood there, not far apart, eye to eye, Ponytail just a tiny bit shorter than Liz. There was smiling and eye contact and yeah. Liz hadn't had a moment with somebody in a long time. She opened her mouth to say something—not that she had any idea what—when the car filled with the sound of her cell phone ringing.

"Better get that," Ponytail said, glancing at her watch. "It's been twelve minutes." With a cute little wink—yes, an actual wink—she turned on her booted heel and headed back toward her shop.

Liz stepped toward her car as the phone continued to ring, hesitated, took a deep breath, and plunged into the driver's seat like she was diving into the ocean, another thing that terrified her. She hit the answer button and closed the car door.

"I'm here. I'm alive. Don't send the cops."

"Girl, I was *this close*," April said, and Liz could picture her, teeth gritted, upper lip curled. "What the hell happened?"

Liz reversed out of her own disastrous park job and pulled back out onto the main drag once again, telling April the story as she went.

"I want to say I'm surprised you almost drove yourself into a building because of a tiny spider, but I can't 'cause I'm not."

"Tiny? Who said anything about tiny? It was the size of a dinner plate, I'm telling you. It might've been an alien spider, now that I think about it."

"Yeah, I've heard there's been an infestation of colossal alien spiders in and around the Adirondacks lately. It's messing with ski season. Said so on the news."

They laughed together as Liz drove herself home. Well, what used to be home. No, it still was. Technically. She hadn't lived there in several years, but she'd grown up there. She drove past the sign that read Brennan House, coasted around to the back parking area, and pulled into a spot. She shifted into park and sat there with the car running.

"You home?" April asked.

"Yep."

"Okay, listen to me, 'cause I'm about to give a good speech, and I don't give them to inattentive audiences, you feel me?"

Liz grinned. "Yes, ma'am. I am all ears."

"You are not a failure. Getting laid off doesn't make you a failure. Needing to return home to help out the family business doesn't make you a failure. And not being quite sure yet what you want to be when you grow up doesn't make you a failure. Those things make you human, just like the rest of us. You're taking a break is all. Help out your mom. Spend time with your dad. Do what you need to do. Okay? Take your time. And I'm here if you need me. Hell, I might even take a break myself and come visit you."

Just like that, Liz felt some of her stress melt off her shoulders. Not all of it, because God forbid she didn't carry at least some stress around at all times. Who would she be if she didn't? But April knew her well and knew just the right things to say.

"What would I do without you, huh?" she asked on a sigh.

"I have no goddamn idea. Let's hope we never have to find out, yeah?"

"Yeah. Thanks, April."

She clicked off but continued to sit in her running car. There were so many memories swirling around this place. Good and bad. Happy and sad. She hadn't wanted to come back, but there was definitely a part of her that was happy to be here. She couldn't deny it. And in that moment, she was reminded of the pretty ponytailed woman who'd saved her, the chestnut hair, the amused smile…Yeah, maybe being back wasn't so bad.

"All right," she muttered as she turned off the ignition and pulled on the door handle. "Let's get this party started."

❖

Well, that was the most excitement Cori'd had in weeks. She shook her head as she climbed back into the window display to finish decorating the Christmas tree she'd set up. She was finding a few things amusing. One, the fear of spiders Liz so obviously had. She'd never make fun of somebody for their phobias, but they were in the mountains in the winter, and as far as she knew, there were no deadly spiders in the area. Two, yes, that was Elizabeth Brennan who'd screeched to a halt on Cori's curb in front of her shop and scrambled out of her car like her ass was on fire. Her very cute and shapely ass.

"What was that all about?" Suzanne Wilmont asked from behind the cash register.

"A spider, apparently."

Suzanne made a face. She didn't love spiders either. "In her car?"

"Yep. I found it and let it go on the tree over there." Cori nodded out the window and toward the leafless tree to her left.

"Big?"

A snort. "According to Liz, it was *massive*." She made air quotes. "But no. It was just a spider."

"Liz? You knew her?"

"We were in high school together." She left it at that. Didn't mention that they weren't friends or that Liz clearly didn't remember her. Because it wasn't a surprise. Elizabeth Brennan had barely noticed her in school. Why would it be any different more than a decade later?

The little bell over the door tinkled prettily as two customers entered the shop. Tourists, clearly. You could mostly tell by the footwear. If they were wearing designer shoes or tall boots that were made for looks and not warmth, they were tourists. Sure, Cori was wearing tall boots right now, but she was dressed for work. Plus, she lived in the little apartment upstairs. If she was going anywhere, she'd scoot up there and change into her Columbias. Nobody around there wanted to get stuck in the snow in boots that were pretty and completely nonfunctional.

The snow began to fall as she continued to trim the tree, and she stopped and just watched. She probably looked silly, standing there in the store's giant window and staring into the sky, but she didn't care. The snowflakes were big and fat and drifted slowly to the ground, and they were beautiful.

This was her favorite time of year. Yes, it was cold. Yes, Crimson Valley became incredibly busy with skiers and snowboarders and snowshoers, but that's what kept her shop open and profitable. But aside from those things, she loved the winter. The coziness. The clean-slate feel of freshly fallen snow. She loved the winter birds and the deer and everything that was beautiful and peaceful.

The bell over the door tinkled again, the same customers leaving with a bag each, and waving over their shoulders at Bear, her lazy golden retriever who was lying on his dog bed near the register, watching the comings and goings like a sentry. Cori was surprised by how lost in her own thoughts she could get that she hadn't heard anything the women had said.

"Two more of your candles, sold," Suzanne said from behind the cash register. "Cinnamon and spiced apple. Inventory is low on those."

With a nod, Cori stepped down from the window display. "I'll make some more this week." Ernie, the cat who once lived in the alley behind the shop and was now Cori's, followed her off the window display, just as he followed her everywhere around the shop.

"Did Ernie do a good job on the tree?" Suzanne asked with a grin.

"Ernie did squat on the tree. He is zero help and should have his pay docked." She swooped him up in her arms where he leaned his head away and pretended to be annoyed but made no move to get down. "But look how cute he is." Scratches and kisses followed, as they always did.

The day went on, customers coming and going, some buying souvenirs, some just browsing. Suzanne took over so Cori could head upstairs to her little apartment for an early dinner. The animals followed and also ate, and then they all tromped back down and sent Suzanne home, and Cori handled the rest of the hours alone until she closed at seven. Once December hit in another few weeks, she'd stay open until nine, pick up the increase in tourists. She didn't mind. Whimsy was her baby, and she loved nothing more than seeing it succeed.

Darkness came early at this time of year. It was the only thing about winter Cori didn't like, the shortness of the days and the long nights. The sun was gone by four thirty, and darkness settled in by dinnertime. But she had a gas fireplace in the corner of the store and another in her upstairs apartment. There was something about a fire, the warmth of it, the mesmerizing flames, that made the world feel cozier, so she wasted no time kicking on the one in the store. It instantly made her feel better about the darkness.

Business was good that evening, and when she finally locked the front door and turned the *Open* sign to *Closed*, it was nearing seven thirty because there'd been a last handful of customers and she never rushed anybody out. She quickly tallied the day's sales, put the profits in the bank bag, and zipped it up, then stuck it in the safe in the back office. She'd deposit it in the bank the next morning once Suzanne arrived.

Lights off, she took the back staircase back up to her apartment, followed by both Bear and Ernie. She poured herself a glass of the Malbec she'd opened the day before, flopped onto her couch, and clicked on the TV. Bear hopped up next to her and laid his head in her lap. Ernie stretched out along the back of the couch.

This was her life. And it was a good one. She was lucky, and she reminded herself of that every day. Was she lonely? Okay, maybe every now and then she'd think about how nice it would be to share this time with somebody. To go to out to dinner or cuddle on the couch with some popcorn to watch a movie. But Crimson Valley was small, and so was its LGBTQ community. If she wanted to seriously think about dating, she'd likely have to sign up for a dating app, and the idea of that was, frankly, exhausting. Maybe one day. But not now.

She laid her hand on Bear's head, then leaned hers back into Ernie. Sipped her wine. Crossed her ankles on the coffee table.

No, this was good.

She was fine.

Chapter Two

W hat was that saying? You can't go home again?
Well, Liz was here to tell you that you absolutely could go home again, and when you did, it would probably be just as crappy as you remembered it.

Okay, maybe that was harsh. Her home wasn't crappy. But it could be stifling. It could be tiresome. It could make her feel like she was wearing a straitjacket that she couldn't get out of and that nobody else seemed to notice.

The basement bedroom of her mother's cottage house had mostly glass block windows with the exception of one—the one that allowed the rising sun to shine through it and stab her in the eyelids as she tried to sleep. She groaned and glanced at her Apple watch to see that it was almost eight. Holy crap, how had she slept that late? She never slept that late.

With a groan and a stretch, she made her way out of bed. It was cold—it was a basement in the winter after all—and on her way to the tiny bathroom, she clicked on the little space heater that had been there since her senior year of high school.

Forty-five minutes later, armed with excellent hair and a travel mug full of freshly brewed coffee, she crossed the property from the small cottage house where her mother and sister lived to the big blue house with the wraparound porch that was a very popular bed-and-breakfast known as Brennan House. The morning was crisp and cold, and she inhaled deeply. One thing that wasn't awful about Crimson Valley was the clean fresh air that could make you feel like you were starting life with a clean slate. She inhaled deeply as she hurried through the fresh snow, following tracks that must've been made by her sister, Lauren. She entered through the back door and kicked off her snow-covered boots, then climbed the four steps into the kitchen. The warm and inviting smell of blueberry muffins filled the air, and her mouth immediately filled.

"Wow, it smells amazing in here," she said as she closed the door to the steps behind her.

"About time you showed up," Lauren said with an annoyed glance over her shoulder. "I thought you came home to help."

Lauren was Liz's sister, younger by three years, and she always seemed to lose her patience when Liz was around. She wore jeans and an apron, her blond hair pulled back in a haphazard ponytail, wisps of it escaping and framing her face, which was devoid of any makeup.

"I know, I'm sorry. I overslept." In no mood to start things off on the wrong foot, she went for the apology instead of the defense. "What can I do?"

Lauren shoved a plate of muffins toward her. "Take these out to the table. I've got a breakfast casserole in the oven and then I need to make some bacon." Her sister turned away and continued to work. She was always better in the kitchen than Liz was. Better cook, better baker, she was great with timing. Liz sucked at all three.

That being said, it was kind of amazing how easily Lauren fell back into the rhythm of running things. Their mom had had gallbladder surgery and would be coming home today, and Lauren had been handling it all on her own for the past couple days. Orders were their mom needed to rest and take it easy for at least the first week, with a total recovery time of anywhere from a couple weeks to six or eight. But it was their busiest season, and there were guests and a weeklong wedding celebration coming up, and there was no way Lauren could handle it all alone, not with their mom not working to capacity. Liz getting laid off and needing to come home couldn't have happened at a better time, demoralizing as it was.

She followed Lauren's terse instructions, and the day flew by, filled with cleaning of rooms, stripping and remaking of beds, loads of laundry, answering the phone to record bookings, guests checking in, guests checking out. Lauren spent much of her time in the kitchen, now that Liz was there to handle some of the easier things, and just after three in the afternoon, their father texted that he'd picked up their mom from the hospital and was getting her settled in her room in the cottage house.

"My pie has fifteen more minutes," Lauren said as she flipped a towel over her shoulder in the kitchen and nodded toward the back of the bed-and-breakfast. "You go see Mom, and then come relieve me and I'll go."

"Sounds good." She hadn't seen her parents in almost a year, and even though the reason she was home was embarrassing, she'd never really lost that excitement of seeing her parents after a long time apart. As she found herself almost jogging across the property to the cottage house, a feeling of overwhelming gratitude washed over her and she stopped for a moment. Standing in the snow, she took in a deep breath, let the freezing fresh air fill her lungs and wake her whole body up, as she sent a silent thank-you out into the Universe. Not everybody was thrilled to go back to their parents' house. Not everybody practically sprinted across the yard to get to their parents' front door. She was beyond lucky, and she knew it.

"There she is," her father said when she burst through the front door, his arms open wide.

Liz flew into them and let herself get lost in his hug for a moment like she was a kid again, taking in everything about him.

Matthew Brennan looked younger than his fifty-seven years. Dressed in a suit and tie, as usual, he looked important. His hair had thinned some as he'd aged, but he just kept it cut short. He was clean-shaven—last time Liz had seen him, he'd had a goatee—and he smelled like Old Spice.

"How's the number one Realtor in the lower Adirondacks area?" she asked him, finally stepping out of his embrace and meeting his blue-eyed gaze.

"Well, he's thrilled to see his eldest child again, that's for sure." He wrapped an arm around her shoulders and held her against him as they both turned to her mother, who was lying on the couch under an afghan in several shades of green that Liz's grandma had crocheted.

"Same," her mom said, and Liz went to her, bent and gave her a gentle hug.

"Hi, Mama. How are you feeling?"

Kristin Brennan held her daughter with surprising strength for a woman fresh out of surgery. Liz could feel how happy she was to have her home. "Ugh. Like somebody was rooting around in my middle. Oh, wait…" They both laughed, and her mother laid a hand against Liz's cheek. "How are *you*, my girl?"

"Ah, you know." Liz straightened back up and shrugged because yeah, getting laid off from your job was a super casual and nonchalant thing. No biggie.

"You'll get back on your feet in no time," her dad said, ever the optimist. "Hey, I noticed you've got a scrape on the front wheel well of your car. You hit a post or something?"

Liz had forgotten about her run-in with the spider until then, and she rolled her eyes. "It's probably from the bike stand I tapped yesterday when a spider tried to murder me in my car."

Both parents blinked at her.

She laughed softly and relayed the story of the enormous spider that had tried to kill her as she drove. "I ended up on the curb in front of that little gift shop. Whimsy, I think it's called? I didn't realize I'd scratched my car, though." She sighed. Because of course she'd scratched her car. That was the kind of month she was having.

"Whimsy," her dad confirmed with a nod. "I've been thinking of listing that building."

"That's the shop the Stratton girl runs," her mom said.

Another nod from her dad. "Yep. D'Agostino used to own it and sold it to me for a song a few years ago. Just quiet, no fanfare. It's been a nice way to pull in a little extra cash, especially with the apartment up above. But now, with that Lattimore Builders wanting to put up a few new restaurants in town, I bet I could get a pretty penny for it. It's in a nice location."

"Wait," Liz said, wiping a hand through the air as if erasing some invisible chalkboard. "Go back. The Stratton girl?"

"Yes. Cori. You went to school with her," her mom said. "She often comes by with things from her shop to help decorate the common room for big events. Weddings. Parties. She makes the most gorgeous-smelling candles…" She turned to Liz's dad. "Seriously? You're going to sell her shop out from under her?"

Liz watched in amusement as her father's cheeks tinted pink. Her parents had been divorced for years, but they'd maintained a tight friendship, and her father still had trouble when scolded by her mother. To his credit, though, he kept his voice firm.

"It's not personal," he said. "It's business."

"Well, I bet she'd think it was personal," her mother muttered. "If you're going to evict the poor girl, you should at least give her a heads-up."

"What? I don't have to do that. It's my building. I own it. I can sell it if I want."

"Matthew Brennan, don't be an ass."

Liz coughed out a laugh at her mother's words, and her father's pink cheeks got pinker.

"I'm not," he protested. "I'm just doing business. I'm a businessman."

Her mother tilted her head to the left and stared at him for a beat. "Then don't be a businessman. Be a human being."

As amusing as it was to watch her parents bicker like the old married couple they hadn't been in a decade, Liz's brain was stuck on Cori Stratton like a film on a loop. She hadn't recognized her. Like, at all. Not even a little. She had to rack her brains but was finally able to call up a fifteen-, sixteen-, seventeen-year-old Cori Stratton. She remembered long brown hair that hung straight and often in front of her eyes. Quiet. Very. Like, hardly said a word. And always a book. She couldn't remember Cori Stratton without some kind of reading material in her hand. Paperback. Graphic novel. Library book. She was always reading.

Reconciling that unobtrusive, very quiet, flew-under-the-radar girl from high school with the sexy, put together, spider-rescuing woman from the gift shop yesterday was a mind-boggling task. How was it possible they were the same person?

"Welp, I've gotta get back to the office," her father said, yanking her out of her head and back into the room. "Unless you need anything else." He raised thick eyebrows and looked at her mom.

"No, I think I'm good." Her mother reached out a hand and grasped hers. "I've got my girls to help me."

Liz nodded and squeezed.

Her father kissed her on the cheek. "Good to see you, Squish," he said, using her childhood nickname. To her mother, he said, "Your prescriptions are on the table. I'll call you later," then kissed her on the forehead.

The door closed behind him, and Liz's mom asked, "So, how are you really?" Her eyes were soft and kind, if not slightly half-lidded, likely from a combination of her surgery, lack of sleep, and the drugs she was on. But before Liz could answer, her phone pinged the arrival of a text. She slipped it out of her pocket and glanced at the screen.

"Lauren's getting antsy. I'd better let her come see you." She bent down and kissed her mother one more time. "We'll talk later, yeah?"

She passed Lauren on her way back to the big house. Her sister had her arms folded tightly across her chest, whether to ward off the cold or make it clear to Liz she didn't want to engage, she wasn't sure. But she nodded and smiled and commented that their mom looked good as she passed, then stomped off her boots at the back door and headed in. There were two chickens just about thawed on the counter, and it looked as though Lauren had been cutting potatoes when she left.

Figuring it would be better for everybody if she didn't attempt any sort of helping with dinner, she shed her coat and headed out to the front desk where her phone pinged again. It was a text from Keith, her old boss. The guy who'd laid her off after she'd worked her ass off for him for nearly three years.

Apologies, Liz, accounting mailed your final check rather than direct depositing. Hope you're well.

So personal. So warm. She sighed loudly, and it morphed into a soft groan. That meant her check would go to her old apartment first, and then she'd have to ask April to send it to her, a good four or five days extra when it should've gone right into her bank account.

"Who still sends checks anyway?" she murmured, thinking her string of bad luck had to stop sometime.

Didn't it?

❖

The back workshop was Cori's happy place. It had originally been used for storage when her mother and her mom's best friend, Annabelle, had run the place. After Annabelle passed away and Cori took over, she'd gotten into doing her own crafts and found she had a special affinity for candle making. She chuckled inside because it made her sound like some froufrou hippie chick who made her own clothes on a loom and never wore a bra—not that there was anything wrong with that!—but there was just something about making candles that centered her. Grounded her. Made her feel valid. Silly and new-agey as it sounded, it was the truth. So, she'd rearranged that back room, organized it so that Annabelle's old boxes of supplies and crap were in their own section, and she ended up with a nice large area with shelving and a workspace for her own crafts.

She liked soy wax for her candles, though she also used beeswax and coconut wax on occasion. All her candles were eco-friendly, something that had become more and more important to her and to her customers over the past several years, because climate change was most definitely a thing.

Because her workshop was her favorite place in the whole world, she could lose herself in there for hours—and had, a couple times. More than once, Suzanne had had to come find her to remind her she had a business. And that her pets needed to eat. And so did she.

She was mostly in there in the evenings if Suzanne was working the shop. They traded off on hours like that so that one of them wasn't working all the nights during the busy season. But she also liked to work on her own creations after-hours. Like now. A glance at her watch told her it was going on eleven, a week before Thanksgiving. They were closing in on the peak of the holiday season, so she wanted to get some more holiday-scented candles on the shelves, replace the ones that had sold out. If she poured them and scented them tonight, she could put them out for sale in the next day or two.

Bear lay on his big, round dog bed in the corner. Ernie had been wandering in and out of the shop through the door she'd left ajar, but now looked like he was making biscuits on his own bed next to Bear's. She sighed with great contentment. "I love you boys," she said.

The shelf to her right held all her fragrance oils—the best sellers, the personal favorites, the new scents. She had a brand-new bottle of apple-bourbon fragrance oil she'd been dying to try out, and she grabbed it, then stirred a small amount into the melted wax, slowly and for several minutes, making sure it was mixed in evenly. She wanted her candles to throw a scent all the way down to the bottom, when the wick was just about gone.

This particular candle was going to have a simple look, a creamy ivory colored wax and a white wick in a clear glass jar. Sometimes, simple was best. Simple sold well to the locals. The tourists, on the other hand, wanted something more than just white in clear. For them, she'd add things like color to the wax or pieces of potpourri or dried flower petals or pieces of dried apple to indicate the scent. Things to give it some kind of substance. Texture. She'd put them in colored jars or ones with distinct shapes. She experimented all the time, working out what sold best, from scent to color to shape.

There was something about filling her melting pot with solid little wax balls and watching them liquify slowly. Something calming. Something steadying. She stood there now, watching the little balls of wax as they oozed into each other until they were a clear, hot liquid. She tossed a few shards of color into the pot and stirred carefully until the liquid became a deep red. It was the holiday season, after all—those frantic few weeks when people got their shopping on—and she wanted to make sure she had plenty of options to offer in festive colors. She'd do some deep greens, too. Maybe a few more ivories.

Her mind drifted when she created. That was part of what she liked about this quiet time. The Bluetooth speaker on the shelf played soft instrumental Christmas music, but other than that, it was quiet, and she had learned to let her mind go. Tonight, it took her back to seeing Elizabeth Brennan the other day.

She hadn't seen Liz in—what?—years? Liz had gone away to college in Syracuse, while Cori had gone to the local two-year school to get her business degree. She'd seen Liz around town here and there during breaks from college, but the last she'd heard, Liz had decided to stay in Syracuse, had taken a job with some large company there.

They'd been very different in high school. While Liz had never been mean, she ran with that crowd. The popular kids. Liz was a cheerleader. Cori paused here as she poured her now very red wax into a bubble-shaped glass holder and let a soft laugh go at how saying somebody was a cheerleader came with a very specific image and kind of conjured up everything you needed to know about a high school girl. It was such a stereotype, but a true one some of the time. So, Liz was a cheerleader and Cori was...not. But they had many classes together, and Cori was always aware of Liz. She knew now that she'd been crushing on her, but back then, as a teenager who had yet to understand her own sexuality, she'd just felt drawn to her without knowing why. How weird that of all the places Liz could've run her car into a curb, she'd done it right in front of Cori's shop.

"The Universe is unpredictable, boys," she said to her animals.

Bear watched her with his big brown eyes. "It does weird things and sends us signs that we mostly never see." That was something she'd learned from Annabelle, and she thought about it often. She liked to think of herself as a person who was aware enough to pick up on things like signs, but she probably wasn't. Like, was it a sign that Liz had run aground in front of her shop? She clearly hadn't recognized Cori, so if it had been some kind of sign, what the hell did it mean?

She gave her head a shake. *Not gonna worry about that.*

The red of the wax was deep and rich. She was pleased with this color and quickly grabbed her phone to jot notes with the specifics of how many shards of which color she'd used to get it. She'd learned this trick the hard way, to make notes about everything if she ever hoped to duplicate happy results.

There was a small window over her work counter, and she glanced up then, noting the softly falling snow. This was most definitely her favorite time of year and a big part of why she couldn't see herself ever living anywhere else but Crimson Valley. She finished the last candle, then went to the back door, unlocked it, and pushed it open. There was nothing behind the building but a back parking area and a small dumpster, but she went out there anyway and just stood, head tilted up to the sky.

God, it was gorgeous. Cold. Crisp. The snowflakes were fluffy. Fat. Slowly falling as if they were being gently sprinkled from the sky. She held out her hand and caught a few in her palm, looking at their unique shapes in the split second before they melted into her warm skin. She heard Bear's steps as he followed her out. He never let her go anywhere alone, and for that, she loved the big lug even more. He stopped next to her, and she laid her hand on his soft head, and they just stood. Listened to the silently falling snow.

It was magical.

Chapter Three

A pparently, it only took one day of oversleeping to make Liz wake up way earlier than necessary. She'd made sure to set her alarm for six, so she'd be up and showered and ready to help Lauren with the continental breakfast at the big house and hopefully avoid any snarky comments from her little sister. But her brain had clearly decided six wasn't early enough. It was now five thirty-one according to her phone, and she'd been lying there in her basement bedroom, wide-awake, for the better part of an hour.

There was a lot to do today, and maybe that was what had her brain firing early. Her mom needed some help getting around. If Liz knew anything at all about her mother, it was that she'd try to overdo it from minute one. So between her and her sister, they were going to have to run the B-and-B and keep an eye on their mother. It would be a fun game of back-and-forth, that was for sure.

Today was also the day Lauren would fill her in on the wedding party that was coming in another week. The bridal party would filter in, taking over the whole B-and-B for a solid week of activities and parties and dinners and rehearsal. And Lauren had already prepared her for their work. In addition to having a completely full house for a solid week—which wasn't unusual, but also wasn't constant—they'd be preparing for the wedding itself, which would take place under a tent out back, with portable outdoor heaters. Apparently, the bride wanted to be married in the snow. Then the reception would move inside to the old barn on the property, which they often rented out for parties and gatherings. But there was a lot to be done in the coming weeks. Liz was both looking forward to it because it would hopefully keep her busy, and also dreading it because it would be nonstop for days and days and her energy was already running short.

She let her brain run free until her alarm finally sounded. Then she showered, dressed, and headed upstairs by seven. She was surprised to see her mother was already seated at the kitchen table, her iPad tuned to *Today*, propped up against the napkin holder, and the scent of freshly brewed coffee hung in the air, pulling Liz toward the pot like it owned her. Which it pretty much did.

"Morning, Mama. How are you feeling?" She kissed her mother's cheek, then poured herself a cup of coffee.

"Sore, but not too bad."

"Did you sleep?" She leaned her back against the counter and held her mug in both hands. Took a sip as if the liquid was life-giving. Which it pretty much was.

"Some. It's hard to turn and move, you know? I was stuck on my back most of the night." Liz made a noise of understanding and her mother held out a hand to her. "I'm so happy you're home," she said when Liz clasped it. "I know it's not the best of circumstances for you, but I'm glad to see your face."

"I know. I'm glad to see yours, too." They smiled at each other for a moment, and then Liz let her go and pushed up off the counter. "What do you need before I head to the house? Mistress Lauren would love an excuse to snark at me, so I don't want to be late."

Her mother snorted a little laugh. "Elizabeth. Be nice. Go help your sister, and if one of you could come back in"—she glanced at the clock on the stove—"maybe an hour and a half and help me shower, I'd appreciate it."

"You got it." She held up her mug. "I'm taking this with me. Don't try to stop me."

"I wouldn't dream of it."

Liz kissed her cheek again. "Text if you need something." When her mother shrugged, she firmed her voice up. "I mean it, Mama. You have to take it easy. No lifting. No chores. No housework. You sit. You watch TV. You let your kids wait on you. Understood?"

"Man, the city has made you bossy."

"Understood?" Liz asked again.

"Yes, ma'am. Understood."

"Good."

Two minutes later, she was zipping across the snow to the big house, ready to submerge herself in the running of a bed-and-breakfast. The morning flew by. Lauren knew exactly what she was doing, and she tossed out orders to Liz periodically. Much as she didn't appreciate being bossed around by her little sister, she had to admit Lauren had the place running like a well-oiled machine, even with the absence of their mother.

By eleven thirty, things had calmed and Liz was ready to help clean rooms. She realized at the same time Lauren seemed to that they'd gotten too caught up in work, and neither of them had gone to help their mother shower. They looked at each other with twin grimaces. "You go," Liz said.

"Okay. Mrs. Adler is already upstairs—maybe you can give her a hand."

Liz nodded. Cleaning the rooms in Brennan House wasn't new to her. Her mother had started the place many years ago when her parents were still married, so she'd been working there in some capacity since she was a teenager. There had been a revolving door of employees— college kids over the summer, various family members and kids of friends—always a new face, often a familiar face. If Liz remembered correctly, Mrs. Adler had been with them for two years now.

She headed up the grand staircase and found her ex-English teacher stripping the bed in room two. "Hey, Mrs. Adler. How are you?"

Mrs. Adler's face lit up. "Liz! Oh, it's so nice to see you, sweetie." She came around the bed and gave her a hug. "How many times do I have to tell you, you can call me Angela now."

"Yeah, I don't think I can," Liz replied with a grin, "but I can help with this stuff." She wrapped up the sheets and tossed them into the hallway. She and Mrs. Adler made an agreement that Liz would take care of the beds while Mrs. Adler cleaned the bathrooms. Then they'd share dusting and vacuum duties. It wouldn't take long, as not all the rooms were occupied yet.

It was easy to fall back into a routine she'd had as a teen, and she didn't have to think. Her phone pinged in her back pocket, and she stopped in the middle of making a hospital corner to see it was April.

Checking in. Surviving?

She smiled, missing her friend terribly in that moment. Not

knowing when—or if—she'd end up going back was an even harder thing to swallow, and her heart ached as she typed.

So far. Big wedding celebration here in a week and a half. Prep work and such. How's Angus? Angus was April's enormous black cat that Liz—not so much a cat person—had bonded with in a big way.

Slept in your room all day yesterday. Misses you. So does his mom. And then a heart emoji followed.

I miss you guys, too. She almost sent a sad emoji but didn't want April to worry, so she sent a kissing emoji instead, then slid her phone back into her pocket and got back to work with a sigh.

The next hour was spent cleaning and talking about books with Mrs. Adler, sharing their love of a good thriller. By the time she'd pushed the last set of sheets down the laundry chute and headed downstairs, her father was lingering near the front desk, scrolling on his phone. Dressed in jeans, boots, and a sport jacket with a puffy ski jacket over that, he looked casually professional.

"Hey, Dad. How's the real estate biz?"

"It's not bad, Lizzie, I must admit. It's not bad at all."

She kissed his cheek, inhaled his familiar woodsy aftershave. "Did you need something? I think Lauren's with Mom."

"She's on her way back here. I'm bringing your mom a late lunch, but I wanted to pop in and say hi first. Hi."

Liz hadn't noticed the bag on the front desk, but the sight and smell of it hit her at the same time, and her mouth instantly watered. "*Ooh*, you're bringing her a Bucky Burger? How do I get in on that?"

"Have your gallbladder removed," her father said with a wink, then picked up the bag and headed for the back door.

"Are there fries in that bag, too?" she called after him.

"Pretty safe bet," he called back.

He and Lauren must've passed at the back door because Lauren came through the kitchen and to the front desk looking back over her shoulder. "Did he have a Bucky's bag?" she asked Liz.

"He did."

They both stood there looking in the direction their father had gone for several seconds before meeting each other's gaze.

"I can't believe he didn't bring us Bucky Burgers, too." Lauren blinked at her.

"So mean."

"We need Bucky Burgers," Lauren said matter-of-factly.

"Not only that, we *deserve* Bucky Burgers," Liz said with a nod. "And fries."

"Duh." Lauren pulled out her phone. "I buy, you fly?"

Liz smiled at her sister, thrilled to have an exchange with her that wasn't tense or filled with quiet snark. "Deal."

❖

Bucky's had been a staple in Crimson Valley for as long as Cori could remember. It wasn't anything special. Just a diner-type restaurant that served breakfast, lunch, and dinner and was open twenty-four hours. Its customer base was a mishmash of every possible type of person. Tourists. Skiers. Truckers. Kids coming in after sports practices or games. Families for breakfast on Saturday mornings. Overserved folks who'd closed the local bars and wanted pie at three in the morning. Snowmobilers. Hunters. And business owners like Cori, who liked to splurge on occasion and get herself a famous Bucky Burger for lunch or dinner. She had no idea what the short-order cook back there did to his burgers, what kind of drugs or magic he put in them, but she'd never had a better cheeseburger in her life. Anywhere. Ever. She was sure they were about a million calories, so she tried to eat them sparingly, but every so often, a craving hit and nothing would satiate her but a Bucky Burger.

She'd called her order in and left Suzanne to mind the shop while she'd dashed across the street to pick it up—the close proximity of Bucky's both a blessing and a curse, as the smell of a fresh batch of french fries in the air could literally wake her out of a sound sleep. It was a bit of a late lunch, nearly one thirty, so she expected it not to be quite as busy as it likely had been an hour before.

What she didn't expect was Liz Brennan standing near the register, clearly also waiting for an order. For a split second, she gauged the distance to the door and wondered how silently she could escape, but then she laughed at herself. Apparently, it was easy to fall back into the habits of a high school girl with a crush. Back then, she'd absolutely have found a way to escape any interaction. But it wasn't back then. It was now, and she was a grown-ass adult, and then Liz turned to meet her gaze and all her thoughts about high school just…stopped.

"Oh, hey there," Liz said through her glossy pink lips. She was dressed simply in jeans and a red ski jacket, her blond hair pulled into a messy bun. "Again."

Cori smiled. "Any more spiders attack you recently?"

Liz laughed, the sound soft and slightly musical. "No, thank God. Maybe the one you let go warned all his friends away from me."

"Let's hope so."

An awkward beat passed, just the two of them standing there waiting for their food. Finally, Liz said, "So, you're Cori, right? I didn't recognize you the other day. I'm Liz Brennan. We went to high school together."

"I remember you," Cori said, and she was pretty sure she'd said it matter-of-factly, but something crossed Liz's face. A shadow of something, and it zipped by quickly.

"Been a while, huh?"

Cori nodded. "Years."

"Yeah." Liz looked past her and out the window. "That's your shop?"

"Mm-hmm."

"Whimsy. That's a good name. I like it."

"Thanks. Me, too."

"What do you sell in there?"

"A little bit of this and a little bit of that," she said with a grin, her stock answer to this question. "We've got the usual souvenir stuff, but then some more unique things. Candles. Jewelry. Lots of stuff from local artists."

"I'll have to pop in and take a look around."

Their conversation was interrupted by the waitress calling Liz's name, then handing over a bag. Liz held it up and said to Cori, "Can't beat a Bucky Burger."

"No, you cannot," Cori said.

"Good seeing you, Cori." And Liz left. And Cori watched her go, enjoying the view—because why not? that was okay, right?—her eyes following her all the way to her car until the waitress called Cori's name and yanked her back to the present.

The day was brisk, temps only in the high twenties with a bit of wind, so even just a quick trip across the street was an exercise in cold. Cori had her boots on and her jacket unzipped and couldn't get back to the shop fast enough. Once inside, she stomped the snow off her feet, then carried the bag to the back room to plate things. She'd relieve Suzanne out front, then reheat her own burger after. She tossed a fry to Bear, who'd followed the scent of meat, as he always did.

"We're gonna have to bundle up for our *w-a-l-k* this afternoon, my boy. It's frigid out there."

Business was good today. Not overwhelming, but a steady stream, and Cori would take a steady stream any day of the week. The candles she'd made last week were selling well. Only three remained on the shelf, and she was glad that there would be room for the holiday ones she'd poured the other night. They were just about set, so she'd get them entered into the online inventory and ready for sale tonight.

Standing behind her register and simply surveying her shop was often a favorite thing to do. She loved to watch people peruse, listen to their conversations about the various items on her shelves. She paid close attention not only to what sold, but to talk about what might be missing, what items people might be looking for that she didn't carry. Whimsy wasn't a typical souvenir shop. No, she liked to think of her stock as a little more creative, artsy, unique. Kind of eclectic. Yes, there was a spinning display of Crimson Valley postcards. Yes, she had a set of shelves in the front corner that held things like Christmas ornaments and mugs that said *Crimson Valley* on them. But she didn't only sell to tourists. The rest of her shop was different, a little classier than your average tourist stop, and she was proud of that. Proud of what she'd done with the place. Proud of all the local artists whose work she carried, displayed, sold. Local folks made up just as much of her business as tourists, and not a lot of gift shops in the Adirondacks could say that.

The bell over the door tinkled happily, and in came Isaac, pulling a handcart loaded with boxes, dressed from head to toe in UPS brown. "Hey there, Cori," he said in his perpetually cheerful voice. "How's your day?"

"Can't complain," she said, smiling back at him. She couldn't help it. Isaac might have been the most cheerful, happy person she'd ever met, and his disposition was contagious much of the time. She moved out of his way as he rolled the cart behind the front counter and unloaded four boxes into a neat pile. He could've just left them inside the front door. He was well within his rights as a UPS driver to do just that, but he always brought Cori's deliveries all the way in and left them neatly stacked for her wherever she asked him to put them. "How about you? Cold out there today."

Isaac made a *pfft* sound as he stacked the last box. "Nah, it's not cold, it's *fresh*. Makes me feel alive." He stood to his full height of somewhere well beyond six feet, and his brown eyes crinkled at the corners with that constant smile. He handed over his computer pad, and Cori signed her name. "Until tomorrow," he said with a salute, then headed out the door, taking his handcart with him.

Suzanne came up next to her and said quietly, her voice tinted with awe, "It's too bad he's not your type because he's beautiful."

"If he was my type, trust me, I'd already be married to him."

They stood quietly, watching him stack boxes onto his cart for the sporting goods store down the block until the sound of a discreetly cleared throat brought their attention back to the present.

"Sorry," Suzanne said to the customer, a woman in her sixties. "Busy ogling our UPS driver."

"I saw him," the woman said with a knowing grin. "Can't blame you there."

"Go eat your lunch," Suzanne said to Cori. "I've got it from here."

In the back room, she slid her plate with the Bucky Burger and fries into the small microwave to heat them up, smiling and shaking her head at the conversation about Isaac not being her type, and that's when her brain decided to toss her an image of Liz Brennan from earlier. Jeans. Casually tousled hair in the messy bun. Fresh-faced. Great ass. Yeah. *That* was her type.

Her snort was loud enough that it pulled Bear's attention from the microwave to her for a split second. It was a pretty safe bet to say that she was not, in fact, Liz Brennan's type. Liz had dated...what was his name? Joshua? Jamie? Justin. That was it. Justin. Justin Page. Liz and Justin had been voted cutest couple and king and queen of homecoming their senior year of high school. No, she had never been Liz's type.

The microwave beeped, announcing that her Bucky Burger was now sufficiently hot, juicy, and ready to eat. She sat down at the small table in the corner and shared her lunch with her best boys. Bear ate several fries and a couple bites of burger while Ernie batted around a piece of the bun for the entire time she ate.

Wrapping up half the burger to save for later, she sighed and stood up. Liz Brennan had always been fun to look at, but that was all, and Cori was totally fine with that.

Which was a good thing because the image of Liz from earlier stayed with her for the rest of the day.

CHAPTER FOUR

Thanksgiving had come and gone uneventfully. There was nobody checked in for the day, though guests arrived the next day for the weekend. It was a quiet affair with just the four of them: Liz, Lauren, and their mother and father…interesting that he chose to spend the day with them. Lauren made a gloriously golden-brown turkey with all the trimmings, and she'd even kept her sarcastic comments to Liz to a minimum.

After they'd checked in the three guests who'd arrived Friday morning, Lauren called Liz over so they could chat about the upcoming wedding party.

"Okay, so they start arriving a week from tomorrow." Lauren had a laptop open on the counter and leaned on her forearms, going over the upcoming week's events, needs, lists for Liz to catch up. "It's gonna be crazed, not gonna lie."

Liz nodded. Maybe this was what she needed, this level of submersion into being busy. Maybe it would help her take her mind off the worry of what exactly was next in her life. Because right now? She didn't have the first fucking clue.

"Everybody should be checked in by Sunday," Lauren was saying. "We'll be fully booked. The groom and his groomsmen are staying up at The Lodge, but the bridesmaids will be here, along with a few other guests." She hit a few buttons and a colorful calendar popped up onto the screen with different days and times marked off for different reasons. It was actually super easy to read, and Liz turned to her sister.

"This is really impressive, Lauren. You're good at this."

"Thanks. Okay, so Monday, they're all doing their own thing, but we're gonna have a few here who've requested dinner, so I'll need your help with that. Tuesday night is the bachelorette party. Not here, but I imagine we'll see them at some point." She sighed. "Bunch of drunk bridesmaids'll be so much fun. Nobody'd better puke in my common room."

Liz grimaced at the thought.

"We'll need to decorate and get things ready on and off all week, in addition to having a continental breakfast out every morning. I've got a design for the whole place for their arrival. Same for the barn. Whimsy's coming to help this weekend with the house and then throughout the week with the barn and other stuff."

"Whimsy?" Liz asked, perking up before she even realized it.

"Yeah, that little shop in town. She's got a great eye and lots of decorating stuff she rents out for parties and things. Lights, flowers, centerpieces, that kind of thing. We use her all the time for events."

"Cori Stratton."

"Yeah. She went to school with us. With you, I think. She's a couple years older than me." Lauren turned back to the calendar and pointed. "So, we'll need to have everything ready to go on Saturday. The rehearsal dinner is in town that Friday night, so that'll give us some time to get things started while the guests are all out."

Liz tried to force herself to focus, yet couldn't help but wonder about how Cori Stratton seemed to be everywhere she looked. How strange that a woman she hadn't seen in years and hardly remembered from school was suddenly around every corner. And would continue to be, by the sounds of what Lauren was telling her.

They spent the next hour dividing and conquering the list of things that would need to be done, dealt with, or taken care of over the coming two weeks. It was a lot, Liz had to admit, and there was a small part of her that hoped she could handle it all. While she'd worked in the B-and-B as a teen when they'd first opened it, she left for college and then moved to Syracuse after graduation, so she'd never been as deeply enmeshed in the business as Lauren was.

"Got it?"

Liz blinked at her sister, took a moment, and cleared her throat. "Um, yeah. Yeah, I think so."

Lauren looked about as confident as Liz felt. "We've got a few part-time employees that will be around to help with cleaning and stuff, but it's mostly going to be on us, and without Mom at a hundred percent..." She left the statement to dangle, making it clear to Liz that she was going to have to step up. "I mean, you and I both know she's going to *try* to be at a hundred percent, but..."

She nodded. "Okay. Got it. I'm here. Use me."

"I plan to." And with that, Lauren snapped her laptop closed just as headlights hit the window in front of them and traveled past the house. "Dad's back."

"You wanna go say hi?" Liz knew her sister had been working all day and wanted to offer a break.

"Nah, you go ahead. I'm gonna make up the batter for the muffins so I don't have to do it in the morning."

"Need help?"

Lauren stopped and met her gaze and held it for a moment. She almost smiled as she said, "No, but thanks for asking."

"Sure."

It was yet another somewhat sisterly exchange since Liz had returned, and it made her smile. She'd take it.

There was something unexplainable about the night air in the winter in the Adirondacks. Liz inhaled deeply as she walked from the big house to the cottage house, her feet crunching in the snow, and filled her lungs to capacity, held it in, savored it, could almost taste it. The freshness. The crisp nature of it. It wasn't something she could describe to another person who'd never breathed in Crimson Valley. But she knew it when she did. She knew the air of her childhood. Of her home.

The TV was on, and her mother was on the couch when she walked in the front door of the cottage and kicked off her boots. Her father was sitting in the recliner next to her, shoes off, feet up, a glass of red wine in his hand.

"Hi, honey," her mom said as Liz bent to kiss her cheek.

"What, did Dad come to drink wine in front of you and rub it in that you can't have any with your meds?"

"I think that's exactly why he came," her mother said with a soft grin.

"Mean, Dad. Mean."

"I don't know what you're talking about," he said, then made a show of slowly and loudly slurping his wine. Liz and her mother both laughed.

"How're you feeling?" she asked her mother.

"Oh, you know. Fine. Sore." Her face was slightly pale, and Liz suspected she was putting on a front for her.

"Did you overdo it again?" Looking around, the house was too clean, and she could envision her mother dusting, wiping, polishing.

A sigh. "Probably," her mother said.

"Definitely," her father said.

"Mama. We're both right here. You need to let us help, okay?"

Her mother made a *pfft* sound and waved her off because they both knew that asking for help was not in her nature.

She shook her head with a smile at her mother's hardheadedness, knowing she'd inherited it herself.

"Your dad brought pizza if you're hungry," her mother offered, pointing over her head toward the kitchen.

She was still full from her Bucky Burger but grabbed a corner piece of the pizza on her way through the kitchen to the basement and took it with her downstairs.

When she'd been a teen, this basement room had been almost like having her own apartment, minus a kitchen, and not much had changed. She was kind of surprised Lauren hadn't taken it over when she'd left but had stayed in her own room upstairs. She flopped onto the bed with her pizza and clicked on the TV.

Liz didn't like this part of the day. Because this was when she had time to think. When she wasn't busy, her brain would shift and refocus, and she'd remember why she was here, why she'd had to come home.

April was continually reminding her that she was not a failure, but a failure was exactly what she felt like. She'd left Crimson Valley ready to take on the world. Ready to get her degree and a high-powered, high-paying job and to live her best life. Instead, she'd graduated and worked three different low-powered, minimally paying jobs in a row that had sucked the life right out of her. How she'd gone from knowing exactly what she wanted to drifting around like an empty plastic bag blowing in the wind, she had no idea. She hadn't seen that coming. At all.

"From most popular to doesn't know what she wants, that's me," she said into the quiet of the room.

A knock at the top of the stairs caught her attention, and her father called out, "Everybody decent down there?"

"Nope. Doing naked yoga."

His chuckle preceded his descent. He was carrying two glasses of wine, and he crossed the room and handed her one, then took a seat in the chair near the foot of the bed. "To my girl being home," he said and held out his glass so she could touch hers to it. "I'm glad you're here, even if you're not." Her parents knew her so well. She tended to forget that little inconvenient fact. Her dad gave her a serious look. "How're you doing, kiddo? Really."

She sighed and munched on the last bite of her pizza and pondered the question. Lifting one shoulder, she said, "I'm fine." At her father's clear head tilt of skepticism, she laughed. "Really. I'm okay." She knew he wanted more, so she tried harder. "I'm adjusting and...just taking some time to figure out my next steps. And staying busy is helping."

"Well, I'm sure your sister appreciates the help."

"I'm sure she'd like it to be coming from somebody other than me, but whatever. This wedding party coming in next weekend...that'll keep me occupied."

"Definitely." He glanced up at the ceiling, then lowered his voice. "Hey, you guys are keeping an eye on your mom, right?"

"I mean, we're doing our best, yeah. Why?"

A shrug. "I just worry she's overdoing it."

"Dad. Have you not met Mom? Of *course* she's overdoing it."

They laughed together, and he pushed himself to his feet. "All right. I'm off. She's in bed watching TV, but check on her in a bit, yeah?"

"I will." She watched him climb the stairs, then set her wine on the little table next to the bed and propped her pillows up so she could lean against them. She should change into her pajamas. The engine of her dad's car turned over, and she heard the crunch of tires on the snow as he pulled away. A couple minutes later, the back door opened, and she knew Lauren had come home.

She lay back, listening to the soundtrack of her youth. Footsteps above her. Creaking spots in the floor. Muffled conversation. Sound from a television. She could follow Lauren's path from the kitchen into their mom's room, then into her own room, the bathroom, and back into the kitchen. The slam of the microwave door and the beeps of buttons being pressed, then the whoosh of it beginning to heat whatever Lauren had popped in. Velveeta Shells & Cheese, if she had to guess. Lauren was a terrific cook but rarely cooked for herself, and the quick and easy, highly processed and freaking delicious macaroni and cheese dish had always been her favorite.

Back in time.

That's how it felt. Like she'd gone back in time, but was still thirty-four years old.

With a groan, she stood and headed up to check on her mom.

❖

She didn't need to be up early on Sunday, but Liz was. It was interesting to note how she'd grown from teenager-slash-young adult who loved sleeping in to a thirtysomething woman who rarely slept past seven. She lay in her bed for nearly an hour before the soft light of the sunrise and the sweet birdsong outside coaxed her out of bed and convinced her she should take a walk before her day got busy. Lauren had breakfast covered, and Liz wasn't needed to help clean rooms until after checkout.

Her weather app told her it was a crisp thirty-five degrees and would be sunny once the sun was fully up. But she didn't mind going out early. She'd get to see the sunrise, something she rarely paid any attention to while living in the city.

It wasn't until she was all dressed in her winter garb and headed out back behind the family's property that she began to realize just how much she actually missed this. The woods. Nature. The quiet sounds of birds and squirrels and other creatures that didn't hibernate in the winter.

Their property backed up to woods, and if you took a walk about a quarter of a mile into them, you'd come out on a nature trail owned by the state. Motor vehicles were not allowed—which meant no noisy snowmobiles would come whipping through—but it was a haven for snowshoers, cross-country skiers, and winter walkers alike. That being said, it was barely seven in the morning, so Liz felt like she was the only person in the world on the trail.

She inhaled deeply, taking the cold, clean air into her lungs and holding it. When she was a kid, she always complained to her mother or father that the cold air was freezing the inside of her nose, creating ice boogers. That became a running joke well into her teen years, and whenever she'd sniffle in the winter, one of her parents would inevitably ask her if she had ice boogers. She smiled and shook her head at the memory as her feet crunched through the snow and the sun began to shoot its rays between the bare branches of the trees.

Sometimes she came out here to think. Sometimes she came out here to forget.

That was the beauty of this trail. And she had to admit, much as she was feeling dejected about being back home, there was something almost magical about these woods, about this trail, about Crimson Valley in the winter. It was part of who she was, deep down in her heart.

So, today she was forgetting. She just wanted to walk along and listen to her own footsteps in the snow, maybe catch sight of a deer or two or maybe a woodpecker. Any of those things was to be expected. What she didn't expect was the big, golden dog bounding through the snow like he was having the best day of his life. He ran right up to her, and something about his soft eyes and the way his tongue was lolling out of the side of his mouth—not to mention the puffy green coat that was Velcroed over his back—told her she had nothing to fear. And she was right. He came right up to her, snuffling and whining his excitement at her, and she couldn't help but bend down to lavish him with attention. She took her gloves off and let him sniff her hand, and there was a love fest, as there should have been.

"Hi there. Hi. Oh, hi. What are you doing out here"—she looked at the nameplate on his collar—"Bear? Are you all alone? I hope not. It's cold out here." The words were barely out of her mouth when she heard a voice in the distance.

"Bear! Don't get too far ahead, buddy!"

Liz was relieved to hear it, and since Bear made no move to return to his mom, she held on to his collar while continuing to pet him and talk to him until his owner came into view. When she saw her, she murmured into the morning air, "You've got to be kidding me."

It was Cori Stratton.

She was hiking through the snow in a black down coat, boots, and matching mittens and hat in a creamy ivory. Her dark hair was down, and when she saw Liz, she did a little stutter-step before continuing forward until she stopped directly in front of her. "It's you again," she said, but in a fun way, and then she smiled, and Liz felt a tingling low in her body.

She held her arms out to her sides as if presenting herself. "It's me again. This guy is super cute and friendly, by the way. I think he wants to come home with me." She ruffled Bear's ears, and he pushed himself against her thigh.

"He probably would, though it would make me so sad."

"Well, we can't have that." There was a moment of awkward, and Liz could've just gone on her way, but she didn't want to be finished talking to Cori just yet. "You walk out here often?" she asked, then winced at how very much her words sounded like a cheesy pickup line. To her relief, Cori laughed softly.

"Original. Yes, Bear and I try to walk at least some of the trail every morning. He chases the squirrels and sniffs all the trees, and I love the quiet. Helps me center myself for the day."

"And here I come, ruining the quiet." Liz shot her a half grimace.

"Not at all. Might be nice to have some company. Walk with us?"

Liz didn't need to be asked twice. "Sure, okay, as long as you don't mind." Bear bounded ahead, then bounded back to them, pushing himself against Liz again.

"Pretty sure we don't mind," Cori said with a grin. They walked along in silence for a moment before Cori asked, "How does it feel to be home? Are you just visiting? I heard you were living in Syracuse."

"It feels…" Liz sighed and it dissipated into the air on vapor. "It feels a lot of different things. I mean, I'm really happy to see my parents. I missed things like this, like walking in the woods. But…" She cleared her throat as she felt a weird sensation of wanting to be honest with Cori. "I got laid off from my job."

"Oh no. I'm so sorry to hear that."

"It's the third job I've had since living there and…" Another sigh. She was doing a lot of that lately. "I don't know, do you ever feel like your life just…isn't what you thought it was going to be?" Immediately, she wanted to grab the question out of the air and stuff it back into her mouth. But Cori seemed to really ponder it, furrowing her brow and pursing her lips.

"I mean, I don't think that's an uncommon feeling. I don't know that I thought I was going to own Whimsy and be crafty, but that's what's happened, and I'm good with it."

"Yeah, I think it's the *good with it* part that makes me struggle." She made air quotes and grinned so Cori would know she wasn't mocking her. "I mean, we have a big wedding coming up at the B-and-B, so that'll keep me busy. Keep me from wallowing for a bit."

"I know. I'll be helping out with decorating the house and the barn for it." They walked for a moment before Cori continued, "I just think that sometimes, we get so caught up in what we think we wanted that we forget to notice what we already have." She gave a little shrug, then sliced her mittened hand in front of her like she was erasing a whiteboard. "Listen to me, getting all philosophical. Ignore me." Her soft laugh was cute, echoing into the morning air.

"No, no. That's a good point." And it was.

Another stretch of silence—which was surprisingly not uncomfortable—as Bear bounded through the snow after another squirrel.

"Has he ever caught one?" Liz asked.

Cori snorted. "Are you kidding? He eats too well to move that fast. Plus, if he did, he wouldn't know what to do. He'd want to be its friend."

Liz laughed. "I can totally see that. He seems to like everybody. Have you had him since he was a puppy?"

"No, I rescued him from the shelter. His family surrendered him after they had a third baby because he was too much." Cori's face darkened. "You should've seen him. He was clearly heartbroken. Didn't understand what had happened. Even after I adopted him and took him home, it took some time before he pulled out of his depression. I felt awful for him."

"That's so sad." Liz swallowed down the unexpected lump that had formed in her throat as they walked. "I'm so glad you rescued him."

"We rescued each other," Cori said but didn't elaborate, leaving a little mystery for Liz to think about. Or obsess over, which was more likely. She nodded instead, and they walked on for another few minutes before Cori inhaled deeply and stretched her arms out and said, "God, I love the morning air." She turned to Liz, dark brows raised in expectation. "Don't you?"

"Sure. Yeah."

Cori stopped walking and gave Liz a look. "Unconvincing."

Liz laughed. "What?"

"That was unconvincing. Come on. Breathe it in!" Cori demonstrated by taking another deep breath. Loudly. "Come on."

She couldn't help it. She laughed some more and then copied Cori, sucking in a huge breath of fresh, cold, clean, crisp Adirondack air. She could almost taste it, and it filled her lungs. And it felt *good*.

"There ya go," Cori said, her voice laced with happiness, and right then, in that very moment, Liz wanted to make Cori's voice sound that happy all the time. She wasn't sure what to make of that feeling, but she liked it. "Again," Cori said, interrupting her thoughts, and she sucked in air once more. "And out." Liz obeyed. "See? Isn't that amazing?"

"It is." Liz had to admit it. "I mean, it's not a foreign concept to me—I did grow up here. But it's been a long time since I just, I don't know, *felt* the mountain air in my lungs." She smiled at Cori with gratitude. "Thanks for reminding me."

Cori held her gaze for a beat, and Liz couldn't tell if her cheeks were red from the cold or she was blushing. Either way, she looked super cute, and Liz had a hard time looking away as Cori said softly, "You're welcome."

They circled around until they were back near the Brennan property. Reluctantly, Liz said, "This is my stop."

"Oh." Was it her imagination, or was Cori reluctant to say good-bye as well? "It was nice walking with you."

"Same. Kinda glad I crashed your party, not gonna lie."

And there was that smile. God, that smile. "Kinda glad too." Bear let out a muffled *woof*, as if he was trying not to be rude but also didn't want to be left out. "And this guy was definitely glad. I'm sure he gets tired of only seeing my face out here."

"Somehow, I doubt that," Liz said softly.

Gazes held again, and another beat went by before Cori seemed to shake herself back to reality. As she began walking away from Liz, she waved to her and said, "Maybe we can do it again sometime. We're out here pretty much every morning. Just FYI."

"I'll keep that in mind," Liz called after her. She stood there for a long moment, watching Cori walk away, her dog at her side, until they crested the hill and descended it, out of her sight. "That was a morning I did not expect," she said softly to the trees and the clouds and the birds. Then she turned in the snow and followed her own tracks back to the cottage house.

❖

For the most part, Suzanne and Cori traded weekends. Cori had a couple part-time employees who filled the in-between hours as needed so that either she or Suzanne would have the entire weekend off. The exception was when Cori had an event to supply. She wasn't technically a party supply house or a party rental place, but she had a room in the back filled with decorations and such that worked nicely for parties, weddings, gatherings of all sorts, and word had gotten around town that she was willing not only to rent out her wares but to help set them up. People thought she had an eye for such things.

She supposed they were right. But more than having an eye or the right vision for a place, she enjoyed the act of designing, of creating the right look, evoking the exact desired mood of a gathering. It was fun for her, yet another creative hobby in her arsenal that she'd learned to profit from. So this weekend, Suzanne would cover the shop, and Cori would begin setting things up for the upcoming wedding week of the guests at Brennan House.

The Brennans' B-and-B was not unfamiliar to her. She knew its colors, the size of both the dining room inside and the barn outside, the textures, all those necessary details. In Lauren's email, she'd also let her know that the bride's chosen colors for her wedding were ruby reds and emerald greens and pearly whites, and really, what else would you choose for your Christmas wedding?

Bear snorfled in his sleep on the hard cement floor nearby. She swore that dog could sleep on a bed of nails. In his defense, though, his morning walk had been extra energetic as he showed off for Liz. And then that had her mind drifting over to those memories. Running into Liz in the woods, the pleasant surprise not only of seeing her pretty face, but the rest of her, bundled up as it was. Cori had crushed on her in high school—that wasn't something she'd try to deny—and it seemed she was destined to do the same thing more than a decade and a half later, now that they were adults. Not that Cori didn't indulge in her fantasies a little more now that she was a grown-ass adult and understood her own sexuality rather than was freaked out about it. Liz was still gorgeous, still fun to listen to, to look at, and she hadn't wanted their walk to end, even as her fingertips and toes started to tingle, heading toward numbness. So, yeah, her attraction was still very firmly in place, and she was going to enjoy it for the time being.

As she packed up several strings of twinkle lights, she sighed, smiling. Life, man. It was so confusing sometimes. Her phone pinged, alerting her to a text. The screen showed her a blond twentysomething making a goofy face, eyes wide, mouth open in an *O*. Her little sister Jo.

Dinner @6

Jo didn't use a single letter more than she needed to when texting. She typed back. *Got it.*

The gray dots bounced for a second or two before Jo's next message. *Don't make me come find u*

Cori chuckled. *Wouldn't dream of it.* Her family did pizza Fridays religiously, every week without fail. It was really the only time both parents and all four kids were ever in the same place at the same time. And there were always extra bodies. Boyfriends or girlfriends. Besties. Work pals. Cousins. Cori's parents ordered a huge sheet pizza and dozens of wings from Calzone's over on Sycamore, set it all out on the table, opened a couple bottles of red wine, sodas, beer, and it was pretty much a party. Her parents were never happier than when they had a huge houseful of people.

It was a lot for Cori.

It wasn't that she didn't love her family. She absolutely did. Deeply. But she was also the outlier. She loved quiet and nature and books. And her family loved parties and games and sports. She was an introvert, and they were all very loud and proud extroverts.

But they were hers.

By six fifteen that night, she was parking out in front of her parents' modest split-level, the driveway already filled with the cars of her siblings and their friends. Grabbing the bottle of Chianti that was her father's favorite, she gave herself several seconds to gear up, then hauled herself out of the car and up the front walk.

A collective "Hey!" burst through the house when she walked in, as it always did whenever anybody entered the Stratton house, especially on pizza Friday. It was kind of funny, really, and Cori smiled as she was embraced by her mother.

"Hi, sweetie," she said, her mouth close to Cori's ear.

"Hey, Mom."

"You're fifteen minutes late," Jo announced as she bounced up to them, her septum piercing glinting in the lamp next to the door. She hugged Cori tightly.

"It was either be fifteen minutes late or forget Dad's Chianti."

Jo nodded. "Oh, the Chianti, definitely. I'll let it slide this time."

"You are a good and kind person, Josephine," Cori said, bumping her sister with a shoulder.

"Yep, that's always been my problem," Jo replied, then ushered Cori forward, toward the dining room and into the belly of the beast.

An hour later, she'd been absorbed into the crowd like a cell, sitting at the table listening to bits and pieces of what seemed like fifty different conversations. Her brother Jeremy was talking about his latest ski run while his buddy Kyle had found a new hiking trail for snowshoeing later in the season. Jo was telling their father about the renovations at the lodge where she worked while her brother Jeff wanted her to make an appointment with him to go over her insurance. And the entire time this endless murmuring took place, Cori's mom sat at her place at the head of the table and just smiled. Sipped her wine and smiled. She caught Cori's eye and winked at her.

"In your glory, Mom?" she asked quietly from two chairs away.

Her mother nodded, face flushed, eyes bright. "You know I am."

She did know it. Her mother was at her very happiest when surrounded by her family. Her husband, all her kids, and even their close friends. Hell, if it was later in the evening, Suzanne would likely be there.

"What's on tap for your weekend?" her mother asked. "Suzanne's working, so it's yours off, yes?"

"Brennan House has a week-long wedding thing coming up, so I've got to start getting ready and then things here and there throughout the week."

"And things are good at the shop?"

A half shrug. "Yeah. Business is good. The holiday season and all that. It's always good this time of year."

"And how is my granddoggy? I can't believe you didn't bring him." Her mother made a show of pouting and looking sad, which made Cori laugh.

"I didn't want to leave Suzanne with no company." That was partially true. The other part, well, two parts were that Bear was still exhausted from the excitement of their morning walk, and also, he was more like her than most dogs, and this was a lot of people. A lot of noise. He wouldn't have been comfortable, and she would've worried about him the whole time. Leaving him at the shop was better for both of them. "She'll send him upstairs to my place when she closes."

Her mother nodded and then somebody must've said something funny because the entire table erupted into loud laughter. Cori smiled and shook her head, the ruckus both uncomfortably loud and also a sign that she was home.

Welcome to the Stratton household.

It was after eleven by the time she got back to her little upstairs apartment. Whimsy was dark, with the exception of the window display lights that they left on overnight. She went in the back door of the building, where there was a flight of stairs up to her place and a doorway into the shop, and found herself diverting from the stairs and heading into the dark and quiet interior of Whimsy.

She loved the shop this way. It was peaceful and silent, the bustle of customers and the electronic sound of the register and the hidden speakers in the ceiling that played whatever seasonal music was appropriate all quiet now, resting for the night. The soft scents of her candles mingled in the night air, cinnamon and sage and pine, making the shop smell homey and welcoming. The shelf of stuffies handsewn by a local artist seemed to watch over her as she wandered, and she ran her fingertips over their soft, fuzzy feet as she passed.

Whimsy hadn't always been hers. Her mother had started the shop years ago, when Cori was a preteen. As she and her siblings had grown and become more involved in sports and various activities, her mother'd found it difficult to run things on her own. Her old friend Annabelle had moved back to town with Suzanne, and Barb had hired them both on the spot, so she could step back and focus on her family. Cut to Cori getting her two-year business degree, Annabelle dying tragically in a car wreck, and now the shop was Cori's.

She was proud of it. Everybody in town knew Whimsy. She'd helped many local artists get their products into the hands of consumers. She'd done art showcases and book signings. She was established pretty solidly in Crimson Valley.

Wealthy, she was not, though. You didn't become rich running a small gift shop in a ski town. But she did all right. She could pay her bills. And more than that, she was happy.

"Good night, Whimsy," she whispered to the empty silence, as she often did when wandering after closing.

Upstairs, she greeted her boys, was relieved to see a note from Suzanne that she'd walked Bear at ten, so she didn't have to, and poured herself a glass of water, content in the dim peacefulness of her small apartment.

Out of the corner of her eye, she noticed the blinking red light of her cordless phone. She rarely used the landline, but her father had insisted she have one in case of...what, she wasn't sure. In case of a global apocalypse that crashed all cell phone towers? Maybe. Anyway, nobody ever called her on it except sales calls.

"Probably somebody wanting to talk to me about my car's warranty," she said to nobody as she picked up the handset and had to think for a moment to remember her passcode.

Took her three tries, but she finally got it to play, and she was half listening while going through her mail until the caller identified himself.

"Hi, Ms. Stratton, this is Matthew Brennan of Brennan Realty. This is kind of an odd call, but I felt I owed it to you to give you a heads-up. I try to operate my business aboveboard like that. Plus, I know your parents and feel like I should be totally transparent for their sake." He paused and took a breath. "As you know, I own the building that houses your shop and apartment and..." Another pause made Cori hold her breath because it was pretty clear where he was going, and she really didn't want to hear it. "Well, there's a company interested in the space. Much of the block, really, and they've made me an offer." He hurried to add, "I haven't made any decisions yet, but I thought it was only fair to give you a heads-up, just in case. I promise to keep you as informed as I can." There was another pause, as if he hadn't really thought about how to end the call. "So. Yeah. Okay. Call me if you have questions." He left his number and hung up.

Cori stood there for a long moment, the handset in her now-sweaty grip, trying to absorb what she'd just heard. She finally managed to set the phone back on its base, and she must've stood still for too long because Bear nudged her thigh.

She snapped herself out of it enough to lay a hand on his soft head as she slid down the wall to sit on the kitchen floor, like the weight of the news was too much for her.

Whimsy did okay, but she didn't exactly have savings. She made enough to survive, but part of that was because she lived and worked all in the same place. The cost of moving the shop to a new location and trying to find someplace else to live seemed astronomical in that moment. Not to mention daunting.

Bear whimpered, lay down next to her, and put his head in her lap, clearly worried about her. She petted him absently, but her brain was whirring like a blender, suddenly overfull and threatening to spew her jumbled thoughts and worries all over the kitchen walls.

Okay. Maybe it wouldn't happen. Matthew Brennan had said he hadn't made any decisions. And there was nothing she could do at this point.

Except worry.

Which she was really, really good at.

CHAPTER FIVE

W e're not staying long, Mama."
It was about the twenty-seventh time Liz had uttered that line to her mother, but she meant it and she wasn't sure she was being heard.

"I know, I heard you the first fifty times," her mother replied with a grin as they got out of the car.

Okay, so maybe she *was* being heard. "You shouldn't be up and around. You should be resting."

"Elizabeth." Her mother slammed the car door and stared her down over the roof. "The doctor wanted me on bedrest for twenty-four hours, then to go easy for the next five or six days. It has now been over a week, and I'm supposed to walk as much as possible."

Liz frowned. "Fine. But promise me you'll tell me if you start to get tired. Okay?"

"I promise, Mother."

Liz gasped in mock horror. "How dare you?"

Her mother laughed and tucked her hand in the crook of Liz's elbow. "Come on, worrywart. I want to buy some crafty stuff."

The Crimson Valley Holiday Festival was a weeklong event that was held every year, the first week of December, in the gymnasium and up and down the halls of the local rec center. Artisans from all over the area drove to Crimson Valley to set up their booths and sell their holiday wares. There were also food vendors and games and raffles, and Liz and her mother used to go every year. Lauren hated it, said it was boring, and bowed out as soon as she was old enough to have an opinion. But Liz loved it, something about the way it was set up, the booths in a huge oval with all the food vendors in the center, the different products you could find, the pride on the faces of the artists as they talked about how they made their products, what materials they used, and how they got their ideas. Liz was great with marketing and advertising but didn't have a creative bone in her body when it came to making something with her bare hands, so the people in these booths fascinated her.

"First order of business: hot cocoa," her mother said, and Liz chuckled as her mother steered her to the right food booth. They always started with a cup of steaming hot cocoa. It was tradition. As they waited in line, her mother turned soft eyes to her and gave her arm a little shake as she said, "I've missed this."

"Me, too, Mama." It was true. She'd missed the past several years of the festival, and only now, actually standing in the gym and listening to the echoed sounds being tossed back at her from the high rafters, did she realize just how much this time alone with her mom meant to her, and how much *she* had missed it, too.

Once they had their hot cocoa in hand, they followed their usual path, starting at the far right-hand corner and working in a slow, counterclockwise circle. Her mother stopped at each and every booth, even if it wasn't something she'd ever buy—string art of a deer's head, anyone? That was the kind of person Kristin Brennan was, though. She was kind and fair and wanted everybody to have a chance. She wouldn't dream of walking past somebody's art without stopping to admire it. Plus, it turned out she knew half the vendors anyway, and their path was even slower than if they'd been walking slowly due to her recent surgery because she stopped to chat with somebody at every other booth.

It was one of the things that Liz both loved and hated about Crimson Valley. Everybody knew everybody. Which meant a lot of the time, everybody knew your business. It could be unnerving, feel invasive. At the same time, there was something comforting about it, about having the people in your town know you and look out for you.

Her mom was chatting with a bearded man selling some odd flutelike contraption made of wood, his Bluetooth speaker tucked in the back of the booth playing endless tunes that all sounded like the beginning of the theme from *Titanic*. Liz would have to throw herself out a window if that music was piped never-endingly through her house. She kept wandering. Her mother would catch up after she chatted. The next booth was filled with Christmas tree ornaments, all hand-painted, some made of wood, some made of clay. She had mixed emotions about not being in her own place—or April's place, as it were—for the holidays. She loved to decorate, and this year, it would be her mother's decorations rather than the ones she'd accumulated in her years on her own. Those were in a box in April's storage area in her basement.

"Why so glum?" The voice was familiar and came from the next booth.

Liz looked up and met dark eyes and a tender smile. "I'm not glum. Just thinking about some stuff."

Cori pointed at her. "No, you were frowning. There was definite glumness on that face."

Liz gave a soft laugh. "Okay, fine. You caught me. I was thinking about my Christmas decorations that I left at my old place in Syracuse. How I won't be able to put them up this year."

"That definitely warrants some glum. However"—Cori held up a finger and then showed her a red candle with berries melted into its surface—"you could light one of these lovely cranberry chutney candles and your place will at least smell like Christmas, even if it doesn't look it."

"Seriously? That's your sales pitch?" Liz laughed and grabbed the candle and shrugged. "Sold anyway." And Cori's smile made it worth every penny. She was paying for the candle when her mother caught up to her.

"Oh, lemme smell," she said, reaching for the candle, then giving it a sniff. "Oh my, Cori. You do make the best smelling candles. Give me two of the pine-scented ones." At Liz's look, she added, "For your grandmothers."

"I didn't know you'd be here," Liz said as Cori wrapped the candles in tissue.

"Every year. Suzanne ran the booth last year, so it's my turn."

Liz took advantage of Cori being busy to look around the booth. So many interesting things. Clay pottery and handmade jewelry and blown glass. "All this stuff is by local artists?"

Cori nodded as she put the candles in a bag and handed it to Liz's mom. "Artists from around the Adirondacks, yeah. I feel like it's important to showcase them. They don't always get much exposure, but some of their pieces are just gorgeous."

"They really are," Liz said as she held a blown-glass paperweight up to the light and watched as the beams broke and refracted inside it. She set it back on the shelf and asked, "How's my friend Bear?"

Cori's smile brightened. "He's great. He said to say hi."

"How did he know I would be here?"

Cori lifted one shoulder. "He just knows stuff."

Liz chuckled. "Well, he does have wise eyes."

"You have no idea."

Another customer and then another stopped at the booth, and Liz knew she should move on, let Cori work. She gave her a little wave, and she and her mother strolled toward the next booth, one with various dips in jars and bowls of crackers for sampling each one.

"Seems to be a little chemistry there between you two," her mother said after a few minutes.

"What? Who?"

Her mother tipped her head to the side as if to say *Who are you trying to kid.* "Just noticing is all."

"Oh, taste this one," Liz said, holding a cracker covered in a mango habanero dip, effectively changing the subject, at least for her mom, but it stayed in her head. There was definitely some chemistry with Cori. No doubt. She felt it every time they were near each other—which seemed to be happening a lot lately. It was unexpected and delicious and absolutely not something she should explore. She had no idea how long she'd be here. Hell, she could decide to go back to Syracuse—a good four hours away—right after the holidays. Or right after Christmas. Or next week. She didn't know.

No, pursuing any kind of dating right now made no sense. The end.

But when she glanced back at the Whimsy booth, she caught Cori looking at her before she quickly looked away.

CHAPTER SIX

The day of the big wedding check-in had come. It was Sunday, and the front desk area and common room with the fireplace were all buzzing with the arrival of new guests.

The bride's name was Regina. She was gorgeous and seemed to carry a sense of entitlement, and Liz disliked her immediately. She wasn't exactly a bridezilla, but it was clear she had requirements and expected them to be met. Like, now.

And seriously, if she called Crimson Valley and Brennan House *quaint* one more time, Liz might punch her in her perfect nose.

Her bridesmaids ran the gamut, though, from those that were just like Regina down the spectrum to the one that was quiet, clearly shy, and wildly uncomfortable. Liz liked that girl. She was naturally attractive and slim but, unlike the other girls, didn't look like a stiff wind could come along and blow her over sideways. She sort of trailed behind the other five bridesmaids. Liz caught her subtly rolling her eyes at any comment or request from Regina that seemed a little…much. Yeah, Liz liked that one a lot.

Regina's maid of honor—a tall blonde named Molly—followed Regina like a shadow, agreeing with everything she said and even parroting her at times. It was almost comical, like the two of them had stepped right out of the movie *Mean Girls*. Regina even had the correct name for it.

Liz and Lauren had been working nonstop since seven a.m. yesterday. Now it was Sunday, and most of the guests had checked in— Regina, all six of her bridesmaids, her parents, and three other couples who were wedding guests and friends of the bridal party. Liz couldn't remember ever seeing the lobby of Brennan House quite so bustling, and she had to admit that, while it was a bit chaotic and busy, it was also excellent for business.

Two of the college-age boys Brennan House employed part-time were hauling suitcases and bags up the front stairs for the last of the bridesmaids checking in.

"Let's all meet back down here in an hour, okay?" Regina called out to her squad. "Justin's gonna come by with the boys, and we'll go get some food."

Murmurs and nods went around, and then, one by one, they filed up the stairs to their individual rooms until slowly, so slowly, the lobby was quiet again.

"Holy crap," Liz said, looking at her sister in awe. "That was…a lot."

Lauren smiled—something Liz didn't see her do very often—and said, "That's just the beginning. They're here all week, remember." She glanced out the front window. "Cori's here. Let's help her unload."

Cori's here. How could those two words set off tiny little butterflies in Liz's stomach? What was that about? She let herself dwell for about two and a half seconds, then shook it off and headed outside to help.

Cori stepped out of a minivan that looked to be about ten years old. Her hair was in a ponytail again, and the sun seemed to find subtle highlights of red in the chestnut brown. She wore jeans and hiking boots and a black puffy jacket and glasses, and Liz couldn't stop staring. Where had this girl come from? The Cori Stratton she remembered from school was absurdly quiet, nose in a book so often that people rarely actually saw her face. That's clearly not who she was now, though. Seriously, even back in high school, Liz knew she was attracted to both boys and girls, and this girl? She would've remembered this girl.

"Morning," Cori said as she pulled the back doors of her minivan open. She sent a smile Liz's way.

"Hey," Lauren said as she reached into the van, and Liz realized the two of them had done this very dance dozens of times. They moved without words, like a well-oiled machine, pulling Rubbermaid containers out, stacking them in the driveway, then carrying them inside. Liz felt a little bit lost but did her best to grab whatever was left.

"Dining room?" Cori asked.

Lauren nodded. "Yep."

Liz followed them, carrying a container that must've had some glass elements in it, judging from the gentle tinkling it made as she moved. Once in the dining area, Lauren opened up each container, then looked at Cori expectantly.

"Go," Cori said, waving her off. "I think I can manage. But..." She glanced at Liz as if trying to decide if she could say what she wanted to in front of her, then clearly decided she could. "I know you mentioned you might need some extra hands this week with your mom on the mend. Still the case?" Another glance at Liz. "I could use the cash."

Lauren didn't hesitate. "Absolutely."

"Great. Thanks."

And that was the entire conversation. Liz began to understand that Lauren and Cori had their own shorthand, that they'd worked together enough times to not have to get into details. It was interesting to watch...and made Liz feel a little bit left out.

"Actually—" Cori said then, just as Lauren had turned to head to the kitchen.

But before she could elaborate, Lauren pointed at Liz. "Give her a hand, would you? I've got to get a few things going in the kitchen."

"Sure." And then Lauren was gone, and Liz was left in the dining room with Cori Stratton. There was a beat of awkward, and then Liz clapped her hands once. "Okay. Put me to work. I have no idea what you do."

Cori smiled at her, and it was pretty. Soft. Nice teeth. Glossy lips. A tiny dimple near the left corner of her mouth. She moved to the open Rubbermaid containers. Inside, Liz saw candles and twinkle lights and flowers and centerpieces. Really pretty stuff, nothing made of cheap plastic or dime-store knickknacks. These were high quality. They looked expensive and classy.

"Wow, this stuff is pretty," she said as she followed Cori's lead, pulled things out, and set them on the table.

"Thanks. I made most of it."

Liz gaped at her. "You *made* most of it? I mean, I knew you made candles, but..." She held up a gorgeous centerpiece of fabric dahlias with green leaves that sparkled as if they were covered with dew. It was delicate and beautiful. "This? You made this?"

"I did." Was Cori blushing? Her cheeks became a lovely pink, and she looked away, focusing on the container at her feet.

"Well. I am officially impressed."

"Thanks." She seemed to hesitate for a second as Liz took the top off a gorgeous red candle and inhaled the piney-cedar scent. "I made that, too."

Liz gaped again. "Seriously?"

"Seriously."

As Liz glanced at her face, she realized that Cori seemed…out of her element. Nervous? Was she nervous around Liz? "Man, you are super talented. I can't make anything."

"Oh, I'm sure that's not true."

"Trust me. It is." She scanned some of the other items in the containers. "I'm not even close to your level of creativity."

Yeah, blushing Cori was super cute, Liz wasn't going to lie. And she wanted to know more.

"So, how did you get into this line of work?"

Cori took a string of twinkle lights and began to thread them around the breakfront against the wall, tucking them under the ledge so they weren't obvious. "Which line of work? Party décor? Or my shop?"

"Yes. Both."

"Well, the shop was my mom's. She started it years ago when I was in school. Then her friend Annabelle took it over when my mom got busy with all us kids."

"I vaguely remember it back then." Liz continued pulling out pieces and setting them on the table.

"I started working there when I was a teenager. Then I got my business degree, and when Annabelle died, I took it over. Bought it from my mom and made it official."

"That's so cool. And you live there, too, yeah? Upstairs?" As soon as the words were out of her mouth, she remembered her father talking about maybe selling the building, and before she could redirect the conversation, she saw a shadow zip across Cori's face.

"For now, I do."

Okay, elephant in the room, might as well mention you. "I think my dad owns your building."

"Yeah."

It was clear from the way Cori's face changed that Liz's father had already been in touch with her, and Liz wished there was something she could do to bring back the smile. The pink tint of the blush. Time to change the subject again.

"So, I'm remembering my Bucky Burger from the other day when I ran into you. How was yours? 'Cause that craving is hitting again." She laughed quietly and moved closer to Cori to help her with the lights. Close enough to smell her. Soft, clean, inviting. Like baby powder with a hint of vanilla.

Cori shot her a glance that said she knew what she was doing by changing the subject, and she also seemed grateful for it. "I mean, have you ever had a bad Bucky Burger?" And she bumped Liz with a shoulder.

Liz made a show of thinking, scrunching up her face, tapping her lips with a finger. "Hmm. Can't say that I have."

"Well, there you go." Cori had a gorgeous smile. The fact hit Liz out of nowhere, and she suddenly wanted to make her smile more. Hell, make her laugh. Because she'd heard that laugh and it was wonderful.

"There you are." The male voice was so out of context in relation to her thoughts that her entire body flinched, and she frowned and took a second to turn around. And then she gasped. Literally gasped.

Justin.

The groom of the wedding was Justin—she had heard that said a couple times out in the lobby. The missing information was that it was Justin *Page*.

Justin Page. Her first love. Her boyfriend of nearly five years. The boy who'd followed her to college. The boy whose heart she had shattered into a million pieces when she'd broken up with him because he'd wanted to come back to Crimson Valley and she'd wanted something…more. She'd been sure success and wealth and happiness were waiting in the city, that she'd be miserable stuck here in their tiny Adirondack hometown.

Lauren couldn't have given her a heads-up?

And then she realized that was likely intentional.

She searched hard and found her voice. "Justin. Oh my God. Hi." There was a beat of awkward before they both took steps toward each other to hug.

"I didn't expect you to be here," he said, clearly surprised.

"Right back atcha," she replied and tried to laugh, but it ended up sounding like she was choking on her own saliva. Was her face flaming red? Because it sure felt like it. Sweat rolled down the center of her back and dampened her armpits.

"You visiting?" he asked. "How's the city? Your job? Your love life? I haven't been back here in a few years. Catch me up."

He seemed honestly happy to see her. Totally cool. Completely chill. Not even close to as uncomfortable as she was. She moved back next to Cori again, could feel her presence and a weird strength coming from her, like heat from a radiator. She was still working on her lights, her arm brushing against Liz's, like she was trying not to listen, even though it was impossible for her not to.

"Oh, you know. The city's busy and loud, but I love it. Work's good. Lots going on there." And before she could even think about what she was doing or why, she ran her hand across Cori's shoulder and down her arm. "As for my love life…" She grasped Cori's hand in hers and entwined their fingers. Cori stiffened just slightly. Liz swallowed and it was loud—she was sure Cori could hear it. She picked up Cori's hand and kissed the knuckles.

Oh my God, what was she doing?

She felt Cori's eyes on her, and she was afraid to meet them. Instead, she gave her hand a squeeze, having no reason at all to think she'd know what that meant, that she was pleading with her to just go along with it for the moment and she'd explain everything.

"Oh. Oh! Wow. Hey. Wow. Well, that's great. That's great. Congratulations." Justin was clearly surprised but recovered himself well, smiled widely, and stepped forward to hold out his hand. "It's so nice to meet you…"

"Cori. This is Cori Stratton." Liz let go of Cori's hand so she could turn all the way around. "Cori, Justin Page."

"I remember you." Cori reached out and shook Justin's hand, and at his look of confusion, she added, "We went to school together. I was in your homeroom."

"Oh, right! Right." He nodded, and Liz got the impression he didn't register Cori at all. Neither had she, so she wasn't surprised. Then he narrowed his eyes. "I think my parents know your parents." At Cori's nod, he added, "Well. Good to see you."

"Hey, honey?" They were interrupted by Regina, who peeked her head around the door frame. "You coming?"

"Absolutely," Justin said over his shoulder, then turned back to Liz and Cori. "Let's catch up later, okay?" And before she could answer or even nod, he hurried after his bride-to-be, leaving the room in quiet.

Liz stood there, her eyes on the empty doorway, mostly because she was afraid to turn and look at Cori.

❖

Cori waited and Liz finally turned to meet her gaze. "What the hell was that?"

Liz held up her hands. "Okay. Look." She kept her voice low, just above a whisper. "I know. That was weird."

"You think?"

"I'm sorry. I just…" She shook her head. "I panicked. He's my ex, and when we broke up, it was so I could go off to the city and become a huge success, and that hasn't happened. I'm back here, living with my parents. No job. No partner. And he's about to get married to this beautiful woman and I just…" She dropped her hands to her sides, her expression a combination of shame and worry as she glanced down at her feet. "I panicked."

Cori just looked at her. Just blinked at her for a moment, and the sadness in Liz's eyes squeezed her heart and wouldn't let her look away. God help her, she wanted to make it better. Somehow.

And then Liz turned. "If you'll just go along, just for a little while, just for this week while he's here, I will owe you so much."

"You want me to pretend to be your girlfriend for the next week."

Liz flinched slightly, as if having it boiled down to one factual statement had surprised her. "Please. Yes."

"What if I already have a girlfriend?"

It was Liz's turn to blink at her, and the shock on her face that told Cori she hadn't even considered that it might be the case both irritated and amused her. "Do you?" Liz's voice cracked as she asked the question, which Cori found very satisfying.

She held Liz's gaze for a long beat before sighing. "No."

The relief on Liz's face was super obvious, and Cori set that aside to examine at a later date. "I would be so incredibly grateful, Cori. I know it's a lot to ask, and this is absolutely a me problem and not a you problem, but…" Liz gazed off into the middle distance and very subtly shook her head. "Please, could you do this for me?"

Cori stood there, staring at her, watching her face, seeing her eyes well up. She tipped her head a little and asked quietly, "Why is this so important to you?"

A beat went by, and for a second, Cori wondered if Liz would make up a reason, feed her some bullshit story.

"I can't be a failure in front of Justin. I just can't."

And somehow, Cori knew Liz was telling her the absolute truth. "Why not?"

"I don't know." That was also the truth, she could tell by Liz's tone, by the shadow of shame that crossed over her features. "But I just can't. Please. Please, Cori."

The begging. That polite begging. Cori flashed back to hearing something very similar in her fantasies as a young lesbian trying to reconcile her crush on the most popular girl in school, and now here it was again, but in real life. Except she wasn't begging for sexual relief. She was begging for Cori's help. And what could she do? She'd known from the beginning she wasn't going to say no, but the unshed tears in Liz's blue eyes and the whispered desperation in her voice sealed the deal. Cori sighed quietly, glanced off into the room for a beat, then growled from deep in her throat. "I'm going to regret this. I just know it."

Liz looked like she'd been feeling around in the dark and suddenly a shaft of light had appeared. "Does that mean you're in?"

Cori shook her head, but said, "Yeah. I'm in." And the next thing she knew, Liz had thrown herself into Cori's arms, hugged her tightly.

"Thank you, thank you, thank you."

It took a second or two, but Cori hugged her, too, then patted her back quickly. "Yeah, yeah. Whatever." They parted and Cori said, "So…what do we do?"

"What do you mean?"

"I mean, have you thought this through?"

Liz stared at her. "What do you mean?" she asked again.

"I mean, have you thought about details? If we have to do this all week, what about others? Your sister? Your parents? People who know you?"

Liz absolutely had *not* thought this through. At all. Cori could tell just by the look of sudden panic on her face. For a moment, Cori actually thought she might scrap it, the whole idea. Laugh and say *Just kidding!* and move on with her day. Ha ha! What a fun joke! Isn't Liz hilarious?

Except she'd already told Justin. Cori could see exactly when that fact settled into Liz's brain, when she realized that the idea of going back to him and admitting she'd lied was just too much to even think about. Liz raised her panicked eyes to Cori. She didn't say anything at all, but it was right there on her face, and all Cori wanted to do was make it better.

"It's okay," she said quietly, taking Liz's hand in her own. "We'll figure it out." The relief on Liz's face was so clear, it was almost funny.

It was only a week. Just a week.

Yeah. They could do this.

Couldn't they?

CHAPTER SEVEN

L iz was daddy's little girl.

    She knew it. He knew it. Lauren knew it.

Liz did feel guilty about that last one, but there were times when she needed to use her status to her advantage. Sometimes, it couldn't be helped.

She sat at a booth in Cal's Diner, perusing the menu that might possibly have been older than she was, and waited for her father. It was just after noon on Monday, and the diner was bustling. She hadn't been there in years, but not a thing had changed. Not the red vinyl stools along the counter. Not the way she stuck to the seat of the booth, no matter what she was wearing. Not the cracked white Formica tabletops. And not Bea, the head waitress who looked like every waitress in every diner in every teen movie and TV series ever made. From her plump figure to her graying French twist, she was a walking stereotype and a fixture at Cal's for the past too many years for Liz to count.

"What can I get you, sugar?" she asked, pulling a pencil and small pad out of the pocket of her red apron.

"I'll have a cup of coffee, and I'm waiting for—"

"Two. Two coffees." Liz's dad appeared behind her, then slid into the booth across from her, eyes on the waitress. "Hey, Bea. How's life."

"Can't complain, Matt. Can't complain." She cracked her gum, gave him a wink, and turned on the heel of her crepe sole.

"Hi, sweetie," he said, his smile wide as he picked up the menu. Liz's dad was handsome. That might be a weird thing to think about your father, but Liz had always thought so. Even growing up, her friends would giggle about *cute Mr. Brennan*, and she would shake her head and roll her eyes, but secretly, she loved it. He kept his sandy hair cropped short, and his temples had grayed considerably over the past four or five years. The corners of his blue eyes crinkled when he laughed. Today, he wore a navy-blue suit with an orange and white striped tie and his camel-colored wool trench coat to protect him against a Crimson Valley December. "How's being home?" He set the menu back down, clearly knowing what he wanted, and folded his hands on the table, giving her his undivided attention. "Doing okay?"

Bea returned with their coffees and two waters in bubbled red plastic tumblers that Liz remembered from her high school days when she'd study in one of these very booths. They ordered—a BLT for her dad, grilled cheese and tomato soup for her—and Bea was gone again, taking the menus with her.

"Well," Liz said, inhaling a big breath and blowing it out. "The weeklong wedding party at the house?" At her father's nod, she told him, "Yeah, it's Justin's wedding."

Sandy brows arched down for a moment before popping up toward his hairline. "*Your* Justin?"

"I mean, he's not *my* Justin, but yeah. And do you think Lauren gave me a heads-up at all?"

Her dad shook his head. "Wow. I haven't seen Justin in years." He dumped three little round cups of Coffee mate into his coffee. "I always liked that kid. Good guy."

"Dad. Can we focus for a second?"

"Oh. Yep. Sorry. Focused." He grinned.

"Anyway, I had no idea, and I felt kind of blindsided. I can't believe she didn't warn me." That was a lie. She could totally believe it. It had been a long time since she and Lauren had gotten along. They were very different people, but why that made Lauren not like her, she didn't understand.

"I'm sorry to hear that." It was clear he wasn't sure what she expected of him. "Did you want me to say something to her?"

"No." She waved him off. "It's fine. I'll talk to her. Eventually." A shift of topic was necessary here because she didn't want to put him in the middle of their sister squabbles. "How's the real estate biz?"

He talked for a few minutes about his agents, how he'd hired a couple new ones, but one wasn't really working, and he was going to need another at some point, and then he mentioned a conference call he'd had with the developers he'd mentioned the other day, and then Bea arrived with their food. Liz took her time crumbling oyster crackers into her soup while her dad popped one of Cal's house-made potato chips into his mouth. Once they'd each had a bite and were happily chewing, she decided it was time.

"Dad." She waited until he raised his gaze from his sandwich and met hers. "I think you're making a mistake with the developers."

His face grew serious and he nodded, then dabbed the corner of his mouth with a napkin. "I got that from your mother. You, too?"

A clear of her throat. She wanted this to stay calm. She didn't want to get accusatory. "I totally understand the appeal. Believe me, I do. But…" She glanced out the window, searching for the right words. "This is a small town. People in small towns look out for each other. If you sell your building to developers, they're not gonna care about the residents here. They're all about the dollar signs. How long after you sell will they move on to the next fixture they want to buy, tear down, and rebuild into something ugly and modern? It could be devastating to Crimson Valley."

Her dad nodded again, and she knew that was a sign that he was thinking, taking her words in and rolling them around. "They really want to get a foothold here in Crimson Valley. Could be really good for jobs. For business."

She nodded back at him. "I know it could. It could also do a ton of damage. It would ruin Cori." She cleared her throat. "Who I'm kinda seeing."

Her father made a face that would've been comical if the situation wasn't so serious. He moved his head in a circle and his eyes went wide. "You're…what? How? You've barely been home three weeks."

She lifted one shoulder and laughed softly. "What can I say?"

"Can't fault your taste. She's a real nice girl. Smart. Pretty. I like her." He took another bite of his sandwich and studied her long enough that she almost started to squirm. "I hear you," he finally said. "Okay? That's all I can offer you right now. I hear you."

"Okay." She honestly wasn't sure if he had, but she was okay letting it go for now.

"Liz." He waited until she looked up from her soup. "You okay?"

She sighed. "Yeah, I'm fine." She sipped some water, her mouth suddenly dry. "I'm just feeling really stressed about the direction my life is headed right now. And meeting Cori has been…kind of a bright spot." Not a lie, that was for sure.

Her dad's voice went soft. "Honey. Why? Why are you stressed? Getting laid off is nothing to beat yourself up over. Happens all the time."

At the tenderness in his voice, she felt her eyes well up. Ugh, damn it. She hated this. She hated how close to the surface her emotions seemed to be lately. "I'm such a failure, Dad. I don't know how I ended up here. I left Crimson Valley with such plans. Such expectations for my life. I can't seem to find the right job. And the ones I do find, I can't seem to keep. I'm thirty-four years old and haven't had a single significant relationship. I don't own anything except my car, which is going to die at any moment." She stopped for a second and dabbed at the corners of her eyes, hoping to prevent trails of mascara running down her face. When she met her father's gaze, she said the truest thing she'd said in a very long time. "I don't know who I am, Dad. I don't have the first clue." She hadn't meant to be that honest about how she'd been feeling, but her father had always been easy to talk to.

"I think you need to take a deep breath and stop worrying about things so much. You're home now. You have lots of time to regroup. All the time you need." He wasn't getting it. That was clear. She sighed and then he added, "Maybe things with Cori Stratton could help with that? You just said it's been a while since you dated, yeah?" He glanced up at her as he ate another chip, his eyes holding a sincerity that warmed her heart.

"Maybe. I guess we'll see." She took a bite of her sandwich, and Cori's beautiful face suddenly filled her mind.

"Does Cori know?" her father asked, looking dubious. "That you disapprove of the sale?"

"No. I haven't said anything to her about it, but it'll definitely come up at some point. You know?" Liz shrugged as she dipped her sandwich into her soup as a way to avoid eye contact. "But she doesn't want to lose her shop, Dad. Or her home."

The rest of lunch went quickly, her father needing to head off to a showing. He paid the bill and left, giving her a quick kiss on the cheek, and his expression seemed more serious than when he'd arrived. She continued to sit in the booth with another cup of coffee and watched through the window as he pulled away.

Maybe she'd gotten through.

Or maybe the profit from the sale was more important to her father.

She took a big, deep breath, then let it out slowly.

All she had to do was get through the week.

April was *not* going to believe this.

❖

"I'm so confused." Suzanne's face emphasized her words. Her brow was furrowed. She blinked a lot. She stood behind the register with one hand on her hip and just stared at Cori.

"I know. It's ridiculous. The whole thing is just nuts. I just…I couldn't not help her. You know?" Okay, maybe she was living out a little bit of her high school fantasy. Not only had the most popular, prettiest girl in school noticed her, but she wanted her to be her girlfriend. For pretend, sure, but still. Was it so wrong to want to hang out in that world of make-believe? Just for a little while?

Whimsy was busy. Of course it was. It was a Saturday, late afternoon, during the holiday season. Three people stood in line to cash out. Another eight or ten milled around, picking things up, studying them, setting them back down. Bear got tons of attention, as he always did. He was such a big lug, lying on his dog bed in the corner and watching customers wander the shop.

The weather had been gorgeous. Sunny and bright. Crisp and cold. Perfect ski town weather. The roads and sidewalks were clear and wet. The snowbanks that lined the streets were tall and fluffy and white. Crimson Valley was like a little storybook winter village, and normally, Cori would be basking in her love for her tiny town.

Instead, she was questioning her own sanity.

Because going along with Liz Brennan's unhinged plan was utterly stupid. She just needed somebody else to agree with her, so she'd told Suzanne.

"You can just back out, right?" Suzanne asked. "Of course you can. Why couldn't you? Right?" She carefully wrapped one of Cori's handmade candle jars in a sheet of tissue lying in the flat drawer under the register. "Just tell her you came to your senses."

"I mean…" Cori sighed and rang up the next customer as Suzanne handed over the bagged candle and began wrapping the next items. She *could* back out. Right? Who would blame her for stepping away from such an inane plan? Nobody, that's who. And just when she had made up her mind, just when she was ready to pick up her phone and send a text to Liz saying this was the silliest thing she'd ever heard of, and she was very sorry, but she was going to have to bow out, her brain would toss her an image of Liz's face. Of her eyes. Those beautiful, big, blue-like-a-summer-sky eyes and the pleading in them, the imploring, and more than all of those things, the sadness. There was a sadness in Liz's eyes that Cori wasn't even sure Liz was aware of, a loneliness that Cori couldn't shake. So, no, she just couldn't bring herself to send the text.

The conversation was shelved as the shop got busier. She and Suzanne had worked well together for years, knew each other like sisters, even though Suzanne was more of a mother figure.

"This candle smells *so* good," a woman said, setting one of Cori's cranberry-cedar jars down on the counter.

"Made by our very own shopkeeper," Suzanne said, waving a hand with a flourish Cori's way.

"Oh my goodness, seriously?" The woman's eyes went wide. "Do you do custom orders?"

Cori looked from her to Suzanne and back.

"She absolutely does," Suzanne said quickly with a big grin. "Let's ring you out, and then you can talk shop with her."

Forty-five minutes later, Cori had a custom order for twenty-five cranberry-cedar candles in slightly smaller jars than her usual for the woman's daughter's January bridal shower favors. She put down a deposit and everything, and by the time she'd left Whimsy, Cori was smiling and flying just a little bit. She turned to Suzanne with a big grin.

"My first custom order," she squealed.

"I told you," Suzanne said, just as giddy, as she squeezed her in a hug. "The first of many, I bet. We need to start marketing you and put something on the website." She frowned. "Or hire somebody who actually knows how to market."

The rest of the evening flew past, and by the time they locked the front door and flipped the *Open* sign to *Closed*, both she and Suzanne were exhausted.

"Whew!" Suzanne said, flopping down into the display chair of stuffed animals wearing skis and goggles. "What a day."

"I love when business is good," Cori said, wandering in from the back room with a bottle of chardonnay and two plastic wineglasses. "We've earned this," she said, pouring. Suzanne didn't move, and Cori chuckled as she crossed the store and handed her some wine, then touched her glass to it.

"All right," Suzanne said after sipping. "I may have been imagining it, but I seem to recall you telling me how you are now in a pretend relationship with Liz Brennan. Or was that a Hallmark movie I saw last week and I'm getting things confused?" Her arched brow said she knew damn well she wasn't confused. "Sit down and talk to me." She pointed at the chair next to her, also full of stuffies.

Cori sighed, set her drink down, and cleared off the animals so there was room for her to collapse into the chair. Bear wandered over and lay down directly on her feet. She took a big gulp of her wine, braced herself, and told Suzanne the whole story, including the part she'd left out earlier about the message she'd received from Liz's dad.

"Wait. Matt Brennan's thinking of selling this building?" Suzanne's brown eyes were wide, filled with surprise and worry, and she gave her head a shake, her dark blond curls bouncing. "I…when?" Cori recognized the panic on her face, even though she was clearly trying to stay calm. Suzanne loved Whimsy just as much as Cori did, and the idea of losing it panicked her in the same way.

"I only just found out. He left me a message. Which he didn't have to do, honestly. He was being a nice guy. And it's nothing definite. It's just a possibility. Might not happen at all."

"A nice guy wouldn't sell your home and livelihood out from under you." Suzanne was mad, and Cori kinda loved it. She was mad, too, but also trying to stay reasonable and calm. Suzanne was being the emotional one for both of them. She sipped again and blew out a long, slow breath. "Whimsy has always been right here. In this spot. Ever since my mom opened it. Annabelle ran it from right here, as you know. And now me. And I can't imagine it being somewhere else. I'm not sure it would *survive* somewhere else. You know?"

Suzanne was quiet for a moment, clearly thinking. "Maybe you can ask your pretend girlfriend if she could, I don't know, talk to her dad? Put in a good word for you? For the shop?"

The words hung in the air, their ridiculousness as clear as if they'd been painted on a wall in bright neon orange spray paint.

"I can't lose this place," Cori said softly. "It's who I am. But I don't know that I want to do that, ask that kind of favor." She shook her head. No, she wouldn't go there. It would put Liz in a terrible position, and Cori would feel like she was blackmailing her. *I'll be your girlfriend for a week if you get your dad to not sell my building.* No, she'd never be able to look at herself in the mirror.

Her expression must have gotten to Suzanne because she was suddenly nodding. Cori could see it in her peripheral vision. "I know. I get it." She reached over and grasped Cori's forearm, and they were quiet for a while, sipping their wine and lost in the silence. Finally, Suzanne said, "So. What does this pretend partnership entail?" She sat up and reached for the bottle of chardonnay to top them both off. "It's kind of meta, you know. The fake relationship trope is very common in rom-coms. *The Proposal* with Sandra Bullock and Ryan Reynolds comes to mind." She let out a tiny gasp. "You don't have to pretend to be engaged, do you?"

"No." Cori chuckled, but it died in her throat. "I mean, I don't think so…?"

And Suzanne started to laugh. Not a chuckle. A full-on guffaw. Cori stared at her for a beat or two before finally joining in because, yeah, the entire thing was preposterous. Totally foolhardy. It would never work. People weren't stupid. She couldn't even believe she'd agreed. But she had because she couldn't bear the sadness in Liz Brennan's eyes. And if there was a chance for *her* to be the one to chase it away? Yes, please. Sign her up.

She was in.

All the way in.

CHAPTER EIGHT

The day was gorgeous, even for a weekday.

The sky was a brilliant electric blue. The sun bounced off the snow so brightly, sunglasses weren't just fashion, they were a necessity. There was a bit more to set up at Brennan House for the upcoming bridal stuff, so Cori had worked the morning shift at Whimsy, then decided to walk to the B-and-B rather than drive. She could use a little fresh air. Maybe it would help her brain stop agreeing to stupid, harebrained things like pretend relationships.

Seriously. What had she been thinking?

It wasn't a far walk from Whimsy to Brennan House. Actually, it wasn't a far walk to anywhere in Crimson Valley. To call it a small town was to grossly overstate the obvious. It was tiny, and like all tiny towns, everybody knew everybody's business. That's how she was pretty sure that she and Liz would never be able to pull this off.

Would they?

Her brain had been a popcorn popper lately, just tossing thoughts and ideas and feelings around in her skull until she found a way to empty it. And then it would start all over again.

"Hey, Cori," Lauren said as she walked in the front door.

"What's new, Lauren? How's life?"

"Same shit, different day." She jerked a thumb over her shoulder. "Dining room's empty."

"Perfect. On it." She made sure to wipe her feet thoroughly on the mat. She didn't want to track snow and salt all over Brennan House's gorgeous hardwoods.

In the doorway of the spacious dining room, she stopped and studied. The twinkle lights were subtle, and that's how she wanted them. You didn't want to walk into a room and be slapped with the brightness of strings of lights. No, subtlety was key, especially for a classy wedding. Just a warm glow lingering in the background that you don't really think about. The centerpieces looked good. Fresh, despite being artificial. She'd bring some real flowers later in the week as they got closer to the actual ceremony and began dressing up the barn.

She did a few odds and ends, just fixing and rearranging things she'd done yesterday. She laid out place settings for the dinner Lauren was cooking that night. She smiled as she thought about what an amazing chef Lauren had become, given she had zero professional training, but how she also had zero clue of how to lay a table correctly. So Cori always scooted by when Lauren had a big dinner planned and set the table for her.

By the time she finished up, the dining room looked like a private room in a posh, upscale restaurant—chargers under the plates, linen napkins in napkin rings, the good crystal, silverware set in the correct spots, all of it. She stood at the head of the table and gave it a last once-over, then blew a chef's kiss into the air.

"Perfecto." She headed out to let Lauren know she was done, and there was Isaac, delivering his UPS packages.

"Oh, hey there, Cori," he said, unfailingly polite, his smile its usual bright and contagious.

"Hey, Isaac. How's life?" Just as she asked her question, Lauren came out of the kitchen and headed toward the front desk, and Cori watched Isaac watch Lauren the whole way.

"It's good," he said, his gaze never leaving Lauren. "It's real good. Hi, Ms. Stratton."

"Isaac," Lauren said, a hand on her hip. "How many times do I have to tell you? Ms. Stratton is my mom, and you know it. Call me Lauren. Please."

"Right, right. Lauren. How are you today?"

Cori had ceased to exist, and it made her grin. She watched as Isaac flirted. It was subtle, but definitely there, and she wasn't sure if Lauren didn't see it or if she saw it and ignored it. But she smiled the whole time, her smile reminding Cori of Liz, and were her cheeks just a little bit pink?

The front door opened, and as if Cori's thoughts had conjured her, Liz walked in. She tossed a wave to Lauren—who ignored her—and then her gaze landed on Cori and she smiled. Right at her. Okay, that was nice, she wasn't going to lie. Having a beautiful woman see you across a room and smile that smile? Yeah, pretty awesome.

"Hey, you," Liz said as she sidled up to her. "What are you doing here?"

"Well, initially, I came to set up the dining room for your sister, but currently, I'm watching the UPS guy practically fall all over himself while he says nice things to her."

"Really." Liz's voice was curious, and together, they moved so they were back in the dining room, but watching around the door frame. They stood side by side and spied on Lauren and Isaac like they were on a stakeout.

Cori lowered her voice. "This is the longest delivery stop in the history of delivery stops."

"So long," Liz whispered. "Oh, he's got it *bad.*"

"I can't tell if she knows."

"Me neither."

They watched for several more minutes until Isaac finally bade Lauren good-bye until tomorrow. She waved at him, then stood there behind the front desk until his brown van actually pulled away.

"I think—"

"She definitely—"

They both spoke as they turned to face each other, and their noses were so close they almost touched. Cori swallowed and it was loud. Liz smiled that smile at her.

"I think she knows," Cori said quietly, not moving.

"I think so, too," Liz said, also staying where she was.

"What are you two doing?" Lauren's voice seemed so loud in their quiet, and they both jumped, popping apart and stepping back.

"Um. Nothing," Liz said. "Just here to, um…" She glanced around the dining room. "See what Cori was doing. Yeah."

Lauren looked at them with suspicion for a beat, then turned on her heel, tossing over her shoulder, "Go check on Mom, would you?"

Liz threw a mock salute at her back, and Cori snorted a laugh. And then they were alone again. Their gazes met, held. "So," Liz said, her voice hushed, "I had lunch with my dad today."

"Oh yeah? How was that?"

"I suggested to him that I thought he would be making a mistake if he started selling property to developers. I mean, Crimson Valley is a small town, and my dad's a pretty well-known businessman here. He'll completely alienate his base if he brings in folks from the big city who'll start dismantling everything that makes Crimson Valley what it is, you know? He listened to me. I know he did. I'm not sure I changed his mind, but I can tell he's at least thinking about it." She shrugged like it was no big deal. But that wasn't true. It was absolutely a big deal.

"Oh my God," Cori said in disbelief, and before she could think about what she was doing, she threw her arms around Liz and hugged her. "Seriously? That's amazing."

Liz smiled at her as she pulled away, and clearly, the Brennan girls were similar blushers because Liz's cheeks had tinted a pretty pink. She shrugged. "Well, like I said, I'm not sure if I actually changed his mind, so maybe we can find another way to convince him. But for now, I think you might have a reprieve."

Cori forced herself to take a subtle step back because, clearly, being this close to Liz was clouding her judgment. But still, she was beyond grateful. "I will take any reprieve I can get," she said.

Liz was quiet for a beat, then said in a low whisper, "So, listen, if we're going to convince people we're dating, we should get started, right? Why don't you come with me to check on my mom?"

"Oh. Yeah. Okay, good idea."

Liz held out her hand. Cori looked at it for a moment. Liz had lovely hands. Soft-looking. Pretty. Long fingers. Nails polished a rich plum. Cori grasped it. Oh, yes, just as soft as it looked. Warm. Strong. She cleared her throat and let Liz lead her from the dining room through the kitchen. Lauren glanced at them, and Cori saw her do a double take as they headed out the back door.

The cold was like a slap, and Cori was glad the cottage house wasn't that far behind the big house, as they hadn't grabbed coats.

Liz snorted a laugh once they were halfway between the two buildings. "I think my sister may have given herself whiplash with that double take she did."

"You saw that, too? Maybe Isaac can give her a neck rub." They both laughed, the vapor of their breath clouding, then dissipating into the winter air. But Cori wasn't cold. At all. There was warmth radiating up her arm and into her core, keeping her toasty. She glanced down at the source.

Liz still held her hand.

"Hi, Mama," Liz said loudly as they entered the smaller cottage house on the property. Cori had never been inside this one, and she looked around, taking in the pared-down size compared to the big house, but also the warmth and the personality of this one. A fire crackled in the small fireplace in the living room where Mrs. Stratton sat on the couch, her feet up, the TV remote in her hand.

"Hi, honey. Oh, hi there, Cori."

Both she and Liz watched as Mrs. Stratton's eyes traveled down their arms to their linked hands, and then her eyebrows rose in clear surprise.

"Just stopped by to see if you need anything. Did you eat lunch?"

Cori felt Liz's grip tighten on her hand. Was she nervous?

"I did. Lauren brought me some soup, and your father's bringing dinner later."

"Okay, good. I'm gonna go over to Cori's for a while, but just text me if you need anything, okay?"

"I will. Have fun." She said the last two words almost as a question, and Cori had to bite her lip to keep from grinning at her obvious confusion. Liz let go of her hand to step forward and give her mother a kiss. Then she grabbed it again and led her out of the house. Neither of them said anything until they were halfway between the two houses and Liz let out an explosive breath as if she'd been holding it since they stepped outside.

"Holy crap," Liz said. "I mean, I didn't lie to her, but it was clear she had questions."

"She so did." Cori glanced at her watch.

"Do you need to go?"

"No. Suzanne has the store covered. I was going to do a little work in my shop…" She let the thought drop off, but Liz picked it right up.

"Could I come help? Or watch? Or just hang out for a bit?" She wrinkled her nose. "Kinda don't want to deal with the third degree just yet."

Cori lifted one shoulder. "Sure. I walked."

"You know what? It's a beautiful day. Let's go in and grab our stuff, and I'll walk you back."

❖

The sun was so bright, walking without sunglasses was nearly impossible. And Liz was okay with that because it helped her feel more secure. Something about Cori not being able to see her eyes gave her a little boost of courage.

And how was it so easy to be with Cori? Aside from the strong physical attraction to her that Liz hadn't expected, everything about being near her, talking to her, walking with her was nearly effortless. Liz wasn't sure how that was possible already. They barely knew each other...which gave her an idea.

"Okay. We need to get to know each other if this fake relationship is going to come across as realistic, right?"

"Right." Cori gave a nod. She, too, wore sunglasses. Hers were Wayfarer style as opposed to the mirrored aviators Liz wore.

"So, let's do a lightning round."

"What does that mean?"

"It means we ask quick, easy questions and we give quick, easy answers so we start to learn about one another. You know? A lightning round."

"Oh, okay. Got it. You go first."

Liz nodded as they walked past the small grocery store in town. "Favorite color."

"Easy. Red."

"Oh, that's interesting."

"It is? Why?"

"Red is bold. Loud. Makes a statement. You're..." Liz swallowed as she realized her mistake here.

"I'm what?" Cori seemed amused, a slight upturn of one corner of her mouth giving her away.

"Softer. I expected you to say something like pink."

Cori seemed to take that in. "Fair. And thank you. I'll take that as a compliment. What about you? Favorite color?"

"Purple."

"An admirable choice and my second favorite color. How about food? What would you eat every day if you could?"

"Pizza."

"Same." And they both laughed.

"I mean," Liz said by way of explanation, "it's versatile. You can eat pizza every day, but with different toppings, so you'd never get bored."

"Agreed. Okay. Most controversial pizza topping?"

"Oh, ugh. Pineapple." She made a gagging sound.

Cori mock gasped. "And just when I thought we could be friends. Pineapple on pizza is delicious."

"Said no normal person ever." They bumped shoulders as they laughed. "And what about you? Most controversial pizza topping?"

"Ugh. Anchovies."

"What?" Liz stopped walking and gaped at her. "How can you say that?"

"Liz. They are fish-flavored salt bombs. That's all. I don't want that on my pizza."

Liz shook her head, still laughing. "You don't know what you're missing."

"I do, though. I'm missing fishy bites of salt. No, thank you."

They laughed some more, their breath dissipating in the air on vapor clouds.

"Where is your favorite place in the world to be?" Cori asked, and her voice was a little softer, and for some reason, this felt like an important question to Liz.

She sighed quietly and took a moment before answering as honestly as she could—because somehow, she still felt like she needed to be honest with Cori. "I don't know." She felt Cori look at her before she actually saw her turn her head, and she met her sunglassed gaze with a slight shake of her head. "I really don't. I think I'm trying to figure that out. How about you?"

"Here," Cori said without missing a beat. "In Crimson Valley, yes, but in my workshop. That's my favorite place in the whole world." The joy on her face was so clear, and Liz found herself not only envious, but wanting to be there with her.

"Then I'm so excited I get to see your workshop. It's behind the store, right?"

"It is. And I'm excited to show it to you. I mean, it's not much. Just a big, messy room with all my crap everywhere."

"That sounds awesome."

And then, just like that, they arrived at Whimsy. It wasn't busy, but there were a couple customers wandering around, looking at things, picking things up and setting them down. Christmas music played cheerfully through unseen speakers—currently Kelly Clarkson was singing about being wrapped in red. As soon as they'd walked in the door, Bear sauntered over, clearly happy to see Cori. She wasted no time squatting down to him and loving all over him. Then she looked up at Liz and said to the dog, "Bear, you remember my friend Liz."

Normally, Liz would've held out her hand for the dog to sniff, but she didn't have to. It was clear Bear remembered her, and his oversized feather duster of a tail wagged furiously as he pushed his nose into her, clearly requesting pets. She'd never had a dog because Lauren was allergic, but she'd always loved them. "Hi, buddy," she said softly as he leaned in to her, and when she put her face in front of his, he gave it a lick.

"Oh yeah," Cori said, standing back up. "He remembers you. Let me just check in with Suzanne to see if she needs anything."

Liz watched as Cori walked away but made herself not stare at Cori's ass—God, it was a nice ass—because she was afraid people would notice. Particularly, the woman behind the counter, who she could only assume was the aforementioned Suzanne, and who was looking at her with what could only be described as curiosity. Liz cleared her throat and moved to stand out of the way, near a shelf holding snow globes and a stuffed cat. She picked up a snow globe with a view of Mount Evergreen in the distance and shook it, then watched the snow for a moment before picking up another. This one was Christmas themed, with an old-timey red pickup truck carrying a freshly cut tree in its bed. She shook that one and watched. And when she put it back *the fucking stuffed cat moved.*

"Holy shit," she said loudly before she could catch herself, and she took a quick step backward, hand pressed to her chest. Out of the corner of her eye, she saw Cori's head snap up and she hurried over. The cat deftly picked its way around the snow globes, not disturbing a single one, which was impressive, she had to admit, even with her heart in her throat.

Cori was there then, chuckling, and she grabbed the cat. "Ernie," she scolded him, "what have I told you about scaring people?" She kissed his gray and black head as he stared at Liz, and she was pretty sure he wore a satisfied grin. Cori looked at her, reached out a hand, and ran it down her arm. "You okay?"

Liz nodded, dropping her hand from her chest where she was monitoring her racing heart. "Fine. I mean, I just lost three or four years of my life, but yeah. I'm fine."

Cori's grin was wide. Amused. She set the cat down.

"You thought that was funny," Liz said to her, pointing.

"I mean...you should've seen your face."

"Your cat tried to kill me. That's the bottom line here." She glared at Ernie, who seriously couldn't have cared less as he turned and sauntered away from them both.

And this time, when Cori slid her hand down Liz's arm, it was her turn to grab her hand. "Come on back to the workshop, Jumpy McJumperson." And she tugged Liz behind her.

As they passed the counter, Suzanne watched, her face also amused.

"I almost died," Liz said to her and pointed in the direction the cat went as they walked by.

"I saw. It was pretty close," Suzanne agreed with a grin and then turned to the customer who approached the counter.

Bear followed behind Liz and Cori as they walked to the back of the store, and Cori opened a door there. They all went through, and then she closed it and the silence was instant and awesome.

And speaking of awesome...Liz gaped at the space. "Wow. This is amazing." She said it softly, almost as if she was afraid she'd disturb the creative vibe that hung in the air. The smells were plentiful and mingled. Melted wax, essential oils, jars of what looked like different dried herbs or flowers. To the left were metal shelves that held all kinds of things, from tools to glass containers of all sizes. There were cardboard boxes on the floor, stacked, some open, some taped shut, and another stack was piled in a corner. To the right was an industrial sink, a large garbage can, and a small lounge area that boasted a beat-up couch, a funky chaise lounge, a minifridge, and a coffee table that might have been older than Liz, she wasn't positive. The floor was concrete and stained with a myriad of colors—probably spilled paint over the years—and a few padded mats covered certain spots. Liz figured they were places Cori stood for long periods of time.

"It's just my workspace," Cori said with a shrug.

"It's a very cool workspace. Do you spend a lot of time back here?" She moved to the shelves and began perusing all the instruments there, tools she'd never seen before. She picked up different sized jars and turned them in her hands before moving on to the next.

"I do. This is where I make my candles and stuff."

Liz's gaze turned to her as she recalled this tidbit. "That's right. I forgot you make those, too."

Cori nodded and pointed toward the door they'd come in. "The ones I sell out in the shop. I made most of those right here."

"Seriously?"

"I mean, it's not a big deal. They're just candles."

Liz shook her head. "No. Don't do that. Don't downplay your creativity." She looked around. "This is very cool. Can I watch sometime?"

"I…" Cori glanced around the room like she was looking for something. "I was actually going to start on some today. I got my first custom order." Her gaze went to her feet and her voice got soft when she said it.

"What? That's amazing!"

Cori's cheeks tinted a very pretty pink, and Liz gave herself a point for causing it. "Wait. You said this is your first custom order?"

"Yeah, a woman bought one of my large candles and asked if I did custom orders. I never have, but I asked her what she had in mind. She wants twenty-five smaller candles for her daughter's bridal shower next month. She wants cranberry-cedar."

"Oh, that sounds lovely. But how is it your first custom order? Do you not advertise that you do that?"

Cori shook her head. "I never have, no."

Liz gaped at her. "Never? Why not? You're just leaving money on the table. You need to make it known that you can do this. Not just here in the shop, but on your website. You could get orders from all over the country."

Cori's eyes had gone a little wider when Liz started talking, and it was honestly the cutest thing. Like she'd never even considered selling her custom candles outside of Crimson Valley.

"I can help you, if you want," Liz said, dialing it back a notch or fifteen. "Sorry. I get a little excited when I see an opportunity like this. Marketing is what I do."

"Oh yeah?"

"Well. It's what I did. Before I got laid off."

"I'm sorry, Liz."

Liz waved a hand and made a *pfft* sound. "No big deal. Happens all the time." And because the last thing she wanted to do was focus on her shambles of a work life, she steered things back to Cori's custom order. "When will you start on the little candles? Where will you make them?" She glanced at the workstation, which was limited in space because of the boxes stacked in the corner. "I can help you make a more functional workstation." She pointed as she spoke. "We could move these and this and that over there. Then you'd have more counterspace and a few empty shelves to put your finished products on..."

And just like that, they began working as a team, sliding shelves and clearing counters. Liz hauled the boxes in the corner. There were four of them, all labeled ANNABELLE in black marker.

"Who's Annabelle again?" Liz asked as she stacked the boxes on the other side of the room. They were labeled, but not sealed, and she peeked into each one as she set them down. They contained all kinds of things—books and what looked like journals, clothing and shoes, some photo albums and framed photos and an old Polaroid camera that Liz pulled out to look at for a moment before putting it back.

Cori was reorganizing the metal shelf to make more room. "She was my mom's best friend. She lived in New York City, I think, and then showed up in Crimson Valley when I was a teenager. She and Suzanne. They were partners, though they kept that kind of quiet."

Liz nodded as she cleared off the countertop.

"She worked here for my mom for a few years and then took it over when we were all in school and Mom got super busy with our stuff. Sports and PTA and band practice and plays. Annabelle and Suzanne ran the place for years for my mom before Annabelle was killed in a car accident a few years ago."

"Oh, poor Suzanne," Liz said softly, her heart aching.

Cori stopped what she was doing and sighed softly. "Yeah, it was rough on her. She thought about leaving, going back to Tennessee where she's from. But I talked my mom into selling Whimsy to me, and I begged Suzanne to stay and run it with me. Annabelle loved it here, and I know Suzanne does, too."

"Clearly, she agreed."

"She did, but it took a lot of convincing." Cori's soft laugh was like little musical notes.

"So, it's just the two of you?"

"We have a couple part-timers who help out during the busy seasons. High school and college kids. Like now, the holidays are usually crazed, so there's one girl who works on the weekends while she's home from college on break. And we have two high schoolers who help out in the evenings when we need them. But yeah, it's mostly me and Suzanne." Cori's hands stilled for a beat, and then she looked to Liz. "Speaking of Suzanne, I have a confession. I had to tell her the truth about our little charade. She knows me really well. Fooling her would have been next to impossible."

Liz didn't like the idea of too many people knowing, but she couldn't argue with Cori's reasoning, so she nodded. "Sure, okay." She stood back, hands on her hips, and surveyed the work they'd done. There was now a clear, empty space for working. Liz pointed it out from left to right. "You can do your work here, melting stuff. Then here, where you put them together. Then here, where you let them dry. Then here to the shelves, where you get them ready to ship. And then here to this table, which can be your shipping station. We get you some boxes and packing materials and tape. You print your labels..." Her voice trailed off as she noticed Cori watching her, grinning. "I'm sorry. I can get a little carried away."

"Are you kidding me? This is incredible. I had no idea how to do this, and you just made me a map. I so appreciate this. And you." She stopped, her eyes capturing Liz's. "Thank you, Liz. I mean it."

"You're welcome," she said back, just as softly. The air between them crackled with...something. Oh, Liz knew what it was, but knowing and admitting were two very different things.

She wasn't ready for either one.

Instead, she clapped her hands together once. "Okay. Show me the magic. Make me a candle."

CHAPTER NINE

L iz groaned when her alarm went off.

She slapped at it, feeling like she'd just gone to bed an hour ago. That was probably because it was oh-dark-thirty and still pitch-black out. She squinted her sleepy eyes at the screen. Four thirty.

"Oh my God," she muttered into her pillow.

No, she didn't want to get up, but she had to. Since she'd bailed on Lauren for the whole afternoon yesterday and barely made it back in time to help with dinner, giving Lauren an extra hour and a half of sleep was the least she could do. So she'd promised to get up early and put the breakfast muffins into the oven. Lauren made the batter last night and gave Liz specific instructions on how to bake them.

Half an hour later, she was showered, bundled up, and crunching her way across the yard to Brennan House, arms wrapped around herself, hair still damp, breath coming out in clouds of vapor that floated off into the darkness. Goddamn, it was cold.

Once the muffins were in, she set a timer on her phone, brewed a pot of coffee, and headed out into the front room to stoke up the fire. Her heart jumped into her chest and she stopped in her tracks when she saw that the fire was already roaring and a woman was sitting in a chair close to it with a book and a cup of tea, judging from the little tag on a string hanging over the side of her mug.

"Oh my God, you scared me," she whispered, not wanting to scare the woman back. It was the bridesmaid she'd noticed when they'd all checked in. The quiet one.

"Hi," she said just as quietly. "I'm so sorry. I hope it's okay that I'm down here. I couldn't sleep, and the fire still had some hot embers, so I threw another log or two on it." She indicated the woodpile with her eyes.

"No problem at all. You actually saved me the job of having to start it back up. My sister's much better at fires than I am." She held up her coffee mug. "Mind if I join you?"

"Please." The woman closed her book and indicated the rest of the room.

"I hope the bed or the room isn't why you couldn't sleep."

"Oh, not at all." The woman tapped a forefinger against her temple. "This is why I can't sleep."

"Understood. More than you know. I'm Liz, by the way," she said as she lowered herself into the matching mate to the woman's chair. A small, round table sat between them. "Sister of Lauren, the one who does most of the work around here."

"It's nice to meet you, Liz. I'm Tanner, stepsister of Regina, the bride-to-be, and only a bridesmaid out of obligation."

"Ouch."

Tanner waved a dismissive hand. "Please. It's the story of your life when you're the younger, plainer, quieter sister of the two, and not related by blood."

"Obligatory wedding stuff is rough."

"It sure is."

There was a moment of silence as they sipped from their cups and stared at the flames. It was surprisingly not uncomfortable sitting with Tanner. She had a calm presence, a quiet friendliness that Liz liked. "What do you do, Tanner the quiet bridesmaid?" At Tanner's smile, she added, "That's who you are in my head."

"Valid. I work in a bank back home in Albany."

"Oh, is that where Regina's from?"

Tanner nodded. "In fact, she met Justin there."

"In your bank?"

"Yup. She was making a deposit, and he was opening an account. Their eyes literally met across the room. It was like a Hallmark movie."

"That stuff never happens to me," Liz said with a soft chuckle.

"Same." There was another beat of silence before Tanner spoke again. Her voice was even softer this time. "Do you ever feel like you thought you knew what you wanted to be and then realized you were wrong?"

Liz smiled as she stared into the fire. "I think I might be in that little bubble right now." She pulled her gaze away and looked at Tanner. "What did you think you wanted to be?"

Tanner gave a little snort. "Like Regina."

"Not so much anymore?"

With a sigh, Tanner said, "I don't know." Then she gestured upstairs with her eyes. "Not *this* Regina, that's for sure. This bridezilla, shouting orders at people, drinking too much, laughing super loud version of her is new. I have always looked up to her, but now? Ugh. And her bachelorette party is tonight, and I really don't want to go." She took a deep breath and let it out slowly. "But I will, because I'm the good girl of the family and I do what I'm supposed to. I just want this week to be over so I can go back home to my quiet little life."

Liz nodded, not having expected quite so much personal information.

As if reading her mind, Tanner looked at her with a grin. "Wow, that was a lot. Sorry about that."

"No worries."

"Could we…keep this between us?"

"Of course. My lips are sealed over here." She held her cup toward Tanner. "To not being bridezillas when our times come."

"I will definitely sip to that." Tanner touched her cup to Liz's, and they both sipped.

Liz's watch chose that moment to beep. "Blueberry muffins are done," she said, pushing to her feet.

"Thanks for listening, Liz. It's nice to have somebody to talk to."

"I'm here anytime." She reached her hand out for Tanner's cup, asked if she wanted more, but she said no, so she headed into the kitchen, empty cups in hand. In the kitchen, she took the muffins out of the oven, then refilled her cup, knowing she was going to need *all* the caffeine today. And through all of that, the conversation stayed with her, and she suspected she'd be thinking about it all day.

Do you ever feel like you thought you knew what you wanted to be and then found out you were wrong?

"Get out of my head, Miss Tanner," she muttered to the warm muffins.

❖

Cori found herself thinking nonstop about the marketing ideas Liz had for her custom candle orders. It was amusing to her how she'd never even thought about it, about marketing her own crafts, other than what she put on the shelves in Whimsy, but now that it had been mentioned, it was all she could think about. All the things she could make. All the things she could sell.

It was much colder today than yesterday, the sky a dull white with patches of gray clouds overhead, and she decided to drive to Brennan House instead of walk. Lauren needed help with dinner tonight. Apparently, all the bridesmaids were eating there before heading out to have the bachelorette party. She'd taken the morning shift at Whimsy, so Suzanne would take over for the afternoon and evening and Cori could make a little extra cash by helping Lauren.

She wondered if Liz would be around.

No, she *hoped* Liz would be around.

And that, she was not going to dwell on right now.

Brennan House was bustling today, and Cori had to take a second to acclimate as she went from her quiet car into a house filled with bodies moving around and the buzz of several conversations and a lot of laughter. She kicked the snow off her shoes—not having worn boots since she drove—and hung her coat up on the coatrack near the door. A handful of women sat in the common area, drinking wine and laughing loudly as the fire roared in the fireplace. As she made her way toward the kitchen to find Lauren, she passed the dining room, and there was Liz, staring at the piles of dishes as if they were things she'd never seen before in her life.

"Those are called *plates*." She overenunciated the word, and Liz looked up at her, wide-eyed.

"Get in here and save me," she stage-whispered, making a rolling gesture with her hand. "I have no idea what I'm doing, and my sister's going to kill me soon."

"Well, we can't have that." Cori joined her, noting the stack of plates. "Lotta people for dinner tonight."

"Yes. All the bridesmaids and the bride. Lauren's making dinner, and she's in her element in there and I don't want to bug her, but I haven't done this since high school and I've *never* done it fancy-like…" She held her arms out to her sides, her eyes still enormous as she beseeched Cori. "Where the hell do all of these go? Why are there so many? Help me!"

Cori couldn't help but laugh at the panic on Liz's pretty face. "Okay, okay. Calm down, weirdo. I got you." She picked up a charger and handed it to her. "This is a charger. It goes under the plate."

"So, two plates on top of one another. Well, that seems silly."

Cori grinned and they set the table together, Cori explaining where everything went and Liz commenting on how nonsensical it seemed— "Why is it called a charger? Can I set my phone on it?"—until they were both laughing so hard, they were crying.

The bridesmaids began to file in at that point, and both Liz and Cori worked hard to pull themselves together. Laughing with Liz was the most fun Cori had had in longer than she could remember, and she didn't want it to end, but it was time for a modicum of professionalism here. Brennan House was a pretty casual place, but Lauren Brennan was a pretty serious person, and Cori respected her, so she did her best to get hold of herself. But every time she met Liz's eyes, laughter would bubble in her belly and threaten to burst out, like she was in a blooper reel for a sitcom, so she tried her best to avoid looking at her at all.

The bridesmaids settled at their seats, and both Liz and Cori helped Lauren serve dinner, pour wine, make sure the women had whatever they needed. Soon everybody was raving over Lauren's broiled salmon with asparagus, the warm spinach salad, and the roasted sweet potatoes. Dessert was a triple berry cobbler that made Cori's mouth water just looking at it as she stood next to Liz in the doorway to the kitchen.

As if privy to her thoughts, Liz leaned close and whispered, "God, I hope there's leftover cobbler."

"*Same*," she whispered back, drawing the word out to three syllables.

"Hey," one of the guests said suddenly, catching Cori's attention because she pointed a fork at her. Was she the bride? She thought so. "Justin said you two are dating, yeah?"

Cori blinked and turned to look at Liz, who seemed just as surprised by the out-of-the-blue question.

"Um, yeah," Liz said just as Lauren walked in with a bowl of freshly whipped cream and did a double take at the two of them. Liz caught it and quickly added, "It's new."

"Well, you're under the mistletoe," Regina said, moving her pointing fork up just a bit. "Duh." The others at the table murmured their agreement as Liz and Cori both slowly turned to look above their heads at the same time.

How Cori didn't realize it was there she had no idea, since she'd hung it herself only a couple days ago. She swallowed hard and met Liz's gaze and held it for a second. Two seconds. Three.

What was it about those gorgeous blue eyes? Why did Cori trust what she saw in them? It made no sense at all to her, but she leaned anyway and met Liz halfway.

Liz's lips were soft. Warm. Tasted just slightly of cherries. It was their first kiss, and it was sweet and tender and it lit a fire in Cori's center that she wasn't expecting. Not even a little bit. *Holy shit.*

They pulled back and the dinner guests applauded, then went back to their previous conversations as if Cori kissing Liz was just a blip in their evening and not the explosion it was for Cori. What in the world just happened? And what was she supposed to do with it?

Liz looked away quickly, her cheeks red. Hell, her ears were red, too. Was she embarrassed? Yes, this had been her idea, but she probably hadn't thought about having to actually do anything physical with Cori.

Except she'd held hands with her yesterday. A lot. So, yeah, there was that.

And then one of the bridesmaids stood up with her champagne flute and tapped on it with her fork to get everybody's attention, and Cori was able to shift her focus. For the moment.

"Okay, you guys know I've been friends with Regina for about a thousand years. Or ten. One of those." The others chuckled at the woman, who was tall and blond and, Cori figured, likely the maid of honor. She turned to look at Regina, her eyes shimmering. "I just want you to know how much I love you and how so very happy I am for you. Justin is the luckiest of men." She bent down and kissed Regina on the cheek. Regina smiled, and it looked slightly pained. "To the bride!" The blonde held up her champagne, and the rest followed suit.

The rest of dinner went by quickly—the group was excited for their evening to begin, or so Cori gleaned from snippets of conversation. They were headed downtown to The Disco Ball for some dancing and drinking and Cori thought she heard somebody say there would be a stripper later. The idea of loud music, loud and drunk twentysomething women, and half-naked men dancing far too close to her made Cori want to find a place to hide. Then she mentally reminded herself she was not part of this group, and her relief was palpable.

"Dinner got so many compliments," Liz was saying to Lauren as they carried dishes in to the sink.

"Definitely," Cori agreed, setting two more plates on the pile next to the sink.

"You look exhausted," Liz said to her sister. "Why don't you go check on Mom and hang there. Cori and I will clean up."

Lauren did look beat—Liz wasn't wrong. Her hair was coming out of her ponytail in several places. Her apron was covered with smears of various colors of food. Her face was a bit drawn. "You're sure?" She addressed her question to Cori.

"Absolutely. Go. We've got this."

"Cool." Lauren whipped off her apron, grabbed her coat off the hook by the door, and stepped into her boots. Once her coat was on, she started to zip it, then stopped and looked at Liz. "Could you do tomorrow morning again? My head is killing me, and I'm gonna have to take a migraine pill tonight. You know what they do to me."

Liz didn't hesitate. "Sure. Go." She waved her sister away.

"Thanks, Liz. I appreciate it." Lauren stepped out into the dark cold, shut the door behind her, and was gone.

"That was nice of you," Cori said as an involuntary shiver ran through her and she rubbed her hands up and down her arms.

Liz lifted one shoulder. "Her migraine meds make her feel like a wet dishrag. She'll need some extra sleep."

They fell into an easy rhythm of cleaning. Cori rinsed a dish and handed it to Liz. Liz loaded the dishwasher, sometimes moving things or rearranging for a better fit.

"You're good at that," Cori said. "Like that old video game with the shapes and you had to make them fit..."

"Tetris?"

"Yes! That one. I bet you'd be good at it."

"You should see me pack a car," Liz said with a waggle of her eyebrows.

They finished with the dishes, then wiped everything down. Liz took the dining room. Cori tackled the kitchen counters. When Liz came back in and tossed her rag and towel down the laundry chute in the wall, Cori parked her hands on her hips and asked, "Now what?"

Liz opened the fridge and peered in. Then she looked at Cori over the top of the door, her eyes and smile both comically wide. "Now, it's time for dessert." And she pulled out the rest of the triple berry cobbler. "Ta-da!"

"Oh my God, I forgot!"

"Seriously? It's all I've thought about since Lauren served it to the guests. Well. That and the mistletoe."

"Holy crap, the mistletoe," Cori said, covering her eyes with a hand. And before she could catch it, she started to laugh. She peeked through her fingers and saw that Liz had started to laugh, too. And then they were looking at each other and their laughter died away until the kitchen was quiet.

"You're a good kisser," Liz said, then gave her a quick shrug and pulled a couple dessert plates out of a cabinet.

"Why, thank you," Cori said, her thoughts telling her to keep things light, not to get too serious. "You're not so bad yourself."

"Much obliged, ma'am."

"Do you think the impending headache is why Lauren didn't question us? Because I thought her head would snap right off her neck the way it whipped around when you confirmed we were dating."

Liz barked a laugh as she cut a piece of the cobbler. "Oh yeah, I'm definitely gonna hear about it. Her headaches wipe her out, so I have a reprieve until tomorrow." With her eyes, she gestured to the wine fridge in the corner. "Wanna pick a bottle? I think we earned a glass of wine after tonight, don't you?"

Ten minutes later, they were seated in the living room in front of the fire, which had died down a bit during dinner. But Liz poked and prodded and added wood, and soon, it was roaring again.

The cobbler was sweet and delicious. The wine was smooth and the perfect complement to it. The fire was warm. Liz was gorgeous.

The thought surprised Cori, but she didn't avoid it because it was true. The firelight made her blond hair seem more golden, and it almost sparkled. Her dark lashes were long—Cori could see them in her profile. And then Liz turned and caught her gaze and held it. They sat like that for a long moment, and something stirred in Cori. Something low in her body. Something sexy.

This is fake. You're pretending. She's *pretending.*

The voice reverberated through her head. Was it her own voice? She wasn't sure. What she was sure of was that it was correct. This was a facade, and the sooner she accepted that, the better off she'd be.

She cleared her throat and held up her empty plate. "I'd better get home to my boys." She didn't really need to. Suzanne always fed Bear and Ernie before she left if Cori wasn't home. But she needed a reason to escape. Being this close to Liz, especially when they were alone, was messing with her head.

"Oh. Okay." Liz was clearly disappointed, and Cori decided to think about that later. Because if she thought about it right now, she'd stay, and she knew she shouldn't. "Will I see you tomorrow?" Liz's eyes were bright in the firelight and her expression hopeful, and Cori had to get the hell out of there.

"Maybe, yeah. We'll see." She stood up with her dish, and Liz reached out to take it from her.

"I got this. Just leave it." She smiled up at Cori, who let go of the plate.

She barely remembered putting on her coat and waving a quick good-bye, but once she was in her car and on the road to home, she blew out a long breath as if she'd been holding it all evening. She had to pull herself together. This was fake. It was *fake.* They were *pretending.* Liz needed her to play this role until after the weekend. At that point, Cori would go back to her normal, quiet, lonely life.

No. No, her normal, quiet life. Just those two descriptors. She wasn't lonely. Liz wasn't filling some void that Cori hadn't even realized was there. No. She wasn't. It's not like she'd awakened Cori to her own solitude. Absolutely not.

Then she sighed again. Loudly.

"Son of a bitch," she muttered.

❖

Liz slept like crap.

It wasn't because she hadn't been exhausted. She absolutely had.

Yesterday had been a whirlwind, and she'd gone to bed late, having sat alone by the fire long after Cori had gone home. But she'd tossed and turned, her brain refusing to turn off and give her some peace, and before she'd known it, her alarm went off, reminding her she'd promised Lauren she'd do breakfast prep.

By the time she'd filled the muffin cups and brewed a pot of coffee, the clock on the oven said it was 4:47 a.m. She slid the muffin tin in, letting the warmth from inside envelop her for a moment before she closed it. She set the timer on her phone, grabbed her coffee, and headed out to the living room to stoke up the fire…which was already stoked and roaring, a figure curled up in the corner of the couch, staring at the flames. Again.

"Oh, hey," Regina said softly before Liz had a chance to turn away and return to the kitchen to hide. What the hell? Was it now her lot in life to sit with strangers by the fire? "I hope it's okay that I'm down here."

"Of course it is." Liz stood there for a moment, feeling awkward and possibly looking it.

"Come sit." Regina indicated the couch next to her. She wore red flannel joggers and a dark blue T-shirt with a teddy bear on it. The outfit and her scrubbed clean face made her look fifteen rather than in her thirties.

"Um…do you want some coffee? I just made a pot."

"Oh my God, you have no idea how much. I thought it was okay to sit by the fire, but"—Regina's smile was sheepish—"I didn't think I should be raiding your kitchen."

Liz ascertained that Regina took her coffee with a splash of cream and retreated to the kitchen to get it. She was nervous, and that annoyed her. *Pull yourself together, Brennan.*

Back in the common area, she held a steaming mug out to Regina, who took it with both hands and sipped greedily, clearly not concerned by its temperature. The second Liz sat down, she could smell the alcohol coming off her.

"How was the bachelorette party?" she dared to ask.

Regina sighed and sat back, as if the coffee had completely relaxed her. "Oh, it was fine," she said, watching the flames rather than looking at Liz. "I was way overserved. No, that's a lie. I drank too much. The serving had nothing to do with it. It was totally on me." Then she turned to Liz. "It's part of why I'm down here. Most people pass out when they're drunk. I'm the opposite. I can't sleep." She took a deep breath and another sip of coffee before adding, "So I threw up in the bathroom of the bar, came home, brushed my teeth and washed my face, made sure my bridesmaids were all tucked in, then came down here."

"And what time was that?" Liz made herself comfortable in the big overstuffed chair opposite the couch.

"One thirty? Two? What time is it now?"

"It's after five."

Regina's eyes went comically wide for a second. "Oh, man, I'm going to be tired today." And then she laugh-snorted and it was cute and made Liz grin. Regina sipped her coffee again and gazed into the fire, and Liz had the sudden understanding that that's exactly what she'd been doing for the past three hours. Just staring.

"Find what you're looking for in those flames?" she asked quietly.

Regina shook her head and kept her gaze on the fire. "Nope. Not even close."

"I'm sorry."

One shoulder lifted in a subtle half shrug.

"Justin's great," Liz offered. "One of the good ones, you know?"

Regina nodded this time. "He is. He's the best. I love him with everything in me."

Liz believed her, and that was a relief because there was clearly something bothering her. Before she could decide whether or not to probe, Regina surprised her.

"You and the brunette—I'm sorry, I forgot her name—you guys seem to have something pretty special."

Liz blinked at her for a beat before responding. "Cori. You think so?"

Regina smiled. "You should see the way she looks at you."

That was interesting.

"Yeah?"

"Oh yeah. She watches you a lot. If Justin hadn't told me you were dating, I would've guessed. Or at least figured she has a thing for you."

"She's pretty awesome."

"How long have you been together?"

"Oh, um, not long. Not long at all."

"Well, if it's new and she's looking at you like that? She's all in. Trust me."

Liz sat with those words all morning and into the early afternoon. While it was true that Regina was still a little drunk during their discussion, she hadn't been drunk during dinner. And since that's when she'd apparently seen Cori looking at her, Liz had to give some credence to it. Didn't she?

"I mean, I don't know Regina at all," she muttered to herself as she headed from Brennan House back to the cottage to see if her mom needed anything. The bridesmaids had gone skiing today, so no dinner was necessary. Lauren was going out with friends for a bit this afternoon, but she'd be back to make a dessert presentation for later this evening when the party was back from skiing. "Maybe Regina's terrible at reading people." She pushed through the front door to find the TV on, but the living room empty, so she headed back to her mom's room. "Maybe she has zero idea," she continued to whisper to herself. "Maybe Cori looks at me with utter disdain, but Regina thinks it's something else." She stopped and knocked once on her mom's closed bedroom door. "Mama?" She pushed it open as she said, "What do you want to do about—" He words died in her throat as she gaped at the sight. "Holy shit!"

Her father flipped himself off her mother, clutching at the covers. They both looked at her, both clearly naked.

"Oh my God!" Liz slapped both hands over her eyes and said it again, louder this time. "*Oh my God!* What are you two doing? What—? How—? *What are you doing?*"

And then there was laughing. Quiet chuckling that started with her father, and then her mother joined in, and then it grew into outright laughter. Liz kept her hands over her eyes as her parents cracked up.

"Honey, come on in here," her father said.

"What? No. In the same room as my naked parents? My naked *divorced* parents? *No.* No way, thank you very much. *Oh my God.*"

They kept laughing. "Please?" her mom said, her voice sugary sweet. Yeah, they were teasing her now.

"This isn't funny," she said. "I can't believe you two! Stop laughing! How long has this been going on? Does Lauren know? What in the—? *Stop laughing!*"

They did not.

She backed up, keeping one hand over her eyes as she felt around for the door frame, then the door. "I think we deserve an explanation at some point, but if you'll excuse me, I have to go bleach my eyeballs first." That made them laugh louder. She shut the door on the sound and stood in the hallway in utter disbelief. Then there was a full-body shudder because she had just seen her parents—her naked parents!—in bed together and nobody wanted to see that 'cause *ew*, so gross.

"Oh my God, I've gotta tell somebody." And then she spun in a circle as if someone would suddenly appear to listen to her. Lauren was out and Liz was bursting and she had to tell someone.

That's how she ended up at Whimsy and found Cori in the back room.

CHAPTER TEN

"Oh my God, they were actually in bed?" Cori laughed at the thought of Liz walking in on her parents, though Liz was less than giddy about it.

"Not just in bed. I think they were in the middle of *actually doing it*." Liz grimaced like she'd just tasted something horrible, and Cori laughed a little bit harder.

"So," she said once she'd collected herself, "I thought they were divorced. Was I mistaken?"

"I thought they were divorced, too." So many emotions had marched across Liz's face since she'd arrived twenty minutes ago. Cori had been headed back to her workshop while Suzanne took over the afternoon shift behind the register. One look at Liz's face was all it took—she'd grabbed Liz's hand and led her to the back room. And now, as she studied Liz's expression, she saw confusion, hope, surprise, joy, and maybe a smidge of anger all swirling around, taking turns clouding her blue eyes. "I haven't even told Lauren yet. Do you think she knows? I mean, why wouldn't they tell us?"

"Maybe they're still figuring it out themselves?" Cori kept her voice gentle, noncommittal. The last thing she wanted was to alienate Liz and her very big feelings right now. "Maybe they didn't want to say anything to you and your sister until they have it worked out?"

Liz was calming down. Slowly, yes, but she was. "I guess that could be it."

"It's good, though, right? If they're back together? Isn't that a good thing?" She poured some wax beads into her melter and plugged it in. "They do spend a ton of time together for two people who are divorced. Even I've noticed that, so I guess it's not that much of a surprise."

Liz dropped into a chair and just stared. Just blinked. It made Cori grin.

"You okay over there?"

Liz groaned and laid her head back and draped her arm over her eyes. Then she groaned again. "I don't know."

"I've got a steel brush over near the sink if you need to scrub the insides of your eyelids."

That made Liz smile, which made Cori inexplicably happy. "I might take you up on that." They were quiet for a moment, then Liz pushed to her feet and came to stand close to Cori. "Part of the custom order?"

Cori shook her head and tried hard not to think about how close Liz was and how it made her feel—heated, nervous, aroused. She didn't mean to clear her throat, but it just kind of happened. "No, not this time. I made some red holiday ones last week, so I'm making green today." She took her color shards off the shelf above her head, a beautiful emerald she'd discovered last year when trying out a new supplier.

Liz took the little baggie out of her hands and examined the pieces inside. "How do you know how much to use?"

Cori half shrugged. "Experiment. I used this one last year, so I kind of have a handle on how dark it gets." She opened the baggie and took out a couple small pieces, then dropped them into the melted wax and stirred with her thick wooden spoon.

"So you just stir until the color melts in."

She could feel Liz's breath on her neck, her ear, as she watched over her shoulder and spoke, and it awakened something low in her body. She nodded because she didn't trust her own voice in that moment. She just kept stirring.

"When does the scent come in?" Had Liz's voice gone a little softer? Cori thought so, and she gave herself a moment to absorb that.

"Now that the color is all melted in." Above the shelf with the color shards was another shelf with bottles of essential oils and scents. "Do you have a scent preference?" she asked, daring to turn her head and meet Liz's gaze. God, her face was close.

Liz's tongue darted out to wet her lips as she squinted at the bottles. "Well, it's a holiday candle, so…" Her eyes scanned until she pointed. "Evergreen?"

Cori handed the small bottle to Liz. "Check and see if you like it."

Liz unscrewed the bottle cap and Cori watched those beautiful hands. She had a flash of memory from high school, of watching Liz's hands as she wrote, pen gripped by her long fingers as she marked on her test paper.

"Oh, that's nice." Liz's voice brought her back to the present. "I was afraid it would be too pungent, but it's not." She held it under Cori's nose, and even though she knew exactly how it smelled, she sniffed dutifully anyway.

"I've been doing this for a while, so I've played with different brands. Some are super strong and some aren't strong enough. I like this brand, though." She gestured to the green liquid she was stirring. "Go ahead. Pour it in. Slowly."

"All of it?" Liz asked. At her nod, Liz tipped the bottle and let the clear liquid dribble into the wax. "How come slowly?"

"You don't want to create any air pockets."

"Ah."

Liz poured and Cori stirred and they stood close, sharing the same air, and…was that air charged with something electric? Something that crackled like static? Cori wasn't sure. What she *was* sure of was that she liked Liz this close.

"Wow, that smells good," Liz said, inhaling a second time. "Christmassy, but not too much."

"That's exactly what we want."

And then the little bottle was empty, and Liz stepped away, and Cori's body nearly cried out from the loss of her body heat.

"Do you want to add any texture?" Cori asked.

"What do you mean?"

Cori gestured with her chin to a shelf on the far wall to the right. "There are some little tiny branches over there. Some dried berries and such."

"Ooh!" Liz hurried over like an excited child, and Cori grinned at her. "There's so much cool stuff over here," she said.

Cori shook her head as she stirred, trying not to think about how perfectly natural and right it felt to have Liz here, in her shop. In her space. In her life.

"Okay." Liz was back next to her, spreading items out on the counter. "I got these tiny pine branches and a few of these cranberry thingies. They seem like Christmassy stuff to me. What do you think?"

"I think they're perfect."

For the next hour and a half, they made candles. Melted, poured, scented, decorated, added wicks. The two of them made a fantastic team—their artistic views were similar, they moved like they were choreographed, never bumping into each other, and they stood close together pretty much the entire ninety minutes. By the time they added a last layer of melted wax to top off the candles and Liz dropped her accessories into it, Cori felt like her whole body was crackling with electricity, like her nerves were all standing at attention.

"And now we wait?" Liz asked, and her enthusiasm was nearly contagious. She was like a kindergartener in art class, in a hurry to see her final project in all its glory.

"Yes. They have to dry for twenty-four hours before they're good to go."

Liz stood there, looking at their finished candles, an adorable grin on her face. It was still there when she turned her gaze to Cori. And then she surprised her by throwing her arms around her and squeezing her in a tight hug. "Thank you," she said quietly in Cori's ear. "I needed this distraction."

Cori hugged her back, took in the fresh, clean scent of her. "Thank *you*," she said. "I didn't realize candle-making would be so much fun with a partner."

Liz pulled back, smiling. "Maybe we can do it again?"

"Definitely."

There was a beat then. Not awkward. Just quiet. Held gazes.

Liz inhaled and blew out a breath. "Okay. I gotta go. Time to deal with the 'rents."

"I'm here if you need to chat," Cori told her. "Or rant. Or vent."

"Careful what you offer," Liz replied with a grin.

And a minute or two later, Cori was left alone in her workshop again. It was the way she'd always worked and created, on her own. Alone. So why did she suddenly feel like she was missing something important?

❖

The conversation with her parents had been almost surreal. The four of them—Liz, Lauren, and their mom and dad—had sat in the living room of the cottage house for less than twenty minutes. She and Lauren had done a lot of blinking and looking surprised. Their parents had done a lot of smiling and shrugging and we're-just-living-our-lives explaining. There were hugs all around before they had to return to Brennan House to serve up dessert and prosecco to the bridesmaids who'd returned from their day of skiing. They'd walked from the cottage to the B-and-B in silence. One of them would look at the other, open her mouth to speak, then close it again and continue walking.

They were in the kitchen hanging up their coats when Lauren looked at her and said simply, "What the actual fuck?"

Liz shook her head. "I know."

This was going to take some absorbing.

Lauren had made two cheesecakes—one traditional with a cherry topping and one chocolate with a chocolate ganache and raspberry topping. They looked like they'd come from a cheesecake shop, and Liz was once again shockingly impressed with her sister's abilities.

The bridesmaids were already back, hanging in the common room where Lauren had stoked up the fire a while ago. Lots of chatter between women, as the prosecco was poured and sipped. Once the dining room was set, Liz went out into the common room and got everyone's attention.

"Ladies, there are two different kinds of cheesecake in the dining room, as well as more prosecco. Please, help yourselves."

Tanner was the first one back, clearly a bit removed from the rest of the pack, as usual. She smiled at Liz. "How was your day?"

"Not bad. How was the mountain?"

"Oh my God, so beautiful. It was a perfect day to ski." Then she took a bite of the chocolate cheesecake and her eyes went wide. "Holy crap. This is delicious." Others had filtered in and variations of the same wondrous joy went around the room.

Back in the kitchen, Lauren was putting dishes in the dishwasher.

"Your cheesecake is a huge hit. You should go out there and listen to those women sing your praises."

Lauren smiled, but continued what she was doing.

"You okay?" Liz asked.

Lauren gave her a nod. "Yeah. Just…" She stood up and gestured back to the cottage house. "So weird, you know?"

"I do. I mean, we should be happy. And I *am* happy. But it's just…"

"Not at all what I expected."

"Exactly." She hung around a bit longer, helping Lauren with any extra cleanup, but just before ten, Lauren told her she'd take care of the rest.

"You're sure?"

A nod. "Yep. Go."

She was exhausted. It settled on her like a weighted blanket as she trudged along the path from Brennan House to the cottage house. But she was also wide-awake, her brain buzzing, feeling overloaded, and there was no way she was going to sleep anytime soon. Stopping halfway between the houses, she pulled out her cell phone and sent a text. Waited. Watched the bouncing dots until a response came.

Meet you there in 15.

Liz changed course and headed for her car and, ten minutes later, was locking it in the parking lot of McElhone's—or Mack's, as the locals called it. It was a local dive bar tucked in a dark alley behind the grocery store. Not a place the tourists knew, but all the locals did. Liz was sitting at the bar taking her first sip of her beer when the door opened and Cori walked in.

Liz's whole body reacted. Her nerves stood at attention. She sat up straighter. And yeah, there was a subtle throb between her legs, like it was just letting her know exactly what kind of reaction this was. Cori wore light-colored jeans with a hole in one knee and a navy-blue hoodie. Her hair was in a messy ponytail, and her face looked scrubbed clean, pink and soft.

"Oh my God, did I yank you out of bed?" Liz asked, putting the pieces of Cori's appearance—cute and delightful, but clearly not what she'd looked like earlier—together and feeling a little guilty.

"I wasn't sleeping, I was reading," Cori said as she slid onto the stool next to her. "You're much more entertaining than my book anyway." She smiled that smile, the one that revealed lovely teeth and that ghost of a dimple in one cheek. She ordered herself a Baileys on the rocks and then turned to Liz. "How did it go with the parents?"

Liz shook her head and took a slug of her beer. "It was fine. Good. Weird. *So* weird. But good. I guess."

"An interesting summary."

Liz gave a soft chuckle. "Right? Well, first, I had to tell Lauren."

"How'd that go?"

"She stood there looking at me, all bug-eyed, like I'd just told her I was actually an alien octopus and there were tentacles in my pant legs and sleeves. She didn't believe me."

"Oh wow. I mean, what did she think you saw?"

"Right? It's not like I could've mistaken what was happening when both our parents were naked in the same bed at two o'clock in the afternoon." Another slug. Then, "So, I dragged her to the house where Mom and Dad were having dinner together. Because of course they were. And I made *them* tell her."

"This is better than TV," Cori said, "and my book. Together."

"And then it really was just simple. Factual. They said it had been going on, *going on* meaning *the sex*"—and here, Liz gave a full-body shudder that made Cori laugh out loud—"and that it had just happened. We asked if they were back together, and they said not technically—whatever the hell that means—and that they're just living their lives and doing what they feel like doing when the mood hits. Making themselves and each other happy. Also, *ew*." Another shudder.

Cori softly laughed through her entire speech. "I mean, they sound like the kids and you're the parent."

"Right?"

"But…" Cori sipped her Baileys, and it left a little creamy shadow on her upper lip that Liz wanted to wipe off with a fingertip but managed to restrain herself. "It also sounds like they're just doing what they're doing and not trying to put any kind of label on it. Which I have to admit, I kind of admire. Don't hit me." She ducked her head to catch Liz's eye. "You know? They sound happy."

Liz sighed because she'd thought the same thing, but hearing Cori say it seemed to solidify it in her head. "Yeah, I guess you're right."

"And seriously, who doesn't want their divorced parents to get back together? I mean, when they're people who get along."

"Yeah, you're right. And they did look happy. I mean, they didn't look ashamed or embarrassed when I caught them. In fact, they laughed."

"Which is hilarious, I'm sorry."

"Have you ever caught your parents having sex?"

Cori gasped and made a face. "God, no."

"Lucky."

"Don't even put that in my head." Cori leaned in to her and bumped her with a shoulder.

"Excuse me, ladies." The bartender was a hulk of a man with a gray beard and kind brown eyes. He slid two more drinks in front of them. "From the gentleman."

Liz followed his gaze until hers landed on Justin, standing up from a table in the corner with several other guys and putting on his coat. He smiled and walked over to them.

"Hey there," he said, his face flushed, and leaned right in to hug Liz. He still used the same aftershave he always had, as he smelled exactly like she expected him to, woodsy and warm.

"You out with your groomsmen?" Liz asked, her gaze scanning over the other guys he was with as they slid arms into coat sleeves.

Justin glanced over his shoulder. "Yeah, just having a guys' night." He inched in a little closer and lowered his voice as he shot a look to Cori that could only be described as apologetic. "Listen, I'm sorry about the wedding being at your parents' place. I thought you lived in Syracuse, and Regina just loved the idea of getting married in my hometown, since we don't get back here that often. She saw the grounds and just fell in love with the whole place and booked it before I even knew where it was." He grimaced and Liz wanted to be annoyed because yeah, that's where he chose to get married? At his ex's family business? But his expression seemed sincere, and it was clear to her that he was still a really nice guy.

"Listen, no worries," she said, just as she felt Cori's hand on her thigh in full view of Justin, and a shot of...something...zipped through her body. She saw Justin's gaze glance down and then back up. "It's a great place for a wedding. I'm happy for you."

"Okay, well." He glanced down again at Cori's hand, and Liz figured he'd had a few beers or he wouldn't be quite so obvious. "I just wanted to put that out there."

Liz nodded.

He gave them both a wave and returned to his boys, and they headed out the door together. Liz and Cori watched them go, then turned back to their own drinks.

Cori kept her hand on Liz's thigh.

Liz didn't mind. At all.

For the next hour, they talked. Just talked, like they'd known each other forever. Liz asked for an update on the candles they'd made. Cori teased her about her parents. Liz mentioned meeting Tanner and also the odd conversation with an inebriated Regina. Cori talked about rearranging her workspace a bit more.

"Tell me about your family," Liz said. "Now that you know all the sexual escapades of my parents, I think it's only fair." She added a *yikes* face that made Cori laugh.

"Well, let's see. There's my parents, and I have three younger siblings."

"Three? Wow."

"Yeah, a sister and two brothers."

"That's so cool. I can't imagine having that many siblings. It's always just been me and Lauren. Are you guys a lot alike? Do you look alike?"

"We look nothing alike, and not one of them is like me." A quiet laugh there. "I have always felt like the black sheep."

"In what way—well, besides looks?" Liz sipped her beer, which had gone room temperature, and was sad when Cori took her hand off her thigh. She watched Cori's face as she stared into her glass—she'd finished her Baileys and moved on to water—turning it with her fingers.

"They're all kind of…" She squinted, seemingly looking for the right word. "Boisterous. Extroverted. They're talkers and singers and dancers and they're always making some kind of sound. I'm pretty quiet. Also, my sister is a bit of a free spirit but also has a law degree, and my brothers are a math teacher and a CPA. All very logical, left-brain people. Me, on the other hand…"

"The artist in the family."

Cori nodded. "Exactly. Even my parents. My mom started the shop. She was great at the business part, but it was Annabelle who chose the artists, who knew what would sell."

"I feel like I vaguely remember her." Liz racked her brain. "Was she a brunette? Kind of slight?"

More nodding from Cori. "Yes, exactly. She was petite. Really pretty. Soft-spoken and so kind. She seemed to really get me when I felt like my mom didn't."

"That's important, feeling seen and understood."

"It really is. Speaking of that…how come it was so important to you that Justin think you're hooked up?" And just like that, the conversation had gone full circle, coming back to the subject of Justin.

Liz pressed her lips together and studied her nearly empty beer, then shook her head. "I…" She blew out a breath. "I didn't expect to be here. I was supposed to be a success story by now. I graduated with honors, you know? Got a scholarship. Was going to have my own business by now. Or at least be something more than a glorified intern, which was pretty much what I was before I got laid off. I had a fabulous roommate, but I'm thirty-four. I should have my own place by now. So I came home with my tail between my legs, and suddenly, there's Justin, looking handsome and grown-up and about to marry this gorgeous model of a woman, and I just felt like such a joke. Such a failure. And I just…panicked. You were there, and I grabbed you and now…" She glanced at Cori and lifted one shoulder.

"I get that," Cori said with a nod. "Panic happens." A shadow of something zipped quickly across her face, but Liz couldn't pinpoint it. "And on that note, I really need to go. I've got the early shift tomorrow, so I can work on reorganizing my workshop in the afternoon."

Liz waved away Cori's credit card. "Nope. My invite, my treat. Well, mine and Justin's," she added with a chuckle.

Cori's smile was soft, and her eyes looked sleepy, and Liz tried not to focus on how cute she was that way. "Big stuff going on at Brennan House tomorrow?"

Liz signed her slip and then put on her coat. "Nope. The brides-maids have a spa day and then dinner out, so we're free after we clean the rooms."

"That'll be a nice break." They headed out the front door together, strolling casually toward the parking lot.

"It will." An idea hit Liz, and she gave voice to it before she could stop herself. "Hey, do you want some help tomorrow?" She flexed her arms like a bodybuilder. "I'm good at moving things."

Cori's smile was all she needed. "I'd love it."

"Perfect. I'll text you." They were at Liz's car, and she stopped, and her voice went soft. "Good night, Cori." She leaned in and placed a gentle kiss on Cori's cheek, then watched as her entire face flushed pink.

"Good night, Elizabeth." There was a beat and then Cori turned and headed to her own car.

Later, Liz lay in bed, wide-awake. Her phone told her it was after one in the morning, and she knew she needed to get some sleep, but her head kept playing her a happy little recording of Cori Stratton tenderly calling her Elizabeth, and it kept her warm all night long…

CHAPTER ELEVEN

The bridesmaids ushered each other out of Brennan House by ten the next morning, a mix of excited utterances floating around them like clouds.

"I so need this."

"I hope my masseuse is a gorgeous man."

"Are we getting facials, too?"

Lauren had served them a continental breakfast, and Liz cleaned it up, filled the dishwasher, and got it running just as the last of the bunch—Tanner—scooted out the door. As she glanced over her shoulder, she made eye contact with Liz, gave a good-natured eye roll, and was off.

"I like that one," she said to Lauren.

"The quiet one?"

"That's how I think of her, too. Her name's Tanner."

Before they could say more, the door opened again, but it wasn't a bridesmaid. It was Isaac, lovesick UPS driver who only had eyes for Lauren. Which became instantly clear again when he looked right past Liz and his gaze settled on her sister. His entire face changed in the moment. Slackened. His smile grew. His neck tinted pink.

Liz needed to start cleaning rooms upstairs, so she opened the closet behind the front desk and took far longer than necessary to get her supplies together so that she could eavesdrop.

"Got a few packages for you today," he said, and Liz heard him set the boxes on the desk. "How's your morning so far?"

"It's actually been pretty good," Lauren responded, her voice uncharacteristically light. "How about yours?"

"It's better now," he replied, and Liz dropped her head back and laughed silently at how obvious he was. "Listen," he went on, "I was thinking of going ice skating at the rink tonight. I go a couple times a week, but it's always better not to go alone." He cleared his throat, and Liz wished so badly that she could see his face. "Would you maybe want to go with me? It's supposed to be a clear night. They have hot chocolate. And snacks."

And now she wished she could see Lauren's face. When there was a hesitation, she knew it was time to step in. Pulling her supplies out of the closet, she kept her voice as nonchalant at possible and said, "I can handle things tonight. The girls won't be back until well after dinner." She shrugged like it was the smallest of all the deals in the world. "Go."

Lauren blinked at her, first in clear surprise and then with something else. Holy crap, was that gratitude on her face? "You're sure?"

"Absolutely. You've been a worker bee this week. I can take over for one night. I'll get Mom, and we'll put up the tree."

Lauren held her gaze for a second. Two. Finally, she slowly began to nod and then turned back to Isaac. "Okay."

"Yeah?" His entire face lit up like the proverbial Christmas tree she'd just mentioned, and if it wouldn't have likely embarrassed him, she would've called him on it. But it was enough just to watch because he clearly hadn't expected her to say yes.

"Yeah."

"Great. Excellent. That's fantastic." He seemed to understand that he should exit immediately so as not to let his excitement turn to awkwardness. He swooped up his electronic pad and turned for the door. Then he spun back around and said, "Oh. Um, I'll pick you up at seven? Here?"

Lauren nodded.

"Great. Dope. See you. Um, tonight. See you tonight. Yeah. Cool." And then he was out the door.

Liz stood next to Lauren for a moment, both of them staring at the closed door.

"Okay, that was probably the most adorable thing I've ever seen," Liz finally said.

When Lauren met her gaze, she was smiling, her eyes soft. "He's cute, isn't he?"

"Are you kidding me? He's cute *and* hot. The best combination." And Lauren's cheeks tinted pink, and Liz was not about to let *that* pass her by. "Excuse me, but is my little sister blushing?"

In response, Lauren blushed harder, bumped against her, and said, "Shut up," with zero venom whatsoever.

It was an unexpectedly nice way to start the day.

❖

Nobody ever cooked Cori's eggs just right. Except for her mother. She liked them over easy with a runny yolk. But the whites couldn't be runny. There couldn't be one speck of runny white, or Cori couldn't eat them. Nobody had ever been able to hit that perfect combination of solid and runny but her mom.

She dipped a corner of her toast into her yolk as her mom sat down across from her with a cup of coffee. Cori indicated it with her eyes. "Second or third cup?"

"Fourth." Her mom grinned, blue eyes dancing.

"You're the only person I know who can have four cups of coffee before ten and not be bouncing off the walls."

"I have four children. It takes more than an overdose of caffeine to rattle me." Barbara Stratton wore her usual daily outfit—jeans and a nice top, blond hair in a ponytail or bun of some sort. Today's top was a lightweight sweater, because she ran hot and if she wore something heavy—even something that seemed appropriate for winter in the Adirondack Mountains—she might possibly, as she so colorfully put it, spontaneously combust. "Hot flashes are a thing," she was constantly saying to Cori. "Just you wait."

This was rare, having her mom to herself. Her sister still lived at home and was often around. But every once in a while, Cori got lucky. It was usually in the morning, like today, and she could usually get a homemade breakfast out of it.

"How are things at the shop?" her mother asked. She didn't stop in often. Once she'd handed the reins over to Annabelle and Suzanne, she'd become more of a silent partner, realizing and accepting that Annabelle and now even Cori were much better at the ins and outs of ordering and selling.

"I got my first custom order," Cori told her, unable to help the smile.

"What? That's fantastic!" Her mom closed a hand over her arm and squeezed. "For? Candles?"

She told her mother all about the order, how surprised she'd been, and how Liz had hit her with a bunch of marketing ideas.

"Liz Brennan? Is she back in town?"

Cori nodded. "Yeah. Last week. We've been…spending some time together." And then her mom got that look. The twinkly eyed look. The matchmaker look. She even waggled her eyebrows up and down. "Mom. Stop."

Her mother laughed. "What? She's cute, from what I remember." Another mischievous look. "Is she still cute?"

Cori's brain chose that moment to toss her an image of Liz standing under the mistletoe just before they kissed. "Yeah. She's still cute."

"Maybe you should ask her out." Her mother looked like she was thinking, then added, "Does she play on your team?"

Honestly, her efforts were so sweet that Cori couldn't be as mortified as she wanted to be. Her parents had never been anything but supportive of her sexuality. She grinned as she finished her toast. "Actually, she plays on both teams."

"Oh, well isn't *that* interesting?"

God, she needed to get off this topic, stat. "So, I was rearranging a bit in the back room. I need to make more space for my supplies and stuff if I want to do more custom orders. There are a couple more boxes of Annabelle's stuff. Should I just give them to Suzanne?"

A quick zap of surprise flashed across her mother's eyes, so quickly that she wasn't quite sure she'd actually seen it at all. "There are more boxes of hers?"

"I mean, it's been a mystery figuring it out. They say *Annabelle* on the side in big letters, but I'm not quite sure…" She made a show of rubbing her chin and squinting.

"All right, smart-ass." Her mom took a playful swipe at her as she pushed to her feet. "Yeah, give them to Suzanne."

"Will do." She finished her breakfast and, as she looked up, caught her mom watching her. "What? Do I have eggs on my face?" She grabbed a napkin and wiped her mouth.

"No. I…" She hesitated for a moment, her expression serious.

"Are you dating, honey? Are you seeing anybody? Liz Brennan? I worry about you being alone."

"I'm okay, Mom. Promise." It was a discussion they'd had before, but it had been a while, and Cori's reaction often depended on her mood. Sometimes, she took the questions as they were meant, a mother wanting to see her child happy and in love. Others, she got annoyed, wanting her mom out of her love life *immediately*. Her thoughts jumped to Liz, to kissing her under the mistletoe, to hanging with her last night at Mack's, to their moment in the dark parking lot as they left. But she couldn't tell her mother what they were doing. She'd be shocked and she'd tell her what a dumb idea it was, and Cori just didn't want to hear any of that today. Plus, she hadn't told her mother about any of the things that had happened or why they might be significant now. Her mother didn't know about the crush she'd had on Liz in high school, which meant she wouldn't understand how rescuing Liz from the spider—and now from her shame, questionable as it might be—was helping Cori work through some of the—she now knew—unresolved feelings around that crush. And anyway, there were only a few days left before the wedding, and then their little charade would be over, and she'd go back to being single.

Why did that thought make her so sad?

❖

Whimsy was hopping on a Thursday afternoon.

Liz was happily surprised as she caused the little bell to ring over the front door. Suzanne and a young guy were ringing out a customer at the counter. Suzanne met her gaze across the store, gave Liz a wave, then gestured to the back, clearly letting her know where Cori was.

Bear stood up from his spot near the register and lumbered over to her for greetings and pets. "Well, hello there, sir," she said as she squatted down to pet his soft golden fur. "I'm here to see your mommy. Wanna come back with me?" Apparently, the answer to that question was yes because he followed her through the store and to the door to the workshop where she rapped on the door a couple times, then turned the knob and let herself and Bear in.

"Is this door made of soundproof material?" she asked as she closed it. "'Cause it really shuts out the noise."

"Right?" Cori said with a grin from her spot at her counter. "I love that about it."

"Hi." Liz smiled at her and crossed the room to run a hand across her shoulders. "Whatcha doin'?"

"Trying out a new color," Cori said as she dropped a few shards of a swirly light green into some melted wax. "And then I'm going to try a new scent and see how it pairs." She glanced up at Liz and her dark eyes went soft. "I didn't expect to see you today. Hi." And then she leaned in and kissed Liz on the cheek, clearly without thinking about it. When she pulled back, her eyes went wide for a moment, like she'd surprised herself. "Oh my God. I'm so sorry. I just..."

And Liz couldn't help it. She burst out laughing.

Cori stared for a total of about three seconds before she joined in.

"Wow, we've just become second nature, haven't we?" Liz said, watching Cori's face carefully.

Instead of looking away in shame or embarrassment, Cori held her gaze, and the air between them was charged. "I guess that just means it feels natural," she said quietly.

"I guess so." They were standing close together, mere inches between their bodies, but Liz had zero desire to move away. She cleared her throat and glanced down at the wax, now a clear green. "And what's the scent for this one?"

It seemed to take Cori an extra beat to get her bearings, but she managed. Then she wet her lips with her tongue and swallowed audibly. "Um. I'm gonna try basil and lemon. I have no idea if it's a good combination but..." She shrugged.

"It works on pasta."

"Exactly what I thought. So maybe it'll work in a candle?"

"Let's find out," Liz said.

They made candles for the next forty-five minutes, working together like they'd been doing so for years, laughing and bumping into each other on purpose. Liz had to work hard to keep from dwelling, to keep from thinking about what a good pair they actually did make, because here they were, together, just the two of them, with nobody around they had to pretend for. And it was awesome.

"I need more space over there," Cori said at one point, her hands on her hips as she studied the corner near her workspace, where the boxes they'd just moved the other day were stacked.

Liz stood next to her and pursed her lips in thought. "Okay, so I saw a folded-up card table or something back there behind a shelf." She jerked a thumb over her shoulder. "What if we moved those boxes to the other corner and set the table up right there? It'd give you more counter space."

Cori nodded. "That's a fantastic idea. I forgot about that other table. I think my mom had it out front in the shop at some point, but it's old and dirty and I didn't like how it looked out there. But it's perfect for back here."

They didn't have to say anything more. They simply got to work. It was a little absurd, just how in sync they were, moving things, dragging stuff, setting things up in a way that made Cori's work easier. Liz moved seven boxes to a different corner. When she set the last one down, the box underneath it buckled, and the top box tipped over and fell, spilling its contents onto the dusty floor.

"Shit," Liz muttered as she watched what had to be a dozen books slide across the concrete. "I'm sorry."

"Please," Cori said with a snort. "No worries. Lemme help." And together, they scooped up the books Liz had noticed last time they moved these same boxes, which she'd thought were journals. She pulled one out, confirming her suspicions.

"These your mom's?" she asked, feeling a little weird when she flipped through and saw the neat, slanted handwriting, but also kind of curious. The first page her eyes landed on was dated February 3, 1990.

"No, I think..." Cori flipped through. "No, this is Annabelle's handwriting. I didn't know she kept journals. I wonder if Suzanne knows these are here." She picked up another journal and flipped through the pages.

"This one's from 1990."

"Really? This one's from 2006."

Liz peered into the box. "There aren't nearly enough to span that whole time. I wonder if some are missing."

Cori took the one Liz had and was flipping through the pages when there was a rap on the door. She set the two journals up on a shelf as she stood. "Come in."

Suzanne popped her head in. "Hey, there's somebody here who might be interested in another custom order." Her grin was wide.

"Really? Okay, I'll be right out. Hey, by the way, this box has

Annabelle's stuff. Some journals, looks like?" Cori gestured to the box by her feet.

"Oh, wow. Journals?" And then Suzanne was hurrying into the workshop. She zipped over to the box and closed it up, did that thing where you tucked flaps under flaps until the box was closed without the use of tape. Liz watched as she closed the box up, swooped it up, and headed for the back door, all in one quick motion. "I'll just put these right in my trunk. Take 'em home."

Both Liz and Cori watched in surprise as the door shut behind Suzanne.

"Well, that was weird," Cori said, her eyes still on the door.

Liz lifted one shoulder. "I mean, you said they were together, right? Maybe she's just being protective of Annabelle's private thoughts?"

"Yeah, that makes sense, I guess." Another beat went by and then Cori seemed to shake herself out of it. "Lemme go see what this customer might want."

"Sell a million candles," Liz called after her.

It was a good fifteen minutes before Suzanne returned through the back door. Her face seemed a little pale, and Liz watched as she wiped her palms down her thighs, then blew out a quiet breath. When her gaze landed on Liz, sitting in an old beat-up chair, her face registered surprise for just a split second, as if she'd forgotten that Liz was there. Then her expression transformed and she smiled, and Liz couldn't help but wonder what had just happened in her mind.

"All good?" Liz asked, as Suzanne seemed to take a moment to think. Then she nodded.

"All good. How are you doing?" she asked, clearly wanting to shift the focus. She gestured toward the shop, then to Liz. "The charade working?"

Liz wasn't sure why the use of that particular word got under her skin, because a charade was exactly what it was, but it did. She literally felt herself bristle, but answered, "Yeah. Seems to be."

"Okay then." Suzanne gave one nod of her head, then crossed the workshop quickly and headed back into the store.

"Nope. Not awkward at all," Liz muttered to herself once she was alone with Bear. Not that she could blame the woman. Suzanne clearly cared about Cori, and what they were doing wasn't exactly…

commonplace. "Ah, well," she said as she stood up and almost stepped on Bear's paw. She adjusted quickly, lost her balance for a moment, but caught herself against the shelf. Her hand brushed against a book, and when she looked, she realized there were two journals from the box that got separated. She picked one up and was looking at the blue vinyl cover of it when the door to the shop opened and Cori came back in, a huge grin on her face.

"And?" Liz asked.

"Custom order for a dozen candles for a book club. Seems like an odd request, but who am I to judge?"

"Fantastic! What kind? When are they due? Are you shipping? I have so many questions!"

Cori laughed, and the happiness looked so good on her. Liz just watched her, just watched her face for a moment. Cori was so clearly in her element, stoked and ready to get to work. Liz found herself both thrilled for Cori and envious. She couldn't remember the last time she was as obviously thrilled as Cori was.

"Whatcha got?" Cori asked, gesturing to the journal still in Liz's hand.

Liz held it up. "Oh. Two of the journals didn't end up in the box Suzanne ran out of here with like her ass was on fire."

"Yeah, that was weird, wasn't it?"

"I mean, I don't know her, so…maybe?"

"I was tight with Annabelle. I'd have liked to read some of those journals."

Liz reached for the second journal on the shelf and handed them both to Cori. "Here you go. Have at it."

Cori smiled at her as she took them and set them on the counter. Then chuckled softly.

"What?" Liz asked.

"The green wax. We forgot all about our candles."

"Damn, we sure did. Basil-lemon, right?"

"Yes, ma'am."

"Well, let's get to it, then."

"Can I ask you a question?"

Liz stopped with the bottle of basil oil in her hand and met Cori's gaze. "Of course you can."

"For two people who are faking a relationship, do you think we spend an inordinate amount of time together when nobody's watching?"

Liz didn't miss a beat. "We totally do."

"I thought so. Wanted to make sure it wasn't just me."

"Good." She gave one nod. "Okay. Let's make some candles."

CHAPTER TWELVE

Cori waited for the water to boil in her kettle. Liz had to get back to Brennan House to check on her mom, plus she wanted to be there when Lauren returned from her date with the UPS guy. As had seemed to be happening more and more, their good-bye stretched out to ten, fifteen, maybe twenty minutes. It was clear to Cori at that point that neither of them wanted their time together to end. After Liz had agreed with Cori about how much time they spent together not pretending to enjoy each other's company, something inside her had shifted. Something important.

She couldn't put a finger on it. She'd been trying for the past hour as she rattled around her apartment, the clock closing in on midnight. She should be exhausted, but her brain was rolling too much around. She poured water into her cup, letting the bag of chamomile steep. It was far too easy to see herself in a real relationship with Liz, and she wasn't sure what to do with that. She had no idea where Liz stood on the subject—and yeah, she should probably just ask her—but first, she needed to fulfill her part of the bargain. It was only a few more days and the wedding would be over, the ex and his new bride would be gone, and Liz would be figuring out when and how to get back to the city. Thinking about anything beyond the end of this coming weekend was stupid for her to do. Incredibly stupid. She had to shake Liz Brennan out of her head. At least for a little while.

She stirred a little honey into her tea, and her gaze landed on the two journals she'd carried up from the shop. Perfect. Those would distract her for a while, get her thinking of something other than what it felt like to have Liz standing so close to her as they poured wax or how she smelled like a mix of vanilla and something spicy that Cori couldn't quite identify or how much she really wanted to kiss Liz…kiss her for real. She gave her head a literal shake. Yeah, maybe reading the journals would take her mind off all that. And maybe reading them would tire her eyes out, make her feel sleepy. Bear was curled up on his big round dog bed in the corner of her bedroom, and while she couldn't see him from the kitchen, she could hear him as clearly as if he'd been right next to her, snoring like a truck driver. She sighed with envy, grabbed the journals, and followed his snuffles.

Once comfy in bed, propped against her headboard with her tea on the nightstand, Ernie curled up by her hip, she flipped open the journal from 1990 and began to read.

❖

Ding!

Was that an elevator?

That would be weird. There wasn't an elevator in her building…

Ding!

Okay, get on the damn thing and push the stupid button already.

Ding!

"Oh, for the love of…" Liz opened her eyes and was very surprised to find herself not in the hallway near a malfunctioning elevator, but rather in her basement bedroom at her parents' house in bed. The lights were still on, and her laptop was next to her on the bed, its screen gone black from disuse. Shit. She fell asleep waiting for Lauren to come home from her date and now it was—she squinted at her phone—almost four in the morning. And the dings she'd heard were in her dream? Nope. A closer examination of her phone showed a trio of texts from Cori.

Hey, I know you're prolly sleeping but I'm freaking.

Liz sat up, wide-awake now, and read the next one.

I don't know who else to talk to.

The third had only come through three minutes ago.

Never mind, I'm sorry, I'm just being stupid. I shouldn't have texted you.

Liz didn't even think about it. She simply hit the call button. Cori answered after only half a ring.

"Liz? I'm so sorry for waking you up…" And then she started crying, the one thing guaranteed to get Liz moving.

"Oh, Cori, what? Baby, what is it?" Liz felt her heart squeeze at the sound of Cori's quiet sobs. "Tell me."

"Can you come over here?" Cori's voice was small, uncertain.

"Of course I can. Let me throw something on, and I'll be right there."

"Oh my God, it's four in the morning." Cori said it like she'd only just realized the time. "What am I doing? I'm so sorry. It can wait. I'm so sorry. Ignore me."

The line went dead.

"Yeah, we're not doing that," Liz said, throwing off the covers and grabbing her joggers and a hoodie. She dressed in fifteen seconds flat, gave her teeth a quick brush, threw her hair into a messy bun, and was out the door, keys in hand.

Her car didn't even have time to warm up before she arrived at Whimsy's back parking lot. She jumped out and hit the little glowing doorbell, and then the door opened, and there was Cori, her face puffy and her eyes red, and Liz simply opened her arms. What else could she do?

Cori fell into them and cried quietly, and Liz gave her a moment or two before gently walking her inside before they froze to death.

"Have you been up all night?" she asked Cori, who nodded.

Upstairs, Liz led Cori to a chair and sat her down. Then she found the kettle, filled it, and set it to boiling because if there was ever a time for tea, it was now. Bear was there in the kitchen as well, not at all relaxed, clearly worried about his mom.

She turned, her back against the counter as the water heated, and said quietly, "Talk to me."

Cori picked up a book from the table, and Liz recognized it as one of the two journals that had been left behind from the box. It now had several colored Post-its sticking out of it, mini yellow, pink, and coral flags. Cori gave it a little shake.

"I was ready for bed and thought I'd do a quick zip through these journals. Like I told you earlier, I was very close with Annabelle. She was like a combination of a big sister and a second mother, and we were tight."

Liz nodded to show she was following. The kettle interrupted them, and Cori stopped long enough for Liz to make two cups of tea, bring them to the table, and sit down across from her.

"So, I started reading the earlier one first." She held up one of the journals. "Remember, the two we had are sixteen years apart."

"Right. I remember." Liz kept her eyes on Cori, not at all sure where this was going, but certain that it was big and emotional and upsetting. True, they'd known each other for a laughably short time, but she'd come to associate Cori with calm and serenity, and this current version sitting across from her was practically vibrating with emotion. It was slightly unnerving.

"Listen to this. It's from January of 1990." Cori opened the journal to one of the marked pages and began to read. "*I'm not sure how I'm supposed to do this. It's so close now. And I'm scared. I don't know how to be a mother. I'm not ready for this. Barb says we're never ready, but Jesus Christ, I'm not just not ready. I'm terrified. I don't think I can do this.*" She looked up at Liz. "She's clearly pregnant, yeah? Is that what you get?"

Liz nodded. "Seems pretty obvious."

"Annabelle didn't have any kids."

"Oh. Okay."

"I mean, not that I knew of."

Liz rolled that around. "Adoption, maybe?"

"Maybe?"

"Who's Barb?"

"My mom's name is Barb."

Liz stared. "Oh. Got it."

Cori held up a finger. "This is from the end of February that same year. *I have to get out of here. I can't stay. I don't want to stay. I need to start fresh somewhere else. If I leave her with Barb, she'll be taken care of, but if she stays with me, I don't know what will happen. I'm so scared. I don't know what's wrong with me. How did I let this happen? She deserves so much better. A better mother. A better life.* That's the last entry in this journal, which is interesting because it was only February." She set that one down and picked up the other one. "This is from 2006, so sixteen years later, and there are dozens of entries that I marked because"—she swallowed audibly—"well, just listen. *We're settled in now. Suzanne seems to love it here already. I knew she would. She's not used to the snow or the cold, but I can tell she's so much happier. I'm glad we made the move.*"

"So, she's back here in Crimson Valley?" Liz asked.

"I think so, yeah. This is from later in the year, in July. Listen. *She's grown into such a beautiful woman, as I knew she would. Barb was the right choice. Thank God I did one thing right in my life. I'm so glad to be able to be close to her now, to watch her grow. She's kind and gentle and creative and so much like me, it's a little crazy.*"

Liz's heart rate picked up because she was getting an inkling as to where this was going. But she stayed quiet. She wanted Cori to lead her there before she said anything.

"And then in August: *She's working at the shop now and I'm so happy to get to see her so often. I wish I could tell her the truth, but Suzanne says I need to think about her and Barb and David and what it would do to them. Not to mention our friendship. And I know she's right, but...I just wish I could tell her that she has my eyes.*" Cori's brown eyes welled up then as she lifted her gaze to meet Liz's. "Both my parents have blue eyes," she said softly. "And I was born on February 4, 1990."

"You think Annabelle was your biological mother."

"I think Annabelle was my biological mother."

"Wow."

"Yeah." Bear had finally settled at Cori's feet but kept his head up as if listening to their conversation, his head turning one way, then the other, like he was at a tennis match. Cori reached down absently and stroked his head. "What do I do, Liz?" she whispered, and her face right then, her eyes, held such anguish. It was clearly a combination of emotions. Shock. Hurt. Confusion. Anger. It all blended into clear anguish, and all Liz wanted to do was make it better somehow.

She reached across the table and clasped Cori's hand in hers. Held it tight. "What do you *want* to do?"

The muscles in her jaw tightened. Liz could see it, see the frustration, the anger. "God, I don't know. I don't know who to be angry at. You know? I mean, I want to march my ass right over to my parents' house and ask them *What the fuck is this?*" She held up one of the journals and gave it a shake. "But…" And just like that, all the wind seemed to leave her sails. "I don't know, Liz. I don't know. And don't get me started on my biological father…I have no idea who he might have been, and I haven't found anything in the journals yet." Her eyes welled up once again, and when she turned them to her, Liz felt her heart squeeze in her chest. "What do I do?" The tears spilled over, trailing silently down her cheeks.

Liz scraped her chair around so she was next to Cori, and she wrapped her up in her arms. "I think maybe you just sit with this for a while, instead of going off half-cocked, as my grandpa used to say."

There was a beat of quiet, and then Cori said, "What the hell does that even mean? Half-cocked? Does it mean drunk? Does it refer to a gun and it's only partway ready to fire?"

"I have no fucking idea."

They shared some soft chuckling before going quiet again, and they sat there like that until their tea went cold.

Cori inhaled and let it out slowly. "I'm glad you're here."

"Me, too."

❖

Friday morning ended up being very snowy.

Gray.

Cold.

Cori was fine with that because it matched her mood. She felt sullen, but also blindsided. Confused, but also so much clearer on many things. Questions she'd had her whole life were suddenly answered. Things that had confused her now made sense. The only thing she didn't understand was why nobody had told her.

Who else knew?

She'd guess nobody. She wondered how her parents had pulled it off. She wondered how Suzanne could work with her so closely every day, but never tell her.

And she wondered why the only person she trusted with her emotions around the whole thing right now was Elizabeth Brennan. What the fuck was that about?

Liz had had to leave to help Lauren with breakfast. It was the last day before the big wedding. The rehearsal dinner was tonight, offsite, but the whole gang was coming back to Brennan House for desserts, coffee, and champagne, so both she and Liz would be there to help out. Until then, she was going to have to limp through her day without letting on to Suzanne that something was wrong. Easier said than done, because Suzanne knew her very, very well, and for the first time in her adult life, she was irritated by that.

"Easier to keep a huge raging secret from somebody if you know them like the back of your hand," she muttered from behind the register. It was almost noon. She had the earlier shift at Whimsy today so she could head to Brennan House later, and she was glad she was alone. Well, alone with Bear and Ernie—who, as she watched, was poised on a shelf and ready to give another customer a heart attack. It was clear Bear knew she wasn't feeling happy today. Normally, he'd lounge in his bed or find some sunbeam to nap in, but today, he stuck close, following her around the store as she dusted and straightened, sitting next to her feet when she rang out a customer. His presence calmed her, and she was grateful.

Her phone pinged from her back pocket. Liz.

Bucky burger?

She grinned, but before she could type, another text came.

I already ordered yours, so you can't say no. Be right over. That was followed with a smiley emoji and one that was blowing a kiss.

She wasn't even a little bit hungry but knew she needed to eat something. At the very least, she'd pop a couple fries into her mouth and save her burger to warm up later. Or tomorrow. Or next week. Or whenever she thought her stomach could handle food again. If ever.

How did she get here?

How had the way she'd viewed her life been so drastically changed in a matter of one evening? In a matter of a few pages of decades-old handwriting by a dead woman?

She had to talk to her parents. They owed her an explanation, that was an inarguable fact. But she couldn't do it while she felt like this. She didn't want to go in guns blazing, no matter how warranted that was. No, she needed to sit with these new facts, absorb them, let herself feel the emotions they caused.

Which all sounded great on paper, but—honestly?—she felt like she was about to crawl out of her own skin.

"Hey there," Liz said, as the bell over the door tinkled with cheer and she walked in carrying a Bucky bag. She came right around behind the counter without hesitation, set the bag down, and wrapped Cori in a tight hug. Which turned out to be something she desperately needed, and she sank against Liz, let her support her, literally. Liz pressed a soft kiss to her temple. "How're you doing? Hanging in there?"

All Cori could do was nod for fear she'd burst into tears. Again. And Liz seemed to get that and said nothing more for a moment.

"Okay," Liz finally said, easing out of the hug. She reached for the bag. "You need to eat. I know you don't want to, but I didn't see you eat dinner last night, and I'm willing to bet a bajillion dollars you didn't have breakfast."

"You would be a bajillionaire then."

"Thought so." Liz took items out of the bag and set them on the counter behind them so they weren't right by the register, and Cori appreciated that. "Cheeseburger. Fries. Chocolate shake. I know you probably won't eat much of this, but eat some. Okay? For me?" Her blue eyes were soft, the color a lighter shade than they were last night. She gave Cori a tender smile and waited.

"Okay," Cori said and popped a fry into her mouth. The hot greasy saltiness of it seemed to wake up her system, and suddenly, she was ravenous. Fifteen minutes later, all that was left were two fries and the edge of the burger. She sucked on the straw in the shake greedily as her gaze met Liz's very satisfied one.

"Feel better?" Liz asked, only halfway through her burger.

"Nothing a Bucky Burger can't fix," she said, though they both knew that wasn't true. She caught Liz's gaze and held it. "Thank you," she said softly. And then there was a customer in front of her and she had to put her work hat back on.

"I've gotta run," Liz said, cleaning up the detritus of their lunch, "but I'll touch base with you later, okay?" Cori nodded as she rang out a customer buying a pair of earrings made by a local artist, a Christmas tree ornament, and a festive red candle that Liz pointed at. "She made that, you know," indicating Cori with her eyes.

"Seriously?" the customer asked.

"Seriously. Ask her about custom orders." With a grin, she ran her hand down Cori's arm, and then she and the lunch trash headed out the front door.

Cori followed with her eyes until the little bell rang and the door shut behind Liz, and when she turned back to her customers, the line had four people in it, two of whom were holding her candles.

CHAPTER THIRTEEN

Cori spent the day ignoring Suzanne.

Okay, not exactly ignoring her, but avoiding her. That was a more accurate descriptor. She turned away whenever Suzanne's gaze ventured near hers. She answered her questions quickly and without looking at her. And Suzanne felt it. Cori knew that, and part of her felt bad about it. But she was afraid if she looked in her eyes, she'd either burst into tears from her shocked sadness and confusion or she'd scream at her from all the anger she suddenly found herself carrying.

She was going to have to talk to somebody. Soon. Address the situation. Suzanne, her parents, somebody. Before she exploded in a ball of hurt.

Liz had been amazing.

Cori had called her—practically in the middle of the night!—and she'd dropped everything and come. Cori wasn't sure anybody else in her life would have. She could almost let herself forget that this whole thing was fake. Pretend. *Artificial*, even though it felt so real. But it was also temporary, and that was probably the more important part. Sure, it was nice now, but Liz didn't want to be there in Crimson Valley. She'd made that clear. She'd done her best to escape this small town, and she'd do it again as soon as the opportunity arose.

Cori would do well to remember that.

She was glad she was due at Brennan House this evening to help with the dessert and champagne because Suzanne was starting to give her looks—looks that said *I know something's wrong, let's talk about it*—and Cori just couldn't. Not yet. She was still absorbing and she was still flabbergasted. Because why? *Why?* Why wouldn't they tell her? Why would they keep something like that from her?

It really did explain so much. She loved her family, she truly did, but she'd always felt a little bit like an outsider. She didn't look like a Stratton. She didn't think like a Stratton. She didn't act like a Stratton. Which made perfect sense now, since she *was not* a Stratton.

She gave Bear a kiss on his golden head, and he looked at her with worried brown eyes. He was so emotionally attuned to her, and he always knew when something was bothering her.

"It's okay," she whispered to him. "Don't worry. I'll be okay." She wasn't actually sure that was true, but she couldn't bear the concern on his furry face. She kissed him again, gave Ernie a scritch on her way past him, then went through her workshop and out the back door, tossing a wave over her shoulder at Suzanne, but not able to look at her. She glanced around the workshop, at the candles that were drying. If she wasn't due at Brennan House, this was where she'd be. Alone. Creating. It was the only thing that could take her out of her own head when she was in danger of getting stuck in there.

The night was freezing, and snow was forecast for later. She loved this kind of cold, when the sky was clear and the air so crisp and brittle, you felt like you might shatter it with your breath. She inhaled deeply, felt the cold go deep down and fill up her lungs, then let it out in a huge cloud of vapor. The sky was midnight black and so peppered with stars that it looked like black construction paper poked dozens of times with a pin, then held over a light. The night was quiet, a few sounds here and there—a faraway conversation, a slice of a song coming from a nearby bar as its door opened and closed, the crunch of snow and slush under the tires of a car. It was the soundtrack of Crimson Valley, of Cori's life, and even when she felt as one hundred percent shitty as she did then, she still loved it. Every note. Every whisper.

Brennan House was quiet when she entered through the front door. The bridal party clearly hadn't returned from the rehearsal dinner yet. It was warm and inviting, though, the fire crackling in the fireplace, the furniture in the common room empty, but fresh. Somebody had gone through and fluffed the pillows, wiped down the tables, and added a vase of fresh flowers in reds and whites and silver accents, which she recognized as coming from Bunches, the flower shop down the block from Whimsy.

She slipped off her coat and hung it up and was kicking the snow off her shoes when Liz came in. She'd changed and was now wearing jeans, a white T-shirt, and a red cardigan sweater. Her blond hair was pulled back in a ponytail, which Cori liked because you could see Liz's sharp cheekbones. Her mascara looked new, making her blue eyes pop, and she was smiling. Refreshed.

"How're you doing?" Liz asked quietly as she approached Cori and ran a hand down her arm.

Cori made a swirling motion near her temple. "Bit of a jumble up here, but I'm okay."

"I can only imagine."

A weak smile was all she had to offer, but she could admit, at least in her head, that Liz's touch made her feel the tiniest bit better. "What needs to be done?"

"Well, Lauren's in the kitchen making the desserts, so she needs us to get the dining room ready."

Cori nodded and they got to work.

This was the kind of work she needed. She realized it as soon as she pulled out the first stack of small plates. Busy work, her mom would call it. Something she could do well without expending too much mental energy, which was good because she didn't feel like she had any to spare. But this stuff, she knew. Small plates and coffee cups with saucers. Silver forks and dessert spoons and linen napkins. Crystal champagne flutes. All surrounded by twinkle lights and evergreen boughs and mistletoe and the scents of balsam and cedar and cranberries. Liz was watching her. She was very aware of those eyes on her, and every time they passed, Liz would touch her in some way. A hand on her arm, fingers across her shoulder, a gentle bump of the hip. Cori understood then that it was Liz's way of helping. Of grounding her. Touch. Cori didn't hate that. Not even a little.

And then a blast of cold air hit, followed by a burst of conversation, laughter, and the stomping of feet. The bridal party had returned, and Cori forced herself to smile. It was the Christmas season, there was going to be a wedding tomorrow, and these people deserved better than her moping around, worried about her own crap.

Lauren came out of the kitchen carrying a tray of desserts that looked like she'd ordered them in. "Heads up. Coming through," she quipped on her way to the table. A New York style cheesecake was dripping with cherries and sauce. Several ramekins were lined up next to it, and when Lauren clicked a tiny blowtorch, Cori realized she was looking at crème brûlée.

"Holy shit, Lauren," she murmured. "This stuff looks amazing."

"You should see these fruit tarts," Liz said, carrying a second tray. She set it down and began unloading the tarts onto the table just as some of the guests began to filter into the room.

"Wow! This looks *uh-mazing*." The woman was clearly overserved, Cori thought, noting her slightly slurred words and wobbly balance. Others followed her in, the groom, some of the groomsmen and bridesmaids, all laughing and chatting and happy. "Look at this stuff, J," she said to the guy Cori remembered was Justin, Liz's ex.

"I see it," he said, then glanced up and met Liz's eye across the table. She smiled at him and he gave her a weak grimace as he held his fiancée's arm, clearly steadying her.

"Isn't it gorgeous?" She swayed a little, but caught herself with a hand flat on the table. "Gorgeous." Her gaze traveled the room, and Cori watched as it stopped on each dessert, the twinkle lights, the bottles of champagne chilling in ice buckets, the mistletoe. Then the tall bridesmaid with blond hair was next to her.

Cori caught Liz's eye across the table and raised her eyebrows in silent question. Liz rolled her lips in and bit down on them, obviously stifling a grin.

"Champagne time," the bride said—what was her name again?—and she was loud about it.

"Maybe you should ease up a little bit, Regina," the quiet bridesmaid said to the bride—Regina! that was it!—and Cori only heard her because they were a mere foot away. "You had a lot at dinner."

"What do you care?" Regina snapped at her, and the quiet one blinked at her, then simply shook her head and walked to the other side of the room. Without missing a beat, Regina's smile returned and she was raving about the desserts again. Using her finger, she snagged a cherry off the cheesecake before Justin could stop her. He grabbed her hand after she slid her finger out of her mouth.

"Sweetie, how about we use forks and dishes?"

Regina giggled. "Oops." Then louder, she called out, "Sorry, Lauren!"

"No worries," came Lauren's reply, but Cori couldn't see where she was.

Cori inched her way back until she was near the doorway and in no danger of being trampled by the intoxicated and happy bridal party for standing between it and its sugar and alcohol.

And then Liz was next to her. They stood and watched, shoulder to shoulder, and Cori felt more relaxed than she had all day.

She leaned close to Liz and whispered, "I think the bride is drunk."

"What gave you that idea? That she can't stand up, that her volume is set on stun, or that she keeps sticking her finger in all the desserts?"

"Yes."

Bridal party members sat and ate dessert. Corks popped and champagne fizzed into the crystal flutes. Liz and Cori stood nearby in case anything was needed and watched.

"You doing okay?" Liz asked, leaning close. She smelled like cinnamon and cloves for some reason, and Cori liked it. A lot.

She nodded, but also lifted one shoulder. "So far." And before she could elaborate, Regina's voice boomed through the room.

"Hey, you guys are under the mistletoe *again*."

And then everybody was looking at them. Cori felt like they were under a microscope. The bride and her bridesmaids and Justin and his groomsmen and even Lauren were staring.

She glanced at Liz, who wore that cute little half smile Cori was getting used to. The one that pulled one corner of her mouth up just a tiny bit and made it seem like she was smiling only for Cori.

"Yeah, kiss her like you mean it." That came from Lauren, who was still staring. Liz held her gaze across the room for a moment and it was charged with something Cori couldn't quite put her finger on. Anger? Challenge? Another beat went by, and it felt like the entire room had frozen, though Cori was sure that was just her imagination. Wasn't it? And then Liz was looking at her again, and she stepped in close and took Cori's face in both hands. And then she kissed her.

Like, *kissed* her, kissed her.

You know how they say *The world faded away*? That's exactly what happened for Cori. All the sound went muted and then silent, the only sound her own blood rushing in her ears. The rest of the world blurred, and the only person in focus was Liz. Liz's creamy smooth face. Liz's soft azure eyes. Liz's full glossy lips. Cori's eyes drifted closed as Liz's mouth pressed to hers, softly at first. Tentatively. Her lips moved over Cori's, and Cori felt her own hands drift up to settle on Liz's hips. She moved her own lips against Liz's and then Liz was requesting entry. Cori didn't hesitate. Her lips parted and Liz's tongue slid in and oh my God, were there fireworks? Because Cori was sure she heard small explosions, saw colors behind her eyelids as her fingers tightened and pulled Liz closer.

The sound came rushing back, so loudly that it shocked Cori, and her eyes flew open. Liz was smiling at her, but it was...off. Somehow. Cori couldn't pinpoint what it was. But the room was loud with the cheers and applause of the bridal party. Cori felt her face heat up as she glanced around, her eyes landing on Lauren, who looked, well, disappointed if she had to give it a label.

And then, just like that, everybody went back to whatever they'd been doing before The Kiss, as Cori's brain now called it, complete with capital letters. Everybody went back to normal.

Except Cori.

Because normal didn't exist for her anymore.

CHAPTER FOURTEEN

B rennan House was abuzz. With activity. With an electric energy.
The excitement in the air was palpable.

It was the big day.

Liz was tired. She'd barely slept, her brain keeping her awake and
tossing and turning over that kiss. What the hell had she been thinking,
kissing Cori like that?

Not that it was bad.

Because it wasn't.

It was amazing. Sensual. Hot. Sexy.

They'd had no time to talk about it, though. The celebration had
gotten rowdier, and then Cori'd had to go home to her animals, and Liz
had to stay to help Lauren.

There were bridal party members milling all around Brennan
House, and Liz had no time to mull over last night. There was too much
to do. And Cori would be here later. She could—no, she *should*—talk
to her then.

The common area was filled with people, some members of the
bridal party, and some who were just guests of the wedding but wanted
to pop in to say hi. Champagne and wine were already flowing as
people sat around the fireplace and chatted. Tanner sat in a corner with
her hair and makeup done, in a robe, but she was smiling, and Liz was
glad to see that, smiled back at her. A couple other bridesmaids were
also in full makeup, hair, and bathrobes and were laughing at a story
somebody was telling. Regina appeared at the top of the stairs, also in a
robe, her complexion slightly drawn, like she was *this close* to throwing

up. Tanner saw her, then met Liz's gaze with her own grimace, set down her glass, and headed upstairs, presumably to help her stepsister, which surprised Liz. She watched as Tanner disappeared up the stairs, then turned and walked right smack into a solid chest. She looked up into Justin's smiling eyes.

"Whoa, well hi there," he said, his hands on her upper arms to steady her. He was smiling and he smelled great. Woodsy with a little spice.

"What are you doing here?" she asked. "It's your wedding day. You can't see the bride!" She pushed against him until he was walking backward into the dining room and laughing at her.

"I can't find my wallet," he said. "I think I might've left it—aha!" He pointed at the sideboard where a black leather wallet sat as if waiting to be found. He crossed the room, grabbed it, and slid it into his back pocket.

"Nervous?" Liz asked him, as she took in his outfit for the first time. His tux was traditional black. Underneath it were a silver vest and tie. His dark hair was styled perfectly, and he was clean-shaven.

He shook his head. "Nah. I'm ready." And he was. She could tell by the look in his eyes. It might have been several years since they'd seen each other, but she remembered a lot about him, and one of those things was how easy it was to read his feelings just by looking at his eyes.

"Well, you look fantastic," she said and meant it. "Regina is a lucky woman." She meant that, too. "I saw her a couple minutes ago. Her makeup and hair are gorgeous and she *does* look nervous."

Justin chuckled. "Yeah. She definitely is. There was so much planning. Man, I don't know how you women do it."

Not rolling her eyes at such a guy statement was no easy feat, but she managed.

"Speaking of women, how's things with you and Cori? Looked like they were pretty good last night."

"Yeah, um, they're good. Things are good. We're good." *Yes, please say the word* good *one more time, Liz*, she admonished herself as she internally rolled her eyes. *That's convincing.*

"Yeah? I'm glad to hear that. You deserve to be happy." He grimaced and shook his head. "Man, I wish I could remember her. You're sure she went to school with us?"

"I'm pretty sure that *she's* sure she did."

He laughed at that. "I mean, she would know, right?"

"She would."

"How long you been seeing her?"

She shook her head. "Not long. It's pretty new." Not a lie.

"And you said your job is going well?"

"Mm-hmm." Yeah, she was lying now, openly lying about both her job and her relationship—neither of which existed—to a guy she hadn't seen in years. God, what the hell was wrong with her? She cleared her throat and jerked a thumb over her shoulder. "I should probably go see if Lauren needs any help back there."

"Oh! Sure. Sure."

"And you need to get out of here. Use the back door."

He gave her a sheepish grin and did as he was told. She watched him go, her heart warm and full at seeing him so happy. She made her way through to the kitchen where Lauren was putting together what looked like a large cheese board.

"Hey, you doing charcuterie now?" she asked as she grabbed a bottle of water out of the fridge.

"Yep." Lauren didn't look up.

"How come? The wedding is catered."

Lauren lifted a shoulder, still not looking at her. "I want them to put something in their stomach while they're drinking wine and champagne and God knows what else." Her voice was matter-of-fact, as if she was answering a stranger.

Liz leaned her back against the counter that was directly in front of Lauren and cracked open her water. "How'd things go with Mr. Hot UPS Guy?" She watched in satisfaction as Lauren's entire face went pink. "Oh, I'm going to take that blush as, *It was super hot, Liz, thanks for asking, and yes we sucked face and I'm totally going to see him again.*"

Lauren continued to blush but also continued to arrange cheese and meat and olives and dried apricots.

Liz inhaled and let it out slowly, debating whether or not she should keep her mouth shut. But the whole thing with Cori and their kiss, not to mention Cori and the Annabelle thing, was taking up a lot of space in her head, and she decided to leave things with Lauren alone. For now. She pushed off the counter.

"Okay then. Gonna go see what Mom wants to do about today, what she needs. I'll meet you back here in time to do a final check." She didn't wait for a response, not that she'd have gotten one. Lauren's near-silent treatment was getting old, and she'd have to address it soon. She trudged through the snow to the cottage house to find her mother in the kitchen pouring herself some coffee. She was dressed in black pants and a white shirt, and even wore makeup. "Look at you, all ready to go," she said.

Her mother held her arms out and did a little spin. "I want to help. I'm feeling great and I finished my book, so..." She gestured to the Nora Roberts book on the table.

"Ooh," Liz said. "Lemme guess—romance and intrigue in the mountains?"

"Nope," her mother replied, then took a sip of her coffee.

"Romance and intrigue in a castle?"

"Nope."

"Romance and intrigue on an island?"

"Ding, ding, ding!" Her mother laughed. "How are things over there?" She used her chin to point in the direction of Brennan House.

"All under control. Lauren makes charcuterie boards now?"

"She does. She keeps branching out." The pride in her mother's voice was evident.

Liz nodded. She wanted to address the obvious tension between her and her sister but also didn't.

"Should be a fun wedding. Lots of out-of-towners, but also lots of locals. Justin's family, friends of his parents. Actually, I think Cori's parents will be here."

"Oh yeah?"

Her mother nodded, then watched Liz's face over the rim of her mug as she took another sip. "I like her. Cori. I can't say I'm not surprised by you two as a couple, but I'm happy for you. Both of you." Her smile was tender, and it made Liz's stomach roil.

"Thanks, Mom. Yeah, she's great." She was quiet for a beat, then said, "She's struggling a bit, to be honest. I can't tell you with what because it's not my place. Suffice it to say that she found something out about her family and it has shocked her to her core."

"Wow, that sounds like a lot. Is everybody okay? I mean, I know you can't give me details, but…nobody's sick or anything, right? Barb and David are all right?"

"They're fine, yeah. Wait, you know them?"

Her mother let a small snort go. "Honey, this town is about the size of a walnut shell. Everybody knows everybody. I don't know the Strattons well, but yes, I know them."

"How long have you known them?"

Her mother pursed her lips as she thought. "Well, they already had Cori when I met them…and I think the next kid, too. One of the boys."

Liz nodded. "Got it." She sipped again as they were quiet for a moment, needing to change the subject. Then her voice went soft. "Hey, Mama? What *is* going on with you and Dad?" No snark this time. No sarcasm. Just genuine curiosity.

"I honestly don't know how to answer that," her mother said, but the tender smile and the softness around her eyes and the light color in her cheeks told Liz all she needed to know. Apparently, everybody was blushing lately.

"Well, whatever it is, I'm glad *you're* happy." She repeated her mother's words back to her and took another swig of her water. "And if you need me to kick his ass, just say the word."

Her mother laughed at that, which made Liz happy. Anytime she could make her mother laugh, she considered it a win. She remembered when her father had first left, how sad her mom had been. Liz had taken every single opportunity she saw to try to get her to smile. Jokes. Pratfalls. Funny sketches. Anything.

Suddenly, her mother leaned forward and lowered her voice to a conspiratorial tone. "Hey, how do you think things went with the sexy UPS guy?"

Liz shook her head and shrugged. "I have no idea. I asked, and she blushed like crazy but didn't say anything. Not that she ever says anything to me anymore. She clearly hates me, and I don't know why."

Her mother smiled but tipped her head in what was clearly pity. "She doesn't hate you."

"I think you're wrong about that." She shrugged to show how much the thing that was really bothering her didn't bother her. "It's… whatever." She pushed herself to her feet. "What do you need? Anything? Did you take your meds? Are you sore?"

"That was a lot of questions at once. Let me see." Her mom squinted, then ticked off the answers on her fingers. "Nothing. No. Yes. Hardly at all anymore." When Liz smiled and rolled her eyes good-naturedly, her mother added, "How's it going at the house? Lauren says it's fine. I'm ready to work. Should we head over to the barn and make sure nobody needs anything?"

"Only if you promise me you'll take it easy today and not overdo it."

Her mother made a *pfft* sound. "Please. I've rested enough. I'm fine."

"Are you sore?"

"No. I already answered that one."

"So, if I come poke you in your stomach, you'd be fine with that?"

"Yup."

Liz headed toward her with her pointer finger out. Her mother let her get alarmingly close before bursting into laughter and catching her finger with one hand.

"Okay, okay! I'm a little sore still."

"Mm-hmm. Just as I suspected. You go easy."

"Yes, ma'am." Her mother shot her a salute.

"Honestly, though, Lauren's been covering stuff pretty well." She didn't add that she hadn't been as much help as she should've been.

"She's very good at running the place. Between you and me, I'm a little sad that she hasn't needed me more." Her mom put on an exaggerated pouty lip that made Liz laugh.

"Bodes well for your retirement."

Her mother gasped and took a playful swing at her. "That's not for years and years and years."

"Mm-hmm."

She left her mother in the kitchen and headed down to the basement. She was exhausted mentally, something she only just now realized. So much in her brain. But there was no time to rest. She needed to put on her black pants and white shirt like her mother's and Lauren's, so she could be identified as somebody who could help if need be. She was buttoning her shirt when her phone pinged, announcing a text. It was April, checking in.

How's it going? Missing u

How was it going? What exactly could she say to April? She started typing.

Going great. Surrounded by an ex and his bride-to-be, a fake girlfriend, and a sister that hates me. Oh, and my parents are fucking.

She barked a laugh and added an eggplant emoji, but then deleted the whole thing before she accidentally sent it. The phone dropped to the bed as she groaned, thinking about so many things at once. Her parents. Her sister. Justin and his wedding. Cori's situation. Cori in general. Cori...

"Gah!" She let out the groan as she pulled her hair back into a ponytail, then dusted on some makeup and touched up her mascara. She was going to be on today. She was going to set her own shit aside for once. She felt a sudden determination that was unfamiliar to her. This mess she was in was of her own making, and it was time to put it on a shelf and focus on other people and other things for the day. Helping her sister. Taking care of the guests for her family's business. Sending out good thoughts to Justin and his bride. Sending love and strength to Cori as she dealt with her own stuff.

She picked the phone back up and sent off a quick text to April.

Going okay. Trying to get my shit together. You know how bad I am at that. She followed that with a smiley and an eye rolling emoji, then added *I miss you too.*

Sliding her phone into her back pocket, she checked her look in the mirror, gave one nod of approval, and took the steps two at a time.

Wedding bells were ringing.

❖

Cori had headed straight to the barn that morning.

Not because she was avoiding Liz, but because she wanted to double-check all the things she'd prepared there—the twinkle lights, the candles, the centerpieces. Okay, fine, and also because she was avoiding Liz.

That kiss had kept her up for much of the night, and honestly it was a stressor she didn't need right now because she was trying to figure out how the fuck to talk to her parents about Annabelle and what she'd found out.

She'd been awake at three that morning, so she'd made herself a cup of tea and reread the journals, specifically the entries about Annabelle having a child. And then she read them again. And then she read them again. Because maybe she was wrong. It was possible. Maybe she was misinterpreting the whole thing and it was all just a big misunderstanding. That was possible, right?

She let out a little snort as she climbed a stepladder and straightened a string of lights that had fallen off their hook at some point. No, it wasn't possible. There was no other way to interpret what she'd read. And she'd very nearly accepted it. Talking to her parents about it? To Suzanne? Yeah, that was a whole other level of stress. How the hell did you ask your mother why she'd never told you that she wasn't actually your mother, but that the woman who you looked up to your entire teenage life was?

Her brain was a mess, a jumble of memories she was reinterpreting and conversations from the past that took on new meanings now, and secrets…God, the secrets. The *lies*.

"Looks fabulous," a voice said from below her.

She glanced down at Mrs. Brennan, and it was the first time she realized how much Liz looked like her mother. Same hair. Same eyes. Same skin tone. Her voice was even similar. Cori didn't look a thing like her mother, and now she knew why.

"Thanks," she said. "Is it straight?"

"Perfect." Mrs. Brennan held the ladder as Cori climbed down, then gave her a sheepish grin. "Can't help it. Moms always think their kids are gonna fall. Then they think everybody's kids are gonna fall. It's built in. You'll see."

She felt Mrs. Brennan's hand on the small of her back as she stepped off the last step. She folded the ladder and took a look around. The barn was gorgeous, large and open and rustic, but also quite modern. The wood was an aged, distressed-looking brown, the grain clearly visible. The lighting consisted of six large chandeliers that hung from the high ceilings, tall beams and rafters giving the place its rustic feel. The floor was also wood, and windows all around let in a ton of natural light. One end was home to an enormous floor to ceiling fireplace made of river rock, and Lauren was squatting in front of it, stoking the flames. Next to it stood a huge Christmas tree strung with white lights, with a glowing silver star on top. Rows of tables were covered in white linen tablecloths, the centerpieces made of red and white flowers with silver accents, designed to match the color scheme of the bridal party. Various people milled around in different levels of uniform, some from the caterer, some from the florist, some from the band. It was busy and festive, and despite her swimming head, Cori couldn't help but smile.

"This really is a gorgeous place for a wedding," she said softly.

Mrs. Brennan nodded, her gaze following the others around as if they were little worker bees. "It really is, right?"

"Was this your vision for the place when you first opened?"

A tip of the head, one way, then the other. "More or less, yeah. The barn wasn't part of my original plan. Just the B-and-B. But the first time somebody asked about getting married here in the winter, the idea formed and I ran with it." She turned sparkling blue eyes so much like Liz's toward her. "Kind of proud of the place, not gonna lie."

Cori smiled back at her. "You should be. It's beautiful. I'd get married here." The words slipped out before she thought about them.

"Maybe you will," Mrs. Brennan said with a waggle of her eyebrows. Then she pointed at somebody and raised her voice to be heard. "No, over there. That goes over there." And she was off, leaving Cori standing there thinking about getting married right here. But to whom?

Yeah, that wasn't something she had room in her brain for right now. Nope. She gave her head a hard shake and got back to work.

❖

It was just about time.

The guests were seated. The pastor was standing in his place. The string quartet was tucked in the corner warming up their instruments.

Justin stood next to the pastor with his best man, looking so handsome and so nervous and so filled with joy. His face made Liz smile and warmed her heart. She looked around at the setup. Why Regina wanted to get married in the snow was beyond her. Yes, it was pretty. You know what else it was? Freezing. But Brennan House had done dozens of weddings, and they didn't mess around. Her mother had seen to that. One thing about Kristin Brennan—when she set her mind on doing something, not only did it get done, it got done well. Portable heaters were spaced around the poured concrete area between Brennan House and the barn, and they kept the guests warm. Or warm enough. Thank goodness there was no wind today. Hopefully, the ceremony would go quickly and they could all adjourn to the barn. The barn, where there was a roaring fire. Her feet were cold, but it was her own fault for wearing the wrong socks, and it was too late for her to run back in and switch them, but she tossed a look of longing toward the house anyway. Her gaze landed on Cori, standing on the edge of the gathering near one of the heaters.

She was avoiding Liz. Liz understood that.

Well, *understood* was probably the wrong word. It was clear to her. Yeah. That made more sense. Cori was avoiding her, and it was probably because of their kiss.

Okay, so she'd gotten a little carried away with that, but it hadn't been on purpose, truly. She'd meant to simply kiss her, just like she'd done the first time they were under the mistletoe. But Justin was there. And Lauren was egging her on. And Regina was staring. And then Liz's lips touched Cori's and something had happened that she couldn't explain. The world went foggy, and all the sound was suddenly muted, and the feel of Cori's mouth under hers was like nothing she'd ever experienced. For those few short moments, it was like there was nobody else in the world except her and Cori and she never wanted to stop kissing her. Never.

And Cori kissed her back. *She kissed her back.* With gusto. There was no denying that.

And now she was avoiding her.

Liz sighed. Why did life have to be so goddamn complicated?

She gave herself a shake, and before she could think twice about it, she walked over to where Cori was standing and stood right next to her.

"Hi," she whispered and gave her a little shoulder bump.

"Hey," Cori whispered back but didn't look at her. Liz wanted to address that, but then the string quartet started to play, and suddenly, there was Regina, hand tucked in her father's elbow, eyes so wide Liz found herself wondering if she'd had too much caffeine. Or too much champagne. Or too much coke, because good God, she looked like she wanted to crawl out of her own skin.

There was a small guest list for the actual ceremony, including many people she didn't know, but also several that she recognized. The guy who owned Bucky's was there, as well as the Italian couple that owned Calzone's. Justin's parents were well-known in Crimson Valley, so it only made sense that many business owners were present. Cori's parents sat in the third row next to Suzanne from Whimsy. Liz was absently wondering which part-timer was minding the store when all the guests stood, and then Liz watched as Regina and her dad walked down the short aisle. He kissed her cheek and passed her off to Justin, whose look of happiness clouded slightly with obvious concern. He whispered something softly to her, but Liz was too far back to hear.

The guests sat, and the pastor began his spiel, and Liz was painfully aware of Cori standing next to her. She could literally feel her presence, sense her, smell her—she smelled like cinnamon today, and Liz wondered if she'd made any cinnamon candles recently. She wanted to turn and look at her, take her in, but knew this was not the time or the place.

She forced herself to pay attention to the ceremony because she'd have to scoot before it was over and meet Lauren, who was standing on the other side of the space, near the barn, but she wanted to see what she could.

The pastor was smiling as he said, "Should anyone present know of any reason that this couple should not be joined in holy matrimony, speak now or forever hold your peace," and Liz found herself wondering if anybody had ever actually spoken up, when somebody actually did.

Regina.

"I have a reason."

Her voice was small, so small that Liz barely heard her, and she snapped her gaze to Cori to see if she'd heard it. Cori's raised eyebrows said she clearly had.

Justin looked stunned. "What?"

The only sound from the guests was a soft murmur that rippled through the rows, as if they, too, were trying to hear.

"I don't think I'm ready to get married, Justin. I'm so sorry."

Justin ran a hand through his hair, clearly shocked, as was everybody else in the place. "I...I don't understand. I thought...I thought you loved me."

Regina put a hand on his arm. "Oh, I do. I absolutely do. I'm sure of that. I just..." Liz could actually see her swallow. "I want to be so

one hundred percent in, and I know I will be. I'm just not there yet."
She looked around, and her gaze landed on Liz and Cori, or at least
where they were standing, and she pointed in their direction. "I want us
to have what they have."

This time, the ripples became rumblings as the entire guest list
collectively turned and looked at Liz and Cori.

"What did she just say?" Cori asked.

"Um…" To say Liz was shocked was a colossal understatement.

"Don't you see how they look at each other?" Regina said, still
looking at them, still pointing. "I don't know that we look at each other
that way."

"Oh my God," Cori said, closing her eyes, and she began to slowly
shake her head. "Oh my God."

"I…" Justin seemed to be at a loss for words. "Baby, I do look at
you that way, don't I?"

"Like the sun rises and sets in my eyes?" Regina was still looking
at Liz and Cori. "Like I hung the moon? No, you don't. And what's
more, I don't look at you like that."

"Jesus Christ," came a voice from their right. Surprise zipped
through Liz's bloodstream. Lauren. "They're not even together,"
Lauren said, waving a dismissive hand in their direction. "They're
faking it. They're like a walking Hallmark movie. God, am I the only
one around here who pays attention?"

Well, that took the wind right out of Regina's sails for a moment
because everybody who was looking at her swiveled their heads to stare
at Liz and Cori instead.

"Oh God," Cori whispered.

"No…" Regina said, stricken.

"Unbelievable," Lauren said, breaking away from Liz's horrified
stare and stalking toward the barn.

"Is that true?" Justin asked, and his eyes were glued to Liz's. She
hesitated a second too long because it was Cori who spoke up.

"Yes. It's true. I'm so sorry." She turned to Liz and repeated her
apology. "I just can't anymore. The lies. I just…God, *the lies*." That
last line was delivered directly to her parents where they stood looking
on in confusion. And then she was headed out, back toward the parking
area, people still staring, still murmuring, still confused.

It was Justin who saved the day, as he turned to Regina and took both her hands in his.

"Listen to me," he said and waited until she met his gaze. "I love you. I've never loved anybody more. But if you have doubts or you're not ready for this step, then we'll wait." He shrugged like it was the simplest thing in the world, like they weren't standing in the middle of a twenty-thousand-dollar wedding that they were about to call off. No big deal. "All that matters to me is that you're happy. I need you to understand that, okay?" He slowed down and enunciated each word. "I want you to be happy. Whatever you need, you got it. Just tell me. Okay?"

Regina's eyes had been welling up the whole time Justin spoke, and now those tears spilled over. She nodded. Vehemently. "Okay." And then she reached up and wrapped her arms around his neck and they hugged so tightly, it brought tears to Liz's eyes.

When they parted, Justin looked at the pastor. "I'm very sorry, Pastor, but I think we're gonna wait on this part." Then he turned to the crowd. "But you guys. Thank you so much for being here. Hopefully, we'll do it again sometime down the road. In the meantime, there's a whole lotta food, a whole lotta alcohol, and a great band over in the barn. Let's party!"

Just like that, the guests pivoted, moving through the rows of chairs to the left and heading for the barn. While Liz was sure some of that speed was because there was a roaring fire over there, she also suspected the bartenders were about to get inundated.

Her feet felt glued to the ground. She wanted to follow Cori, who she suspected was upset by more than just their deception being exposed. Cori's parents were still there, looking uncertain as to what they should do. Suzanne looked the most concerned, and when she met Liz's gaze over the nearly empty rows of chairs, Liz swallowed, finding it hard to get a handle on her own emotions. They swirled around like her head was a blender—shock, concern, shame, anger—all of them spinning so fast, she couldn't seem to grab any one of them to allow herself to focus.

That's when she saw Lauren walking across the yard from the barn toward Brennan House.

She didn't even think about it. She knew she needed to talk to her parents and explain. Explain to Justin—she owed him that. But both those thoughts were shoved aside as she very nearly chased her sister across the yard, through the back door, and into the kitchen.

"What is your problem?" she blurted at Lauren the second they were both standing in the kitchen.

Lauren acted like she didn't hear, pulling cream out of the refrigerator, then pouring it into a white pitcher on the counter.

"You have been just *rotten* to me since I got home." Liz felt her anger go from a simmer to a bubble. "You're dismissive. You're snarky. You're downright *mean*. What the hell did I do to you?"

Lauren stopped pouring, placed both palms on the counter, and seemed to give herself a moment. Liz could see her jaw muscles working as she ground her teeth. When she finally spoke, her voice was level and steely. "Do you have any idea what it's like to be your little sister? To live in your shadow? The shadow of Elizabeth the Golden Child? The homecoming queen? The straight-A student? I've spent my whole life there. In the shade. In the dark. Not being seen because everybody's too busy looking at you." She stopped for a beat and wet her lips. Liz was too stunned to speak, and Lauren went on. "I was so relieved when you left for Syracuse, and even more relieved when you decided to stay there. I was able to breathe. I worked hard on this place. Helped Mom make it successful. Earned myself a reputation. A good one." She inhaled slowly, then let it out. "And then you came breezing back, and all anybody could talk about was Liz this and Liz that and I could feel that shadow starting to block out my sun. Again." Finally, she turned to meet Liz's gaze. "You're so selfish. You're so fucking selfish. You show up late for work here. You disappear all the time to do whatever you want, leaving me with all the work. Which isn't a big deal—I do all the work anyway. It's the principle, Liz. And then the Justin thing? The Cori thing? You always get what you want, even if you have to lie to get it. Jesus, what the fuck is wrong with you? Do you need attention that badly? Does it make you happy to hurt everybody who cares about you? What the actual fuck, Liz? Who the hell are you?"

She didn't wait for an answer. She grabbed the pitcher, pushed past Liz, and headed out the door, leaving her big sister standing there in stunned silence.

CHAPTER FIFTEEN

Cori knew she was in bad shape when even being in her workshop brought her no joy.

Whimsy had been pretty busy when she'd arrived, surprising her part-timer, who hadn't been expecting her back for another two or three hours. She didn't want to send the poor girl home and cause her to lose her hours—she was a college kid home for the holidays, trying to make money any way she could—so Cori simply nodded to her and headed straight through the store and back to her workshop, Bear on her heels.

She'd stood in front of the work surface, hands on her hips, but there wasn't a drop of creativity trying to emerge. Not one. She had hoped to silence her brain by making something, but it was clear now that wouldn't be happening. With a sigh, she dropped her hands and turned to the couch in the little lounge area, where she flopped down like her skeleton had suddenly liquified, facedown, one arm hanging off the side so she could pet Bear, who lay down on the floor right next to the couch, clearly concerned about her.

"What a fucking shit show of a day," she said quietly, not really to Bear, but since he was the only one there to listen, yeah, maybe to Bear. "I mean, I knew it would all come crashing down, but I had no idea it would crash so spectacularly, in front of a crowd. Wow."

Bear watched her face, tipping his head like he was actually listening to her.

"I don't know why I went along with it. Lying is always such a horrible idea. I knew better." She sighed a big, deep, bone-weary sigh, and then her phone buzzed in her pocket. She'd turned it to vibrate once the wedding had begun, and it had been buzzing pretty steadily since she'd left. With a groan, she pulled it out and glanced at the screen. Seven missed texts and three missed calls, all in some variation of her parents, Suzanne, and Liz.

She didn't read them. She didn't have it in her right now. She knew she couldn't wait too long because she wasn't hard to find and it would only be a matter of time before somebody came knock—

Knock, knock.

The person rapping on the door of her workshop didn't wait for a response. The door opened, and there was Suzanne. Still dressed in her wedding clothes, she looked very pretty, despite the obvious look of worry on her face.

"Hey," Suzanne said softly. "Can I come in?"

She'd never asked for entry before, so Cori knew this was about to be some kind of a heart-to-heart. Maybe it was better to just grab this bull by the horns. "Sure." She pushed herself up so she was sitting. Bear sat up, too, looking like he was preparing to moderate a debate, but was clearly on Cori's team.

Suzanne sat down in the beat-up chair that was angled toward the couch. "So." She slapped her hands on her thighs and rubbed them slowly up and down her navy-blue dress pants. "Can't say I've ever been to a wedding quite like that before." Her laugh was a clear attempt at lightening the mood, but it just sounded forced. Which it clearly was.

Cori gave her a small smile, but that was about all she could manage.

"I guess the fake relationship is done, then?" Suzanne asked.

"Seems like it."

"Have you talked to Liz since?"

Cori shook her head.

Suzanne nodded slowly and looked around, like she was gathering up her nerve. "I kind of think there's more to this"—she waved her hand in Cori's general direction—"sad, brooding thing than that, though."

Cori swallowed but couldn't look at her, and that irritated her, so she forced herself to make eye contact.

"I know which journals you have."

The statement was surprising and also not at all. While she'd never actually witnessed Suzanne reading Annabelle's journals, it only made sense that she would, every so often. They'd been partners. Lovers. Why *wouldn't* Suzanne want to read them now and then?

"Annabelle was my mother," Cori said, startled by the factual tone of her own voice.

"Yes." And because Suzanne didn't hesitate, didn't falter, simply answered the question, it was like a gag order had been lifted and Cori suddenly had so many things to say, so many questions to ask, starting with the most obvious and likely the most expected.

"Why didn't anybody tell me?"

Suzanne glanced down at her feet, then back up. "Annabelle wanted to." Then she wiped her hand in front of her face like she was erasing her words. "No. I don't want to do that. I don't want to sound like I'm defending her—or me—and blaming your parents. I'm not. It was their call. And your mother told me she was planning to tell you when you were an adult."

Cori raised her eyebrows and held out her hands as if presenting herself. "Hello? Thirty-four now. How much more of an adult do I have to be?"

"I know. I'm sorry. It just...once Annabelle was gone, I didn't feel it was my place."

"I'm not okay with that answer."

"I know." A beat passed, and Suzanne's voice was barely above a whisper. "It's the only one I have. I'm sorry."

Cori shook her head but had no more words.

Suzanne waited quietly for what felt like a long time. Finally realizing she wasn't going to get any more from Cori, she apologized one more time, pushed to her feet, and left her alone.

Cori counted to ten after the door had closed, just to make sure she wasn't coming back. It was only after that she allowed herself to cry.

❖

"Fake? The whole thing was fake?" Liz's mother and father stood in the kitchen where Liz had been since Lauren had unloaded on her and then stomped off. She hadn't been able to move. It was like her shoes had grown roots and burrowed into the linoleum, and this was where she lived now.

"I'm sorry," she said, surprised by her mother's ire.

"You're sorry?" Her mother's eyes flashed. "You're sorry?"

Her father calmed her mother with a hand on her upper arm. He pulled her gently back, and they switched places so he was standing in the front, her mother tucked behind him as if she needed to be held there.

"Can you tell us why?" her father asked. He was much calmer than her mother, his voice soft, his eyes gentle. "Why would you need to fake a relationship?"

Liz's eyes were swimming. They had been since Lauren left, tears brimming. Now, she blinked and they spilled over. "I don't know," she said on a whisper, feeling like a four-year-old who didn't have the language to explain exactly why she'd done something, so she just claimed ignorance instead.

"Was it the stuff we talked about?" her dad asked. "The failure stuff?"

A nod, and then some words arrived. Thank God. "I was already feeling awful about myself, about my life, about how not successful I am at my age. And then there was Justin, about to get married, happy in his career, in his life, and he asked about my love life and Cori was right there and...I didn't even think. I just grabbed her and pretended we were together, and then I realized we'd have to fake it for the entire week the bridal party was here and"—she grimaced as she looked at her father—"she agreed to play along and...we just—no, *I*. I just got carried away."

"And because of your *pretend* chemistry, Justin got left at the altar," her mother said, clearly disgusted with her, and that hit her right in the gut.

Her father held up a hand. "Now, hang on for a second." He shot her mother a look that clearly registered because her face relaxed a bit, and she gave him a subtle nod. "First of all, whether or not Liz and Cori have chemistry and whether or not it's fake, they are not responsible for what happened out there." He pointed in the general direction of the wedding, which had obviously kicked into some kind of high gear, given the beat of the bass that could be felt in the pit of Liz's stomach. Dancing had clearly ensued. "Second of all, regardless of everything I just said, you owe that boy an apology for lying to him. Third, speaking of apologies, you also owe one to Cori. Despite agreeing to go along, she got sucked into this blame thing, too. And fourth..." He stopped then and took a breath, as if the list had taken all the air from his lungs. "While we are disappointed and pretty confused as to why this was the path you chose to take, you know we still love you. Right?" He opened his arms.

That was it. A sob tore out of her, and she fell into her dad's embrace, telling him she was sorry over and over again. He held her and rubbed her back, and then she felt a kiss on her cheek. When she cracked open an eye, her mother was standing there. "Can I add one more thing?"

Liz swallowed and nodded and braced herself as she said, "Yeah."

Her mother lowered her voice to a whisper. "I'm not entirely convinced the chemistry was fake."

Liz felt her father's shoulder move as he let go of a small chuckle. "Yeah, I thought the same thing," he said.

Somehow—Liz didn't understand it at all—but somehow, that made things just a teeny tiny bit less horrible, and she hugged her father tighter.

Three hours later, and despite the ludicrous happenings at the altar, the wedding was shockingly in full swing. People were crowding the dance floor, and dinner had been eaten and enjoyed. The cake had been shared, despite not being cut by the bride and groom because they hadn't actually gotten hitched. Booze was flowing, and laughter filled the air, and Liz was fucking exhausted. She'd kept her head down, helped Lauren in every way humanly possible, as she tried to figure out how to patch things up with her sister. And now that all the food had been eaten, and music was being played, and slowly, oh so slowly, guests were beginning to leave, there was nothing more for Liz to do until they were all gone. She needed to sit. She needed to use the bathroom. She needed to change out of the shirt she was wearing, which she'd sweated through despite the steadily dropping temperature outside. She told Lauren she'd be right back—not that Lauren cared—and headed for the house, for the basement. Once in the bathroom, she checked her phone. Nothing from Cori—that was going to take some face time—but several texts from April. She owed her a call. But she wasn't up for it. She didn't think she could tell another person what had transpired. Not even April.

She changed her shirt, then went back out into the fray and hung back on the fringes, keeping her eyes peeled for messes to be cleaned up, guests who might need something, or any other thing she could take care of. Lauren was on the other side of the barn. Her mother was standing near the bar, chatting up one of the bartenders. Much as they'd tried to keep her from doing too much, she'd worked just as hard as the rest of them.

"There you are." A deep voice registered just as she felt a hand on her elbow. She turned to look into Justin's dark eyes, and any sense of calm she'd established flew right out the barn window, telling her she was on her own as it exited.

"Hi," she said and did her best to force a smile.

"So," he said, looking out over the crowd and then taking a sip of the drink in his hand, which looked like a scotch on the rocks. "Hell of a day, huh?" He'd lost his jacket and his tie and was now standing there in his dark pants, white shirt, and silver vest. His sleeves were rolled up to reveal his forearms, covered with dark hair. She watched his hands for a beat. She'd always loved his hands.

Pulling her gaze up to his, she said, "Understatement of the year. Possibly of the decade. Maybe even the century. Jury's still out."

They spent a moment watching people attempt the Macarena before he asked, "Are you okay, Lizzy? 'Cause it seems like you're struggling. And believe me, I'd know." He waved the hand holding his drink toward the dance floor, indicating Regina, who'd changed into leggings and an oversized T-shirt that hung off one shoulder, looking very much *not* like a bride. Or even a bride-to-be. The corners of his mouth turned down as he reminded her, "The woman I love and thought I was going to marry today decided she didn't want to marry me. And much as I understood everything she said, and even though I'm sure we will get married in the future, it hurt like a son of a bitch." He looked her in the eye. "So, I get struggling."

Liz nodded. "I guess you do, huh?" She took the scotch from his hand and took a slug, wincing as it burned its way down her throat. When she handed it back to him, she looked him in the eye. She owed him that. "I'm so sorry, Justin. I'm sorry I lied to you."

He made a *pfft* sound and lifted one shoulder.

"No," she said. "I'm serious. You didn't deserve that. At all. Don't ask me to explain because I'm not sure I get it myself, but please…just know that I'm really sorry."

He nodded, still watching the dance floor, and took a moment before he told her, "Regina doesn't believe it, you know."

"Doesn't believe what?"

"That you guys were faking it."

"Really?"

His eyes locked with hers. "Neither do I." Then he grinned that cat-that-ate-the-canary grin of his, kissed her cheek and said, "Gotta go dance with my not-bride-still-fiancée." And then he bounced his way to the dance floor, leaving her standing there with his words and his disbelief hanging in the air where he'd been standing.

CHAPTER SIXTEEN

It was almost weird the way Brennan House went from packed to the rafters to completely empty in the space of one day. Yesterday, the not-so-bridal party had spent the morning recovering from the night before. The group that had checked out was so incredibly subdued compared to the group that had checked in, it was almost laughable. Everybody was clearly exhausted, most of them hungover.

Regina, however, was all smiles. The happiest of the bunch. She walked around taller, like a weight had been lifted from her shoulders and she was able to stand up straight for the first time in months.

She'd surprised Liz by hugging her as she was checking out, thanking her for making her see things clearly. Liz had no idea what she'd done, but she hugged Regina back and wished her well.

Tanner had given her a soft smile on her way out the door, along with a little wave, and then they were all gone, and Liz spent the day with Mrs. Adler, cleaning the rooms, washing sheets, putting new ones on, and tidying up the first floor. It had been Lauren's day off, and she'd slept in, and then Liz had seen her car drive by the main house and onto the road, and she didn't see her again all day. She'd texted Cori several more times but had gotten no response back, and honestly, she was starting to get a little frustrated about that, but with Lauren gone and Liz not wanting to leave everything in her mother's hands quite yet, she'd been tethered to Brennan House for the day.

Now, it was Monday. Three rooms would be filled by the end of the day and four more tomorrow, as it was not only the holiday season but also ski season, and most people who stayed at Brennan house in December and January were there to ski. She'd checked in two guests, and the third wasn't due to arrive until the evening. She headed back to the kitchen where Lauren looked like she was working on a menu, her laptop open on the counter as she scrolled.

"Hey," Liz said.

Lauren glanced up at her and lifted her chin in what Liz assumed was a greeting, but then her gaze went back to her screen.

"Can I talk to you?" Liz swallowed and wondered if her sister could hear it. They hadn't spoken—aside from Lauren grunting a few commands at her—since the blowup on Saturday, and Liz was over the silence. "Please?"

Lauren sighed. It was quiet, but not quiet enough, and Liz heard it. "Sure." She closed the laptop, leaned against the counter behind her, and waited.

"I'm sorry," Liz began. Now that she was in it, she was having trouble finding the right words. "I mean, I know you're mad at my presence here and believe me, I didn't want to be here either, but I don't have a choice right now. If I could get out of your hair, I would."

Lauren was shaking her head. "I don't need you to do that."

Liz narrowed her eyes. "*Okay*," she said, drawing the word out. She thought for sure telling her sister she was leaving would help things, but she hadn't expected Lauren's response.

Lauren pushed herself off the counter. "I actually like having you home, believe it or not."

"I don't believe it," Liz said but added a quick bark of a laugh.

Lauren grinned. "Yeah, I've disguised that pretty well."

"You definitely have."

"You know what I really want?" Lauren asked, and with the question, she leaned forward slightly, her gaze steady on Liz's.

Liz shook her head.

"I want you to respect my job here. To respect what I do and respect the work I need you to do while you're here."

Okay, that wasn't what she was expecting. Not after Lauren unloaded about living in her shadow. She started to mention that, and only managed to get "But…" out before Lauren held up a hand, stopping any more words.

"I know. I know. I ran through it all with Isaac yesterday, and he helped me to understand that my issues with your success, whether in school or life or whatever, are mine. They're my issues, not yours."

Her voice softened. "You're my big sister, Lizzy. *Of course* I'm happy you're home. I've missed you."

Was Liz's head spinning? It sure felt like it was.

Lauren went on. "But, yeah, if you're gonna work here, I need you to *work here*. Okay? That's all. Mom's slowly sliding back in, but I don't want her to rush it, so I need your help." A beat went by, and she chuckled as she added, "I can see by the wide-eyed look on your face that this wasn't the conversation you were expecting to have." She laughed.

"No," Liz said with a soft laugh. She'd been braced for a fight. Or at least for some harsh words. She hadn't expected *I'm glad you're home*. At all. Not even a little.

"Also…" And here, Lauren glanced off into the room, then down at her feet. "I owe you an apology for what happened at the wedding. "I know that the truth is always the right path, but the middle of somebody's wedding is definitely not. I'm sorry. That was so not cool of me." She made a *yikes* face, and her cheeks went red, and Liz knew she was being absolutely sincere.

"It's okay," she said. "Despite the way it happened, it's probably better everything's out in the open. And I can definitely be better about the work. I'm here to help. Promise." She was talking to her sister. Really talking to her, and it felt like it had been years since they'd had a real conversation like this. She didn't want it to end. "So…Isaac, huh?" Lauren's face turned red so fast, Liz burst out laughing. "Oh wow. You really have a thing for this guy, huh?"

"Almost as big a thing for him as you have for Cori." Liz bit down on her bottom lip and it was Lauren's turn to laugh. "Yeah, I thought so. Nobody's that good an actress."

Denying it was useless. "Yeah," she said with a slow nod and a grimace. "But she hasn't returned my texts or my calls. She has some other things going on, a personal matter, but I wish she'd talk to me."

"You're gonna have to storm the castle."

Liz laughed because she'd been thinking the same thing. "I think you're right."

"Then go do it."

Liz tipped her head. "Excuse me, weren't you just saying I need to be more focused on my work here?"

"I was. And I'm the boss, and I'm giving you the rest of the day off." She made a shooing motion with her hand as she pulled her laptop open again. "Go. Go."

"Okay!" Liz said with a laugh. But in the doorway, she stopped and turned back.

"Oh my God, now what? I have things to do, Elizabeth."

Liz crossed the space between them in four steps and threw her arms around her sister, hugging her tightly. "Thank you," she whispered and gave her a kiss on the cheek.

Lauren looked her in the eye as she whispered back, "Welcome. Now go get the girl."

The snow had come down steadily all day, and it had gone from big, fluffy, slowly falling flakes to the wind picking up, whipping the snow sideways so it stung Liz's cheeks as she hurried from her car to the front door of Whimsy.

It always smelled so good in the store. She'd noticed it the very first time she'd come in. Was there an air freshener in some obscure location? Was it Cori's candle display that scented the whole place? She couldn't tell. But she always inhaled deeply within her first couple of steps in.

Suzanne was behind the register ringing out a customer. Bear was nowhere to be seen, and a scan of the shelves revealed Ernie sitting atop a shelf of knickknacks, likely waiting to scare the bejesus out of some poor unsuspecting customer. She met Suzanne's gaze, and Suzanne used her eyes to indicate the workshop. Liz gave her a nod and headed that way.

The door was closed, so she rapped lightly on it. When there was no answer, she rapped again. "Cori? It's me." Nothing. She knocked again. "Cori? It's Liz. Can we talk? Please?" Silence on the other side.

Liz sighed, not sure what to do. Could Cori have stepped out without telling Suzanne? She pulled her phone from her pocket and called Cori's number. A second later, ringing came from the other side of the door. She hung up and knocked again. No answer. She tried the knob. Locked. She blew out a breath of dejection. She was about to give up when Suzanne appeared next to her, eyebrows meeting above her nose in an expression that could only be described as irritation. Without saying a word, she stood on tiptoe, reached to the top of the trim above the door, and came down with a key. She handed it to Liz, then turned and went back to the shop.

"Okay then," Liz muttered and slid the key into the doorknob lock.

Cori was surprised when the door opened, judging from the way her whole body flinched. Liz closed it behind her and set the key down on a table. Cori glanced at it, frowned, and went back to whatever she was doing.

Bear got up from his bed and sauntered across to Liz, his fluffy tail wagging the whole time. She squatted down and lavished him with attention and kisses on his head for several minutes while she worked out what she wanted to say to Cori. Because she'd been so anxious to get here, she hadn't thought about what she'd say when she did.

And now, here she was.

"Hi," she ventured.

Cori didn't look up from her candles. "Hey."

"You haven't returned any of my texts. Or my calls. Or more texts." She went for a little humor, but fell far short.

"No."

Okay, so this was how it was going to go. Liz nodded slowly to herself. Cori had barely glanced at her so far, but when she had, Liz had noticed how exhausted she looked. Her face was drawn, her hair in a haphazard ponytail. She wore baggy pants and an old, worn-out sweatshirt, the sleeves pushed up to her elbows. She had wax melting and jars set out and was clearly making candles. Must've been how she kept her mind busy.

All right. Liz could get behind that. She gave Bear a final pat on his head, then pushed up her own sleeves, grabbed a jar from the shelf, and took the spot next to Cori. She said nothing when Cori's head turned and those dark eyes finally met hers. Liz felt her stomach clench at the amount of anguish she saw in them, but it was also clear Cori didn't want to talk yet. So Liz simply smiled, then looked to the shelf above them at the essential oils and made herself focus on the scent she wanted to put in her candle.

They worked silently for a long time. Liz lost track of how much. They simply made candles. Cori's stance—rigid and prickly when Liz had arrived—eased as time went on. Her shoulders dropped, and her face seemed to relax. That was good. Liz was grateful for even that small acceptance of her presence.

The knock on the door of the workshop startled both of them, and they flinched in tandem, which made Liz smile.

Suzanne stuck her head in. "Shop's closed up. I'm gonna leave this open for Ernie."

Holy crap, what time was it?

Liz pulled out her phone and glanced at it. Nearly nine thirty. They'd been working in silence for hours, just being in each other's presence.

"Okay. Thanks." It was all Cori said, but she attempted a smile and sent it Suzanne's way. Suzanne returned it, though hers was clearly pained.

Once Suzanne was gone and they heard her car start up outside the back wall of the building, Liz took in the work they'd done. "These look good," she said with a nod. "I should probably get home now, but I'll be back tomorrow." She didn't ask. She didn't check Cori's schedule. She just promised she'd return. Somehow, she understood this was the course to take.

Cori nodded and said, "Okay," very softly.

Liz rubbed her hand down Cori's arm, wanting to do so much more. Wrap her up in a tight hug. Kiss her cheek. Kiss her mouth. But something told her she needed to go slow right now. Take baby steps. So she gave her arm a gentle squeeze, gave Bear some love, and headed out the door. Once she was in her car and letting it warm up, she let out a long slow breath. God, that had been harder than she expected. She'd wanted to talk. To talk, to discuss everything that had happened, to hash it all out and maybe talk about next steps. Because Liz had ideas for next steps, and she was anxious to talk about them, to see where Cori stood after she heard them, but...

She shook her head and frowned. Cori was not in a place to talk about such things right now. Liz knew she'd been selfish from the second she'd returned to Crimson Valley a few weeks ago, and that needed to stop. She didn't know when it had happened, when she'd become so focused on her own crap at the expense of everybody else's, but Lauren had been right.

She shifted her car and headed home.

It was time for new leaves and turning them over.

❖

Cori listened to Liz's car as it pulled away. Only then did she let her eyes fill with tears. God, she was a mess. She felt like she'd been hit by a bus, which then had reversed and run over her again, just for good measure.

She was so angry.

Not an angry person by nature, this constant state of wanting to punch things, throw things, scream into the void, was new to her. She felt like a pressure cooker with no way to let the steam out, so it was just building and building and she was going to explode soon. She just didn't know when.

Liz's presence had calmed her somehow. That was unexpected. When she'd arrived, Cori had thought about asking her to leave. She didn't want to talk. She didn't want to go over things, discuss her situation with her parents or what a stupid idea it had been to pretend to be together. She didn't want to deal with any of it, and Liz was a talker, so Cori had been ready to send her packing.

But Liz had surprised her.

She'd been quiet. They'd made candles for hours, standing side by side, choosing colors and scents and textures without words.

It had been exactly what Cori hadn't known she'd needed.

She cleaned up her workspace and headed upstairs to her apartment, both Bear and Ernie following behind her. She was exhausted. Emotionally. Mentally. She'd spoken to her parents, and they'd been simultaneously sorry and defensive, and Cori had walked out midconversation. She was angry with Suzanne as well but couldn't avoid her due to the shop. So she'd basically told her to leave her alone and to keep her parents away for the time being.

A glance at her phone told her she had sixteen missed calls from her mother, and that's why she'd locked the door to her workshop. Her mother had come, knocked, left, come back, knocked some more, left. Cori found it interesting that Suzanne didn't give the key to her mother but gave it to Liz.

Liz.

She was coming back.

Cori felt her tension ease at the thought. Liz was coming back. Good.

Her stomach rumbled loudly, reminding her that she'd barely eaten all day. Funny how it growled to let her know she was hungry, but then revolted as soon as she ate anything of substance. With a sigh, she popped a slice of bread into the toaster.

Liz was coming back.

How was it that a simple statement of fact calmed her from the inside?

She had no idea, but it did. She buttered and ate the toast and had a cup of tea, and her stomach didn't send it all back up again, thank goodness.

Sleep had not been her friend the past couple of nights, despite her extreme level of exhaustion. She'd had trouble shutting off her mind, and it spun endlessly, wildly out of control, and she'd woken up just as tired as she'd been when she'd turned off the lights. Maybe, with some food in her tummy, tonight would be different.

She tidied up around the house, did her nightly things in the bathroom, and slid beneath the covers of her bed. Ernie settled on the pillow next to her, and Bear hopped up to lie against her hip. Her phone pinged an incoming text, and she sighed. Probably her mother. Again.

But it wasn't. It was Liz.

Sweet dreams, Cori. I'll see you tomorrow. Followed by one simple heart emoji.

Cori let out a long, slow breath of relaxation.

Liz was coming back.

CHAPTER SEVENTEEN

For the next three nights, Liz went to Whimsy as soon as things were taken care of at Brennan House. Her mother was back to almost full-time, and Liz never left without checking with Lauren first to make sure she wasn't needed.

"What's happening over there in candle land?" Lauren asked her in the kitchen on Thursday night as Liz got her coat and boots on.

"Candles. Candles are happening."

Their mother was loading the dinner dishes into the dishwasher and turned to look at them, clearly taking in the conversation.

"That's it?" Lauren asked.

"Yeah. That's it." Liz gave a nod, surprisingly okay with the way things were going. "It's what she needs."

Lauren nodded, her expression one of approval. "Cool. For how long?"

Liz lifted one shoulder as she pulled her hat on. "For as long as it takes." She glanced at her mother, who gave her a smile and a subtle nod. Then she headed out to her running car, which was warm when she got in.

Suzanne had worked the early shift, so Cori was behind the register when Liz got to Whimsy. They'd fallen into a bit of a routine that week. If Cori wasn't working, Liz would just head back to the workshop. If she was, Liz would hang around the store, dusting shelves or neatening displays, not because Cori asked her to, but because she wanted to help. Once the store was closed, they'd head back to the workshop to work on whatever craft Cori had going.

Something Liz had learned: the number of candles Cori made was directly proportional to the amount of stress she was feeling. She'd made dozens on Monday. Now that it was Thursday, she was down to a handful, and that filled Liz with relief. Clearly, Cori was processing. While Liz wished she'd do some of it out loud, she was glad nonetheless.

They were working on a few more holiday candles—they'd been flying off the shelves this past week, tourists wanting something not only to remind them of their stay in Crimson Valley, but also for the holiday—and Cori had thanked Liz more than once for her help.

"These smell so good," Liz said for about the hundredth time since they'd started using their usual blend of evergreen and cranberry oil three nights ago.

Cori gave a small laugh, a new sound that warmed Liz's heart. "You say that every time you come in here."

"Because it's true." She held a finished candle under Cori's nose as if she'd never smelled it before. "Sniff. Isn't it divine? So Christmassy?"

"*So* Christmassy." Cori rolled her eyes teasingly.

"It's less than two weeks away. Christmas."

Cori let go of a small sigh. "Yeah." Liz thought that was going to be as far as the conversation went, but then Cori said, "Do you have any traditions?"

"For the holidays? A few small ones, yeah. My mom always buys us matching pajamas."

Cori laughed. "Even now? For her grown-ass daughters?"

"Even now. She will give them to us on the twenty-third so we can wash them and then wear them on Christmas morning. On Christmas Eve, we have dinner together and open one gift, then the rest in the morning when we stay in our jammies all day and eat like pigs and drink mimosas and are just...together." She smiled, a warmth filling her heart at the memories. "I honestly haven't even really thought about Christmas lately. I need to get some gifts. Yikes." She let a beat go by, then asked, "What about you?"

"We have some traditions, yeah. Similar to yours." She glanced at Liz. "Without the cute jammies."

"Don't pretend you're not jealous."

"I usually have dinner with my family, but I'm also usually the first to leave."

"How come?"

"They're loud."

Liz laughed. "Ah, got it."

"And then I come home and hang with my boys. Sometimes I watch a movie. Sometimes I play music. Sometimes we just sit and watch the snow."

"Holiday movies?"

"Yup."

"What ones do you like?"

Cori poured some melted ivory-colored wax into three jars. "Oh, I like a lot. *Elf*, *A Christmas Story*, *It's a Wonderful Life*, *The Polar Express*, *The Grinch*, *The Family Stone*, *The Holiday*...so many. It depends on my mood which one I pick."

"Those are all good ones. *Die Hard*?"

"I am not debating whether *Die Hard* is a Christmas movie with you."

"Of course not. 'Cause it is." Liz shrugged and made a show of squinting at the bottles of oil above them.

Cori pushed playfully at her. "You know what I wish? I wish Crimson Valley had a movie theater. I know driving a half hour to the nearest one isn't terribly far, but I'd love to watch one of my favorite Christmas movies in a movie theater setting, you know?"

Liz nodded. "I do. That'd be awesome, wouldn't it?"

"Oh well." Cori refilled the melter with more wax pellets. "A couple more?" She looked at Liz, eyebrows raised expectantly.

"Let's do it." They got to work on one more batch of candles. Liz waited until they were stirring in a deep indigo shard before she asked her question. "Will you be okay for Christmas? I mean, I don't know where you're at with your parents." It touched on the subject they'd been avoiding, and Liz found herself bracing for Cori to shut down.

She didn't. Cori inhaled a deep breath and seemed to hold it for a few seconds before letting it out slowly. "Yeah, it'll be okay. We haven't really gotten into it because I told my mom I just needed some time to sit with everything. It took her texting me a kajillion times and me not answering before she accepted that." She gave Liz a grimace that might have been a little self-deprecating. "But she loves the holidays so much, and I don't want to completely ruin them for her. So, I'll be there. I'll do my best."

It wouldn't be easy for her. Liz knew that.

"Well, I'll be around if you need to text or call or escape or whatever."

Cori's smile was soft. She'd been doing that a bit more lately, smiling softly. Not her usual big, bright smile, but after the past few days, Liz would take whatever smile she was willing to give. "Thanks. I'll keep that in mind."

As they continued to work, a tiny seed of an idea formed in Liz's brain, and she tucked it away to examine later. For now, she just wanted to bask in the comfort that was being creative in Cori's workshop.

❖

Cori didn't see Liz on Christmas Day.

She hadn't expected to, but it still bummed her out that she didn't. They'd texted. A lot. Cori had managed not to fight with her parents, but only because of the day. She was still grappling with her lineage, wanted to talk about it, but didn't know how without getting overly emotional.

The twenty-sixth of December was sunny, but super cold, unsurprising for the Adirondacks at that time of year, but Cori bundled up and took Bear for a good long walk in the woods. She'd left him home the day before, knowing there'd be upward of a dozen people at her parents' house, and it would be better for him to be lazy in her apartment for the day. And it had been, except he'd woken up a little stir crazy the next morning, and Cori knew he needed to burn off some energy with a romp through the snow.

She stopped midwalk just to take in a big, deep lungful of fresh mountain air. There truly was nothing like it. She'd been to cities. New York. Boston. Philadelphia. And they were always fun to visit. The hustle and bustle was such a change from Crimson Valley that it was easy to get sucked in. But inevitably, during every visit, it would only take a few days before she was longing to be home again. To the quiet. To the calm. To the slower pace of the mountains. It's the thing people liked most when they visited Crimson Valley. Countless tourists who'd come through her shop had told her how much they liked the slower pace, the feeling that they never had to hurry.

When you grew up in that slow pace, though, you often wished for faster. For bigger and brighter and newer. Not many graduates of Crimson Valley High stuck around and settled down here. Most left for that bigger-better-brighter. Cori was one of the few who had never wanted to leave. She was happy here.

She'd taken Bear off his leash once they'd hit the wooded path and there were no worries about him being too close to a road. He bounded ahead of her, then bounded back as if to say *You still with me, Mom? Still coming?* Once he was sure she was, he'd bound off again, his golden ears flapping as he went.

Now, he was over a slight ridge so she couldn't see him, but when he started barking, she heard him with no problem. It wasn't his warning bark, so she didn't worry he'd run into an animal or was chasing down a deer. It was his play bark, and as she crested the ridge, she could see who Bear had found.

Liz.

She wore a puffy black coat with red mittens and a red hat, and she was smiling, and Cori was so ridiculously happy to see her that her eyes welled up a bit as she walked toward her. She did manage to blink away any threat of tears by the time she got to Liz and Bear, but she knew her smile was huge. She could literally feel it stretched across her face.

"Well, hi there," she said, and without stopping at all, she walked right into Liz's personal space and wrapped her arms around her. "Merry Christmas," she said, her lips close to Liz's ear.

Liz's arms tightened around her as she said back, "Merry Christmas to you." When they parted, Liz smiled at her and said, "I was hoping I'd run into you out here."

"Yeah?"

"Why else would I be wandering through the woods in twenty-three degree weather?"

"To breathe in the fresh air," Cori said, throwing her arms out, leaning her head back, and making a show of taking a huge breath in.

"You do that many more times and your lungs'll freeze," Liz said.

"It's a chance I'll take." She watched Liz give Bear some more love, squatting down to meet his eyes, ruffling his ears, his fur, scratching his butt.

"Can I walk with you guys?" she asked, looking up at Cori.

"We'd love it."

Liz fell in step beside her as they walked. "So, things went okay yesterday, judging from your texts."

Cori nodded. The only sounds in that moment were their voices and the crunch of their feet on the snow. "Yeah, it was fine. We didn't talk about the giant elephant in the room because I don't think my sister and brothers know anything about it. And I didn't want to sabotage everybody's holiday with my own crap, you know?"

"I get that." They walked in silence for a bit longer before Liz added, "But you're gonna talk to them soon, right?"

"I need to. Yeah. It feels weird between us now, and I don't like it. It's been a rough couple of weeks." She glanced at Liz, felt a strength radiating off her. "I feel like my whole life has been a lie, you know? My parents aren't my parents. Somebody I loved as a friend and mentor kept the biggest secret possible from me. I have zero clue who my actual dad is. Even you and me. We were a lie, too."

Liz nodded but didn't say anything, and Cori couldn't tell if she was upset by the inclusion of their fake relationship or if she was simply being a good listener.

"So, yeah, there's a lot to discuss," she went on. More silence. More crunching of feet. "How are things with you and Lauren? Still better? And your parents?"

Liz nodded, and her face brightened a little, as if she was grateful for the change in subject. "Lauren has really been great. I'm on my break, actually. We've got a few guests checking in today and staying through the new year. My parents..." She sighed. "A little bit of a different story. My dad's okay. And just as a side note, he hasn't said anything about the developers in quite a while, so maybe you and I should revisit the idea of you making him an offer. My mom is...I don't know. I think she's still disappointed in me for lying. About you and me."

"And you talked to her about your reasons?" Cori stepped carefully. While she still didn't quite understand why Liz had felt she needed to go to such extremes to save face in front of a high school boyfriend, she was in no headspace to delve in. Not yet. She would need to, but not yet. And now the idea of buying the building was simmering in her brain again. God, it was all so much.

"I did. I think she just needs some time."

"Maybe after the holidays are over, you can sit down with her, just the two of you."

"Maybe." They got to a spot on the path where they mutually agreed to turn back. After a moment of retracing their footprints in the snow, Liz turned to her. "Hey, what are you doing New Year's Eve?"

Cori bumped her with a shoulder. "Aren't you supposed to sing that to me?"

"Trust me," Liz said with a snort, "the last thing you want is me singing to you."

"Can't carry a tune?"

"Not even in a bucket. That's what my dad would say."

Cori gave a dramatic sigh. "Fine. No singing, then. I currently have no plans for New Year's Eve. I'm closing the store at six and sending my employees on their merry ways. Then I will probably head upstairs to my place and hang out with my boys. What about you?"

"We're doing up a little champagne and charcuterie for our guests, but once Lauren and I have it all prepared, she just needs to set it out, come nine or so. I know Isaac is coming over to be with her, so she told me I was free to go out if I want."

"The Isaac thing is going well?"

"I think so." Liz smiled and added, "It's nice to see her so happy, and he seems like a super nice guy."

"I don't know him on a personal level, but I can tell you that he has never once, in the three plus years he's been delivering stuff to my store, showed up without a smile. Also, he's fucking hot."

Liz barked out a laugh. "Oh my God, right? The man is beautiful."

"He's the only guy who's ever made me take a second to think about my sexuality."

"But only a second, right?" Liz asked, her blue eyes sparkling.

"Only a second. Then it's right back to girls."

"Oh, whew." Liz wiped a hand across her brow in a dramatic depiction of relief. They were quiet for a while longer, and then Liz asked, "Do you think maybe you'd like some company at your place on New Year's Eve? We could open some wine. Eat some munchies. Watch the ball drop or whatever..." Her voice sort of trailed off in uncertainty, and it made Cori grin.

"Are you asking me to be your date for New Year's Eve, Ms. Brennan?"

Liz's cheeks blushed, and it had nothing to do with the cold. "I mean...yeah. I guess I am." When her gaze landed on Cori's, it was slightly wide-eyed, like she couldn't believe what she'd just asked and worried she'd be turned down.

"I think I'd really like that."

Liz's face collapsed in relief. "Yeah?"

"Yeah."

"Excellent. I'll text you during the day, see where you're at in your schedule."

"Sounds perfect," Cori said, and it really did. Any trepidation she might have had over what her feelings might actually be for Liz were tamped down solidly by the joy of not ringing in a new year alone.

And don't get her started on the joy of Liz's huge smile and bright eyes. 'Cause, yeah.

"Okay, this is my stop," Liz said a moment later as they reached the area where they'd met up. "Gotta get back to work. Boss is a hard-ass. Text you later?"

Cori nodded. "Suzanne is working now, so I've got the late shift."

Liz chuckled. "You sound like you work overnights."

"I have the later of the two shifts. Better?"

"Much." And then Liz surprised her by leaning close, and she kissed her on the cheek. "Have a great rest of your day." She ruffled the fur on Bear's head, gave Cori one last grin, then left them in the snow.

Cori stood there for a long while, watching Liz walk away, until she could no longer see her at all. Only then did she let out a long, slow breath that floated into the air on an icy cloud. "Oh, Bear-Bear. What am I going to do about that woman? Am I going down the exact same path as high school? Is it going to end up the same? She leaves town and I don't see her again for years? I suppose I should expect that." Her tone was calm, and it matched how she felt—fine. Maybe a slight bit of concern, but nothing absurd. She looked down at her dog, who looked up at her with soft eyes before he shifted his gaze back to where Liz had been as if he was feeling the exact same feelings as his person. "What am I going to do about her?"

CHAPTER EIGHTEEN

The week had gotten a little hectic at Brennan House. A couple last minute bookings put them at almost capacity by New Year's Eve Day. Luckily, none of the guests planned to dine there that night. Most were skiing or snowboarding for the day, then eating wherever they were, but almost all would be back at some point in the evening, so Lauren was sticking with the champagne and charcuterie New Year's Eve for them. Isaac was still coming over, and Liz's mom and dad were also around, so Lauren was still fine with Liz taking the night off.

And thank fucking God for that, because Liz had *plans*. Serious plans. Plans that were going to take some sneaking, some subterfuge, and a little help from Suzanne.

She'd made some calls. She'd gotten most of her supplies and put most of them in her car so she was almost ready to go. There was one box in her room still.

"You looking for something in particular?" her mother asked as Liz stood in the dining room in front of the small wine rack in the corner, trying to decide on a bottle.

She tapped a finger against her chin. "What wine goes best with chocolate? And popcorn?"

"Hmm. Chocolate *and* popcorn? Well, you've got a sweet and a salty, so that's a tough call. What kind of chocolate?"

"I mean...milk? Like, candy bars?"

"Okay, well, for a red, you'd want a pinot noir or a merlot. And just regular popcorn?" At Liz's nod, she said, "It's good to balance the saltiness with something crisp and white, like a sauvignon blanc or a chardonnay." She pulled a couple bottles out as examples. "You got big plans?"

"I kinda do, yeah." She wasn't ready to go into detail yet. Not with her mom. Not with anybody, really. She was too nervous. Too uncertain.

Her mother looked at her for a beat before saying, "Okay then. No details for Mom. Got it." But she seemed more amused than anything else, and she smiled at Liz.

"I promise to fill you in if all goes well."

"And if all goes sideways?"

"Mom! Why would you say that? Out loud? Oh my God." She snatched the bottles of wine from her mother's hands and stomped down the stairs into her basement room, her mother's laugh following her the whole way.

The wine went into the box she'd packed, and she looked through the contents one last time. Everything she needed was there. Her phone told her it was nearing five o'clock, and she opened her text stream to April and typed.

It's time. I'm headed over. So nervous. She added six wide-eyed emoji to demonstrate just exactly *how* nervous.

The gray dots began bouncing immediately as April typed back. *Don't be nervous. It's romantic and sweet and she's gonna love it. You got this!*

That was the simple boost she needed. She pulled in a deep breath, filled her lungs as much as they would allow, and then let it out slowly. She shook out her arms like a prizefighter preparing for a match. Then she scooted into the small bathroom and tidied her hair, touched up her makeup, and brushed her teeth. Back in the room, she used the full-length mirror in the corner to check her outfit. Soft navy-blue joggers. A blue-and-white striped button-down with the sleeves rolled up. Her hair was down and wavy. She had small silver hoops in her ears and her silver ring on the middle finger of her right hand. That was it. Simple, casual, and comfortable, but nice. "And a little sexy," she whispered, as she unbuttoned one more button. "A little peek without giving away the farm."

Then she stood there for a moment. She was nervous, yes. Her hands were a little clammy. Her mouth was dry. With another shake of her arms, she said to her reflection, "Okay. Let's do this."

She slid her arms into her coat, stepped into her boots, put on gloves and a hat, and hoisted the box up in her arms. Once it was tucked safely into the back seat of her car, and the car was running to warm up, she scooted across the yard to Brennan House to double-check on Lauren, who was in the kitchen.

"All set?" Lauren asked.

Liz nodded. "Just wanted to see if you needed anything else before I go."

Lauren shook her head. "All good here. Go. Have fun." A beat passed before she looked up at Liz and waggled her eyebrows, which made Liz burst out laughing.

"*Ew*, stop that," she said, shutting the door behind her, but laughing softly. She got to her car and was about to pull the door open when she heard the soft crunch of snow and glanced off to her left in the direction of the woods.

Two deer were making their way across the snow, probably looking for some food. It had gone dusk, but the snow made it seem brighter out than it was, and she could clearly see the two animals, walking slowly, nibbling at trees. They were so calm and so regal and so gorgeous, and Liz simply stood there watching them for what felt like a long time. One of them stopped and looked in her direction, its big marble eyes scanning for danger, but Liz kept still and they went back to eating.

Deer were a good sign. They always had been for her. She loved them, and whenever she saw one, everything within her settled and calmed, and that happened now. Her nervous heart eased up on the pounding. Her buzzing nerves seemed to suddenly smooth out, and her breathing became deep and even. She sent out a silent thank-you to the deer as they wandered back into the woods, then got into her car and headed out.

❖

Cori was the only one left at Whimsy.

She'd sent her last employee home about an hour ago, as business was slow. Bars and restaurants were hopping, with both tourists and locals celebrating, anticipating the ball dropping, the bidding farewell to the year and welcoming in the next, but the shops were pretty much empty by now. And that was okay. Cori was ready to be done working.

When she'd relieved her at noon, Suzanne had given her a hug. A big one. A tight one. She'd whispered in her ear that she was sorry for keeping such a secret from her, that she missed her, and that she hoped they could talk—really talk—sometime soon. It was only as Suzanne was walking out the door that Cori realized she'd pretty much been giving her the silent treatment for the past couple of weeks. She'd spoken to her when it was about a customer or something to do with the store, but other than that, she'd been pretty much unapproachable. She'd *made herself* pretty much unapproachable, and not only to Suzanne, but to her family as well. She answered her mother's texts and her father's calls, but all conversation had been kept at surface level. She understood why—she was hurt. She was hurt, and she needed time to sit with that, to figure out what her next step was.

She sighed now as she flipped the *Open* sign to *Closed* and turned off the front lights. What a year. It had started like any other. It had been a good one. It had all been fine until December, really, until those damn journals had made themselves known. And then everything had gone to shit.

Cori was struggling and she knew it. The smart thing to do was probably find a therapist, somebody who was completely removed from the situation that she could talk to openly and not be worried about hurting feelings or being angry or bursting into tears. In fact, she'd done a Google search earlier that day when things had slowed down in the store, and she'd found a couple of possibilities. She'd read reviews and check Yelp tomorrow. Right now, she wanted to close up shop, take her boys upstairs, pour herself a glass of wine, and collapse on her couch, hopefully with Liz.

As she locked up the store, turned off the main lights, and headed up the stairs with Bear and Ernie on her heels, she pulled out her phone and typed a text.

All closed up. You coming over?

They'd planned to ring in the new year together, and neither had wanted to be out with a bunch of loud strangers, but Liz had been hard to get in touch with today.

The first thing she noticed when she opened her apartment door was the glorious smell of freshly popped popcorn. Strange. She closed the door behind her, stepped into the kitchen, and stopped short. "What in the world?"

Liz sat behind a small table, smiling. "Hello, ma'am. Welcome to the movies. Do you know what you'd like to see tonight?" Waving her arm with a flourish, she indicated the wall next to her, where six movie posters had been printed on regular letter-size paper and taped to it in three rows of two.

The Holiday, A Christmas Story, and *The Family Stone* were playing at six thirty.

Die Hard, The Santa Clause 2, and *Elf* were playing at nine.

Cori blinked in disbelief at the posters, then turned her gaze back to Liz. That's when she noticed the stacks of candy on the counter. Reese's Peanut Butter Cups, Milk Duds, Skittles, and Snickers bars were lined up with a little makeshift sign in front of them that said *Five Cents Each.*

"I think I'd like to start with *The Holiday,*" Cori said, then grabbed a Reese's, "and one of these."

Liz gave one nod, clearly trying to stay in character even as Bear nudged her for attention. She handed over a square of red paper that had a big *ONE* on it with *The Holiday* in smaller, handwritten letters below it. "Your ticket. Would you like any of our concessions besides the peanut butter cups? There's also popcorn, soda, and wine."

Cori had so many questions but decided to play along for a bit longer. "I'd love a large popcorn and…wine, you said?"

"Yes, ma'am. Something crisp to offset the saltiness."

"That sounds great."

Liz stood and, again, indicated with a flourish of her arm. "If you head right in to the theater, I'll bring your snacks in momentarily." As Cori took a step, Liz added, "Oh. There's also a change of clothes in there, off to the left. We thought you'd be more comfortable in cozy clothes." With a wink, she turned toward the pot on the stove, which Cori now realized was full of popcorn.

"What is happening?" she asked in wonder.

Liz smiled at her as she scooped popcorn into a big bowl. "I'm taking you to the movies," she said simply, and something inside Cori melted. Just melted.

She turned away quickly because her eyes had welled up and headed into the living room, where she again stopped short. Everything had been moved, and it looked like there was a giant tent in the middle of the room. As promised, off to the side on a chair were her cozy soft black leggings and her favorite Crimson Valley Ski Club sweatshirt that she'd cut the neck out of so it fell off one shoulder. While Liz rattled around in the kitchen, she quickly peeled off her work clothes, always shocked by how good it felt to get out of her jeans and bra, and slipped on the cozies.

It was time to figure out this tent thing. It was her TV on a table, but then sheets were attached to the sides and stretched out over a whole bunch of cushions and pillows, and Cori realized that those were where they'd lounge and watch the movie. It was dark and warm and cozy inside and more perfect than she could've imagined. As she crawled in and got herself all situated, she realized there was also room for Bear to squeeze in, should he want to. The TV was on, and the title screen for *The Holiday* was up. Liz must've set it from her phone or a laptop or something. Before she could wonder anymore, Liz appeared, crouched down to enter the tent.

"Ma'am, your order." She handed a big bowl of popcorn sparkling with melted butter to Cori, followed by a glass of white wine. "Can I get you anything else?"

"I mean, there's clearly room in here for two."

Liz pointed next to Cori. "That seat is reserved, ma'am."

"Oh? For who?"

That's when Liz finally broke character, gave her an enormous grin, and said, "Me." She crawled the rest of the way in, stretched out next to Cori, and got comfortable, leaning the pillows against the bottom of the couch, which was at their backs. "What do you think?"

The lump in Cori's throat was big, and it took her a couple of tries to swallow it down before she could speak. "I can't believe you did this. It's…" She shook her head. "It's amazing. It's perfect." She had more she wanted to say, but her throat threatened to close up again, so she simply turned her face to Liz's, smiled at her, and hoped the words were there in her eyes.

They must have been because Liz leaned toward her and kissed her softly on the lips. It wasn't lost on Cori that this was their first real kiss. Their first kiss that wasn't for show. She brought her hand up to Liz's face and cradled it as she kissed her back softly.

When they parted, Liz said, "Yeah. So that just happened."

Cori gave a soft laugh. "So it did. Our first not-fake kiss. It happened."

"It'll probably happen again later."

"I hope so." Their gazes held for a beat and in that moment, everything was so perfect, Cori wanted to take a snapshot, something to keep, to remember. She scootched closer so she could lay her head on Liz's shoulder. She popped some popcorn into her mouth and waved at the screen. "It's six thirty-seven. Let's get this party started."

"As you wish," Liz said, picking up her phone, and started the film.

❖

By the time Kate Winslet and Jack Black were dancing on New Year's Eve with Jude Law and Cameron Diaz, Cori had relaxed far more than she'd thought possible just two hours earlier. Her belly was full of popcorn and wine—she was saving the peanut butter cups for the next flick. She was warm and cozy in the movie tent. Bear was curled up at their feet and snuffling softly. Sometime during the movie, she and Liz had moved closer, and now her leg was thrown over Liz's, the nearly empty bowl of popcorn balanced between her thigh and Liz's. Liz had lifted her arm and draped it over Cori's shoulders at some point, and now they were just a comfy, cozy little blob of girl.

They'd chatted a bit for the first half hour or forty-five minutes of the movie, but then they'd gotten quiet and watched. It was such a favorite of Cori's, and she loved everything about it. Plus, it was so romantic. As the credits rolled, she turned her head to find Liz looking at her with hooded eyes, and there was something there Cori couldn't quite define any more solidly than to say it was a combination of desire and hunger. And it didn't scare her. At all.

"What was—" Liz had to clear her throat and try again. "What was your second movie choice?"

"I don't care," Cori said, moving the popcorn out of the way. Nothing mattered right then except Liz. Not how they'd gotten there. Not the other crap in her life. Not her store or her candles or her parents or even Annabelle. Only Liz.

She stopped. Looking down at Liz, looking in her blue eyes, so darkened with arousal, easily went straight to the top of her list of most incredible things she'd experienced, ever. They were similar in size. Liz was a little shorter, but also more muscular. Cori was a little taller, but slight in build, and their two shapes were super complementary. Braced on her forearms, she took a moment to simply look. Simply stare.

"You have no idea how beautiful you are," Liz whispered to her as she reached up and swooped Cori's hair off her face, held it there. "And that makes you even more beautiful."

Cori felt the gentle tug and let Liz pull her head down until their lips met. Gentle at first. Soft, like the earlier kiss before the movie. Almost tentative. Yes, they'd kissed before. They'd even kissed deeply, but always with others around, always for show. This? This was different. In so many ways. Cori pressed a little more firmly and felt Liz's hand slide through her hair, behind her head, her grip tightening just a bit.

Kissing Liz was like nothing Cori had experienced before. She was no novice—she'd had girlfriends. Nothing super long-term, but she wasn't inexperienced. That being said, kissing Liz, lying on top of her like this, feeling every inch of her body under her own, was... beyond any pleasure she'd ever had. Her blood heated, her heart rate picked up, and her body went from zero to about a hundred and fifty in three seconds flat. Soft and gentle went out the window as she pushed her tongue against Liz's lips and was granted entry instantly. Liz gifted her with a sexy moan that came from deep in her chest. Cori could feel it vibrate beneath her body.

Using her hands, she pushed herself up so she could once again gaze down at Liz. "For the record," she said quietly as her fingers worked the buttons on Liz's top, "big fan of this shirt. Big fan."

"Yeah?"

"Oh yes." She unbuttoned the rest until she was able to push the material to either side, exposing Liz's torso, her creamy skin, her simple white bra. Wasting no time, she laid her hand flat on Liz's stomach and felt how smooth, how warm she was, felt the gentle rise and fall of her chest, slid her hand up until she cupped one breast in her hand, gave it a soft squeeze, and Liz's sharp intake of breath caused a surge of wetness between Cori's legs. She returned her gaze to Liz and frowned. "I want to go slow," she whispered, "but I don't know if I can. God, I want you so much."

Liz's smile was tender, and it lit up her whole face. "Well, guess what? I want you, too. And we have all the time in the world to go slow or go fast or whatever. Because I've got news for you. This may be our first time, but it won't be our last." And before Cori could respond, Liz pulled her head down and kissed her. Hard.

Fast was the way it went that first time. Clothes flew off until they were both naked in the tent. The only light was the blue glow from the television screen, and it was perfect, almost emulating moonlight. In the middle of a searing kiss, Cori found her position flipped, and suddenly, she was on her back, Liz hovering above her, letting her eyes rove over her naked body, stopping at her neck, her breasts, the apex of her thighs. Bear sighed, clearly annoyed by all the movement, and nosed his way out of the tent. Cori and Liz grinned at each other before Liz dipped her head, took a nipple into her mouth, and sucked.

Cori's head dropped back to the pillow and her hips jerked as a bolt of electric arousal shot from that nipple down to her center, pulling a whimper from her throat. She closed her fingers in Liz's hair as Liz went from one nipple to the other and back, giving equal time, and sending Cori's arousal status off the charts.

All sense of time dissipated like steam in the air. Cori had no idea how long Liz worshipped her breasts. Might have been a few minutes. Might have been a few hours. But by the time she began moving down Cori's body, her nipples were swollen, thick and dark pink, incredibly sensitive. She was also pretty certain she was soaked.

Liz moved down her body slowly, truly the only time they'd done anything slow tonight. She used her tongue, stopping to taste around each of Cori's breasts, her shoulders, her sides. When she'd made her way all the way down, she pushed Cori's legs apart, draped them over her shoulders, then looked up her body until their eyes met. That gaze held. It was filled with so much. Things Cori recognized. Things she wasn't sure she was ready for. But they were there. Then Liz smiled at her and dipped her head.

She began on the insides of Cori's thighs. Light kisses. Warm tongue. Up and down one thigh, then the other, then back. Cori's body continued to prepare itself, her wetness reaching unheard of levels. With each switch from one thigh to the other, Liz moved up the tiniest bit. By the time her tongue was tasting so near Cori's center, but not quite there yet, Cori thought she might pass out. Or implode. Or burst into flames. Her entire body was on fire in the best of ways. The anticipation in her center was immeasurably high. If it all hadn't felt as incredible as it did, she'd have grabbed Liz's head by now and pushed it to where she needed it. But everything she was doing was *so good*. Yes, she wanted more. Also, she never wanted this to end.

Liz's patience was astounding. Wasn't she the one who said they didn't have to take their time this first time? Because she was doing the exact opposite of going fast. The throbbing between Cori's legs was epic, and she absently wondered if she might have an orgasm just from what Liz was doing, without her ever having actually touched her center.

There wasn't time to wonder much longer, though, because Liz paused, as if giving Cori time to catch her breath, but only for a beat or two. Then she finally released her. With one swipe of her tongue, from bottom to top, Liz sent Cori careening over the edge. Her hips came up off the cushions, and a cry was ripped from her throat. Liz took that moment, with her hips in the air, to slide her fingers inside, sending Cori impossibly higher and grasping for anything she could reach. The pillows. The cushions. Liz's hair. Anything. And she hung on for dear life, pretty sure that if she let go, she'd fly off into space and simply float away, never to be heard from again.

But what a way to go.

Liz used her fingers and her tongue to keep Cori flying, until she finally stopped all movement, but kept everything where it was, her fingers still inside, her tongue still pressed to Cori's center. Cori waited until the colors exploding behind her eyelids calmed before she slowly let her hips drop back down to the cushions. She'd meant it to be gentle, but her entire body felt boneless, and everything just dropped. Liz's tongue left, but her fingers were still inside. Cori loved the sensation of them, that sense of being filled by Liz. She draped an arm over her eyes as her lungs heaved for air. She wanted to speak, but words failed her, so she simply took a moment to breathe.

Finally, after she had no idea how long, she opened her eyes and peeked down at Liz, who was smiling at her with the warmest, yet most mischievous grin.

"Well, hi there," Liz said softly. "That was gorgeous."

"You're gorgeous," Cori replied, and with a crook of her finger, added, "Get up here."

Liz slowly removed her fingers, pulling a gasp out of Cori along with them, then moved up her body on all fours until their lips met. Cori loved the slickness of Liz's, the way she could taste herself on Liz's mouth, and she was shocked to find herself ratcheting up again with barely any recovery time. Suddenly, she wanted Liz like nothing else in the world. More than air. She reached up and cupped the back of Liz's head, shoving her tongue into Liz's mouth with dominance, satisfied when she heard the slight hitch in Liz's breath. Then she slid her hand down Liz's front to the warm copious wet between her thighs, and without any preamble or warning, pushed her fingers in.

Liz wrenched her mouth away on a small cry, her eyes wide in surprise. Cori still held the back of her neck while she watched her face, moving her fingers slowly in and out. Liz's breath became ragged, and she pushed herself up on her hands, looking down into Cori's eyes as she began moving her hips. Up and down, up and down, sliding on Cori's fingers, increasing her pace.

The eye contact was delicious. There was no other way to describe it. Cori watched Liz's eyes, felt a connection there like she'd never known, as Liz continued to push herself down onto Cori's hand, then pull herself up, then slam back down. Cori uncurled her thumb, and on Liz's next push down, it hit exactly the right spot. Liz's eyes squeezed shut, but Cori gave her hair a little tug. "Look at me," she commanded.

Liz did as she was told, opened her eyes, and stared into Cori's until she came, even *as* she came, even as she pushed herself hard down onto Cori's hand and ground her body against it, even as a strangled cry tore from her lips, she never looked away.

And that connection? That eye contact? Was devastating in its beauty.

Moments later, they lay in each other's arms, ragged breathing the only sound. Well, that and Bear's gentle snoring coming from just outside their little tent. They cuddled in silence for a while before Cori pressed a kiss to Liz's forehead and said quietly, "I've never had sex in a movie theater before."

Liz's shoulders shook in soft laughter. "Glad to have given you a first."

Cori turned so she could look into Liz's blue eyes, hooded a bit.

She looked adorably wiped out. "You've given me more than that." She tightened her arms around Liz, felt her snuggle in closer, and closed her eyes, knowing sleep was going to claim them both momentarily. A quick glance at her watch told her it was a new year, and she didn't even care that they hadn't seen the ball drop. They'd rung in the new year in the best possible way.

CHAPTER NINETEEN

The first week of the year was the best Liz could remember in her adult life. Yes, much of that was due to Cori. She knew that. They saw each other almost every day. They smiled shyly at each other. There were little touches all the time—a hand across a shoulder here, the squeeze of an arm there. And they made out a lot. Like *a lot*.

In fact, making out was exactly what they were doing when the door to Cori's workshop opened, startling them apart.

"Mom, what—?" Cori's words both answered Liz's question of who was this person bursting in, and also told her things were about to get tense, judging from the way her voice sort of just…stopped.

Cori's mom looked tired, and the fact that it was obvious to Liz, who didn't know the woman, said a lot. She looked tired and sad and—also?—angry. She was about Liz's height, and blond with light eyes. Cori didn't look a thing like her.

"How long is this going to go on, Corina?" she asked, then blinked as her gaze focused on Liz as if noticing her for the first time, even though she stood mere inches away from her daughter. "I'm sorry," she said then, her eyes on Liz. "I just need to talk to my daughter."

Liz gave one nod. "Sure." She began looking around for her things, feeling the sudden need to escape, but Cori grabbed her arm. When Liz met her gaze, her eyes were pleading.

"Stay?" she asked softly.

"You're sure?" Liz whispered back. At Cori's nod, she relented. "Okay."

"I'd like Liz to stay. She knows the details."

Cori's mom looked slightly surprised by that little fact but didn't address it. Just gave Liz a head bob and said, "If that's what you want. I'm Barbara, by the way."

"It's nice to meet you, Barbara," Liz said, then swallowed a wince because this was certainly *not* a nice way to meet somebody.

"Can we sit please?" Barbara asked, then moved to the lounge part of the workshop without waiting for a response and seemed to collapse onto the couch. Again, Liz thought how tired she looked.

Cori moved to sit at the other end of the couch, and Liz perched on the arm behind her. Cori seemed to want her close, so she did her best to stay within reach.

"Look," Barbara said, her eyes on her hands. She inhaled and let the air out slowly, then brought her gaze up to look at Cori. She was very pretty, Liz saw now. She looked younger than she was, her skin very smooth and creamy for a super busy woman with four kids. But her eyes were sad. Anybody could see that, and Liz remembered something her grandmother said once about motherhood, that a mother is only as happy as her saddest child. "I know you're angry," Barbara went on. "I get that. You have a right to be."

"You think?" Cori said, her tone carrying an edge. Liz laid a hand on her shoulder and squeezed gently, silently telling her to take it easy, to give her mom a chance. Cori clearly felt it because she immediately said, "Sorry. I'm sorry. Go ahead."

"It was always our intention to tell you. And when Annabelle died, it seemed even more important that you know one day." She glanced back down at her hands as she scraped at the plum-colored polish on one thumb. "But I also knew once we told you, I'd lose something. A part of you. Even if it was just small, I didn't want that. I didn't want to lose any of you. Annabelle may have been your biological mother, but you are *my* daughter. From the moment she left you with us and walked away, you became mine. Do you know how hard it was to have her come strolling back into our lives? Don't get me wrong, I loved her, she was my best friend, but she could also be so selfish sometimes. Your father and I had to sit her down and explain to her how hard it would be on you for her to just blurt it out, which is exactly what she wanted to do. Even Suzanne knew better." She stopped as if she needed to catch her breath, and maybe she did. Or maybe she was regrouping. Liz didn't know her, so she couldn't tell. Barbara picked at a thread on the couch cushion for a moment before continuing. "I'm not here to bash

Annabelle. Like I said, I loved her. She was my best friend for a long time. But she could also be a bulldozer when she wanted something or thought she knew best. Suzanne was the one who convinced her to let us sit down together to find the best time to tell you the truth. And then…" She grimaced.

"And then she died," Cori said.

"And then she died." Barbara nodded. "And we were devastated and heartbroken, so we set that part of her aside so we could grieve." Her eyes became shiny with unshed tears. "And time went on and you thrived and took over Whimsy and were doing so well that we just…" A shake of her head. "We didn't want to upset things." She seemed to get what a weak excuse it was, but Liz somehow got it, too. She squeezed her hand on Cori's shoulder, as if hoping to radiate some strength and maybe some understanding through the touch. "I'm so sorry, Cori. We are all so sorry. We should have told you. We know that. We're not disputing that. And we intended to. We did. But time just…it got away from us." She held up a hand as Cori opened her mouth to speak and added, "It's a terrible excuse. I know it is. We know it is. I'm trying to be honest with you here. That's all."

Cori seemed to take it all in, to sit while the words her mother spoke landed on her skin, and her body soaked them in like a sponge. She sat quietly for a long time before Liz felt her take a deep breath under her hand. "I won't lie and tell you it hasn't been a bit…disconcerting to feel so different from my siblings. From the entire family, really. And I sometimes feel like nobody in my family gets me."

Barbara shook her head sadly. "I hate that you feel that way. For the record, I happen to think I do get you." She went for a smile, but there was a sadness to it.

"I mean, yeah, you of all people do seem to understand that I'm different. The others, though, are just like you and Dad. You're all…" She waved a hand around as if hoping to bat it out of the air. "Loud."

Barbara grinned at that. "True."

"And you all process everything out loud. And you're all so vocal, and you all love big gatherings and parties. And there's nothing wrong with any of that. But I have felt so…different. And weird. And like I don't fit in. And because of those things, there's an insecurity that I've never understood and haven't been able to shake. Don't get me wrong. Please. I love you all more than anything. It's just, knowing the truth about Annabelle, about my dad, that might have helped me with some of those feelings. You know?"

Barbara nodded, and her expression was a clear mix of sadness and guilt. "I'm so sorry, Cori. That's all I can do or say, unfortunately, but I wish there was more."

"Does the rest of the family know?"

Barbara shook her head. "No. Just me, your father, and Suzanne. We've never told anybody. As far as we were concerned, you were ours. You still are. I hope you feel the same way."

"What if..." Cori cleared her throat, glanced up at Liz as if drawing strength from her, then back at her mother. "What if I want them to know?"

Barbara didn't hesitate. "Then we'll tell them. Together."

"Yeah?"

"Absolutely. We will do whatever you want. We'll handle this however you wish."

Cori's seemed to take that in and roll it around. "Okay. I just..." She wet her lips. "I need a little bit more time. If that's okay."

"Of course it's okay," Barbara said, and Liz could tell by watching her body language that there was relief. Her shoulders seemed to relax a bit, and some of the tension looked like it flowed away. And then she scooted closer to Cori, close enough to reach out and touch her. She closed her hands over Cori's, and Liz could see the tears in her eyes once more. "I'm so sorry, honey. I never meant to hurt you. I hope you know that."

"I do." And then Cori and her mother were hugging, and Liz felt her own throat close up, worried that she might cry right along with them.

"I love you, my sweet girl," Barbara said into Cori's shoulder.

"I love you too, Mom."

They parted, both wiping their faces and sniffling. "If you want to learn more about Annabelle, you have the best source right out there, you know." Barbara jerked a thumb over her shoulder. "Suzanne knew her better than anybody. Your father and I swore her to secrecy. But now, I'm sure she'd be happy to tell you anything you want to know."

Both Cori and Barbara stood up, and the atmosphere in the room had changed enough that Liz could feel it. The tension, the anger, the trepidation that had hung in the air upon Barbara's arrival had all been diluted. It wasn't completely gone, but the air felt clearer, cleaner somehow. Cori walked her mother to the door of the workshop that led back out into the store, said her good-byes, and closed the door behind her. Then she stood there for a moment with her hand on the door.

"You okay?" Liz asked quietly.

Cori inhaled slowly, then let it out little by little, and finally turned to look at Liz. "I think so?"

Liz opened her arms. "Come here."

Cori walked into her embrace, and Liz held her tightly. They stood like that for a long while. "Thank you," Cori finally mumbled against Liz's shoulder. "For being here. For not running away during the crappy stuff."

Liz pressed a kiss to her temple. "You're welcome."

Cori glanced at the clock on the wall in the corner. "Babe, you've gotta go if you're supposed to relieve Lauren so she can go on her date with sexy Mr. UPS."

Liz sighed. "Yeah, I better scoot. You gonna be okay?"

"I am. Promise."

Liz looked in her eyes, studied them for a moment, and decided she believed her. "Okay. Good. Text you later."

A quick kiss and she was off.

❖

Cori Stratton took up a lot of space in Liz's head now. A lot of space. That had become her life, and she wasn't mad about it. A fake relationship had blossomed into a real romance. She was a living, breathing Hallmark character. And again, not mad about it.

She was punching some information into the computer behind the front desk when Lauren came out from the kitchen dressed in a coat and pulling her hat on. "Stop grinning like a dork. You're gonna scare the guests." But there was no venom in her voice. In fact, she was smiling.

"You should talk," Liz said, pointing at her. "What's going on with your face? I mean, it almost looks like a smile, but that would be so unusual…"

Lauren rubbed at her nose with her middle finger but kept smiling as she pushed out the front door where Isaac was already waiting for her in his car.

"Nice to see her so happy, isn't it?" Liz's mom had come down from upstairs, followed by Mrs. Adler. They'd been cleaning the two empty rooms.

"It really is," Mrs. Adler said. "I was beginning to think she didn't know how to smile."

"I mean, her face could still crack," Liz said with a shrug.

"Elizabeth. That's enough." Her mom shot her a look but was more amused than anything.

Liz watched through the window as Isaac's car drove off, and her gaze was pulled away by her phone pinging the arrival of a text. She grinned at the thought of her sister actually smiling—like, on a regular basis—and glanced down at her phone. It was a text from April.

Hey, bitch, how's life? Sorry I haven't gotten up there to visit yet, but I am coming soon. I have a line on a job—call me!

"Holy crap," she muttered, but nobody was around to hear her. Wasting no time, she dialed April's number. The phone was answered after half a ring.

"That was fast," April said with a laugh. "How are you, woman? Holidays okay?"

"Seriously? You want to small talk me right now?"

"My holidays were great," April went on as if Liz hadn't spoken. "My mother overdid it on the wine, but that's nothing new. My dad and brother did not get into a fight, which was a true Christmas miracle…"

"I will punch you right in the face," Liz warned her, but she was laughing, knowing April was teasing her. Mercilessly.

April mock gasped. "You would never punch my gorgeous mug."

"I will if you don't tell me about this job thing."

"Lies." April chuckled. "Okay, fine. I'll tell you all about it if you tell me one thing first."

Liz playfully spoke through gritted teeth. "What?"

"What do you recommend at this diner place? I hear the Bucky Burger is good, but I don't know for sure."

"Oh my God, are you here? In Crimson Valley?" Liz all but shouted and literally jumped up and down behind the front desk.

"Is that the name of this place? It's charming. I like it."

"I can't believe you came all the way here and didn't tell me!" Liz couldn't stop laughing, and the wave of happy relief she felt whoosh through her was so strong, she needed to sit down. Her mother joined her behind the desk, clearly wondering what was making her daughter so happy. "It's April," Liz told her, and couldn't stop smiling. "She's here."

"*Here* here?" her mother asked.

"She's at Bucky's right now."

Her mother laughed. "Go," she said, waving a dismissive hand. "I've got this."

"You're sure?"

"*Go*." She shooed her away.

Before she could do anything more, she glanced up to see a nondescript black sedan pull in and roll to a halt. Her father got out, as did two other men in suits. They stood chatting for a bit, and then her father shook hands with both men, who got back into the car and turned it around. Her father pushed the front door open, chuckling and shaking his head like he was remembering a funny joke.

"Hi, Dad." She grabbed her coat and slid her arms in.

"Hey, sweetheart. How's life today?" He stomped the snow off his feet and glanced around the room until his gaze landed on Liz's mom. Then everything in his face relaxed. It was cute, if not still a little weird for Liz.

"Life is not bad at all, if I'm being honest." She decided not to say anything to anybody about the potential job until she had more details. "Hey, who were those guys?" She indicated the window with her chin.

"Oh, those were a couple gentlemen from Lattimore."

The way Liz's thoughts came to a screeching halt, she would've been completely unsurprised to hear a record-scratch sound, as if she was in some modern-day teen comedy. "The Lattimore guys? Why? Why are you talking to them again?"

Her father met her gaze, and his thick and sandy eyebrows met in a V above his nose. "They want to buy my building. I told you."

Liz's mother was watching them as well. Liz could see her stop what she was doing and turn her gaze their way. "I thought you were considering not selling," Liz said.

"Well, yeah, but they want to make me an offer." He looked from her to her mother and back, clearly baffled by Liz's disapproval. "I mean, I need to hear them out."

He wasn't wrong. That was the first thought that went through Liz's mind. She'd known he was thinking about what she'd said, but he'd never promised he wouldn't sell *at all*. But still. He'd met Cori. He knew her. He liked her. More importantly, he knew Liz liked her. Was he really going to do this?

"Matthew." That's all her mother said. Just her father's name. His full name, which she only used when she was disappointed in or angry with him. He met her gaze across the room, and Liz watched them have a silent conversation using only eye contact. Then her mother shook her head, made a sound of disapproval in her throat, and headed for the kitchen.

Her father looked from Liz to the kitchen door, then back at her, groaned quietly, and followed his ex-wife into the kitchen, leaving Liz standing there in disbelief.

He was still going to sell Cori's building to a big city builder? Seriously? Her brain reminded her that it was business, that it wasn't anything personal against Cori, but you know what? It was now not only personal for Cori, it was personal for Liz, too.

And Cori would be crushed.

CHAPTER TWENTY

Y ou know that I'm sorry, right?" Suzanne's face was serious, her mouth set in a thin, straight line, her brow slightly furrowed.

Cori held her gaze and watched in fascination as Suzanne's eyes welled up.

"I don't want to blame anybody else," Suzanne went on, "but I told Annabelle she couldn't just go blurting something like that out. It was too important. I thought she should talk to your parents, figure it out together. And when she died, your parents asked me to give them a chance to find the right time, and…" She shook her head as tears spilled over. There was no sound—Suzanne was clearly a silent crier—but she looked so sad and miserable that Cori couldn't stay angry with her, couldn't stand to see her like that. She went behind the counter and, without a word, wrapped her arms around her. "I wanted to tell you," Suzanne said through her tears. "I just…" She pulled back and wiped her face, seeming almost embarrassed that she'd cried. "It wasn't my secret to tell."

"I understand," Cori said and did her best to make it sound genuine. The truth was, she didn't fully understand, and she wasn't sure she ever would. But holding it against her parents or Suzanne for the rest of time just seemed pointless. So she'd decided to do her best to move forward, but with a caveat. "Do you think…" She swallowed the sudden lump in her throat. "Could you answer questions about her? About my dad?"

And Suzanne's face lit up as if she'd just seen the most beautiful rainbow in existence. "Are you kidding? Cori, I would *love* to answer your questions. I'd be honored. You deserve to know everything about her, about them, and I would really, really love to talk about her."

That's how the week had started, which meant that's how the *year* had started. The phrase *New Year* was the most understated of understatements in Cori's life because she was basically a different person now. Not physically, but definitely emotionally and mentally. She now knew things about herself that she'd never known, and that meant she understood things she'd never understood before. Life was different now. Now, she'd be going about her day and somebody would walk through her store wearing the unmistakable scent of patchouli, and Cori could walk over to Suzanne—or send her a text if she wasn't around—and ask, *Did Annabelle like patchouli?* And Suzanne would respond immediately, *Oh, God, she despised it. With the fire of a thousand burning suns, she hated that smell.* And Cori would smile and feel warm inside and tuck that little factoid away with all the others she was learning, because she too hated the smell of patchouli.

She now had a list in the Notes app on her phone. A list of things about the mother she never really knew. Things they had in common. So far, it included all the likes they shared: cheese, animals, Cheerios, HGTV, salt and vinegar potato chips, documentaries, onions on their burgers, the sound of rain, and girls.

The other day, she'd asked Suzanne if Annabelle was creative, and Suzanne's face had shifted into a sad smile as she nodded. "She drew. Sketched. Beautifully. She never thought she was that good, but I did. She would kind of shrug off my praise, but I know drawing was a way she relieved stress." Then she held up a finger and said, "You know what? I think I still have some of her sketches packed away somewhere. I'll see if I can find them."

This is my life now. The thought zipped through her mind as she stood behind the counter of Whimsy. She watched as a handful of customers browsed the shelves. She'd always been pretty happy in general. She had a good life. Her business didn't have her rolling in money, but she did well enough to pay her bills and put a little bit away. She glanced toward the front of the store just in time to see Liz pulling the door open. She gave herself a shake on the mat—it had just started to snow—and then looked up and met Cori's gaze, and Cori felt that warmth, that contentedness that she seemed to feel now.

"What's the smile for?" Liz asked as she walked behind the counter and kissed Cori's cheek.

She shook her head. "Just…adding up all the pieces of my life that finally feel like they fit."

"Yeah? What pieces are we talking about?" Liz leaned her back against the counter and gave her a smile. Was it slightly strained? Cori wasn't sure, and a customer approached before she could ask.

The customer bought a candle, a discounted Christmas tree ornament, and a cute little clay raccoon who was ready to hit the slopes if his skis and goggles were any indication. Cori took her time wrapping the raccoon up in tissue to protect it from breakage, making small talk with the customer, as she often did. Next to her, Liz felt weird somehow. She knew that was a strange thought, but that was the only way to describe it: Liz felt weird.

The customer thanked her and left with her bag. Cori turned to Liz and waved a hand in front of her. "What's going on?"

Liz shook her head and, for a minute, frowned, inhaled a deep breath, then let it out slowly. "Nothing. I'm just tired. I haven't slept much lately." She waggled her eyebrows in a comically lewd gesture that made Cori grin.

"I guess I should let you sleep more."

"Oh no, I'm not saying that." Liz gave her a soft smile and said quietly, "Please don't."

"All right. Fine, but only because you asked nicely." She wasn't convinced but let it go.

Liz gestured to the workshop. "I'm gonna wait for you back there." Without waiting for a response, she turned and headed to the back. In a stunning show of betrayal, Bear got up from his dog bed and followed her.

Cori had no idea what was up, but she was pretty sure it wasn't fatigue. Suzanne was due to relieve her in half an hour and was always at least twenty minutes early, so she'd be there any moment. She let the next few customers distract her, and then Suzanne arrived, twenty minutes before her shift, as predicted.

"You know, Suzanne and I have this easier feeling now," she said as she entered the workshop and found Liz on the couch playing with Bear. "It's, like, lighter or something."

"I'm glad to hear that," Liz said with a smile that didn't quite reach her eyes.

Cori plopped down next to her. "Okay. What's up? I can tell by your face that you're worried about something."

Liz sighed and kept her gaze on Bear as she ruffled his fur and played with his ears. "My dad is talking to the builder guys again."

Cori felt her stomach drop. "About selling my building again?"

Liz nodded.

"Shit."

"I know."

She sat back and exhaled, feeling like a deflating balloon.

"But…I have an idea, kind of."

Liz met her eyes then, and Cori could see so much in them. Worry. Shame. And a spark of…something. "Tell me."

"Make him an offer." Liz let the words settle, kept her eyes on Cori's face and waited a beat before she continued. "I mean, could you? I have no idea what your finances look like, but…could you?"

"I mean…" She made herself really think about it. "I don't have a ton in savings, but I have decent credit. I could probably get a small business loan. That being said, I don't know that I can match what a large builder is willing to pay him." Ugh. This was awful. While she didn't want to let on to Liz that she was as worried as she was, it was hard to keep herself from panic. But then Liz's hand was on her thigh and she was looking in her eyes and everything…calmed.

"How about you see what you can do? Figure out what you can handle financially, and I'll talk to him. Yeah?" The wheels were turning in Liz's head. Cori could almost hear them.

She nodded. "Okay. I'll go over to the bank in the morning."

"Good." Liz opened her arms. "Come here." She wrapped her up tight and pressed a kiss to her forehead.

Cori nestled in, loving Liz's presence, her scent, something kind of woodsy and natural. She let her breath out slowly and relaxed into Liz's arms, and it was almost perfect. It almost made her feel better. But there was something *tense* about Liz. It surprised Cori a bit that she thought she knew Liz well enough already to detect this…whatever it was, but she did. She could feel it. Liz wasn't stiff. Didn't seem uncomfortable. It was subtler than that, just slightly off. Either Liz was more worried about the sale of the building than she was letting on, or there was something else bothering her.

Both of those things made Cori nervous, but she had enough on her mental plate already, so she let herself burrow in a little farther, let herself feel the warmth and the joy of being held by Liz.

She'd get to the bottom of things tomorrow.

❖

Cal's Diner wasn't terribly busy on a Thursday morning. At least not at the not-so-bright-and-early hour of ten thirty. Liz and April sat at a booth in the front by the windows because it had been the only one available when they'd arrived two hours ago, but now the place was nearly empty, and still they sat. Their plates were long gone, their stomachs full of pancakes for Liz and a Denver omelet for April.

"I can't believe you drove all the way out here," Liz said for about the dozenth time.

"I told you, I've been needing to meet with my client in person and having this thing crop up for you was the nudge I needed." April sipped what was her third cup of coffee, then grimaced and put it down. "I am going to be jittery all the way home if I keep drinking this. But damn, it's good coffee."

"I told you. I don't know what kind of sorcery Cal works back there, but his coffee is famous around here for being fire."

"It definitely is."

There was a comfortable lull in the conversation, and it was literally the first one since April had arrived the previous day. After a few moments, Liz looked at her friend and gave her a smile. "Thank you so much, Ape. For everything."

"Listen, all I did was pass on the information from my friend's sister. You're the one who's gotta impress during the Zoom." April's gaze moved from Liz's face to something over her shoulder, and when Liz turned, she was shocked to look into the face of Cori.

"Hey," Cori said, looking from one of them to the other. "I was just walking back from the bank and saw you sitting here." She held out a hand to April. "Hi. Cori Stratton, friend of Liz."

"Oh, Cori, hi. I've heard so much about you." April smiled widely and took Cori's hand. "I'm April Washington, Liz's roommate in Syracuse."

"Oh, right, hi. It's so nice to finally meet you. I didn't know you were going to be in town." Cori's eyes moved from April to Liz.

"Well, I kind of surprised Liz here. I have a client with a vacation home here, and I don't see him in person very often. Then this job thing cropped up for Liz, so instead of calling, I thought I'd surprise her and see my client. Two birds, one stone, you know?"

Cori's face blanched, but April didn't know her well enough to see it happen. Liz did. "The job thing. Right." She was nodding but kept on nodding, and Liz could almost hear the wheels in her head grinding away as she tried to make sense of this big news Liz had kept from her.

"Yeah, I was going to come talk to you about it later," Liz said, forcing a grin, then wondering if that grin was maniacally wide, because it sure as hell felt like it.

"Oh, okay. Good. Well, you know where to find me." Cori was blinking a lot. Like, an inordinate amount of blinking. "It was nice to meet you, April."

"Same."

And then Cori turned and left, not looking at Liz again, and Liz felt her stomach churn, all those delicious pancakes threatening to make a reappearance. "Wow, she's gorgeous," April said, just as Liz muttered, "Shit."

"What?" April asked, pulling her eyes from Cori's exit and refocusing on Liz. "What's wrong?"

"I didn't tell her yet."

April frowned. "You didn't tell her what?" Then her expression shifted as pieces seemed to fall into place. April was always great at puzzles. "About the job possibility? Was I not supposed to say anything? I'm so sorry! I mean, you didn't tell her you were going to stay here, did you?"

Liz sighed. "No, but…I haven't said I was leaving either."

"Okay, but did she think you wouldn't keep looking for a job in your field?" April's tone carried more empathy than accusation. She was being gentle, and Liz appreciated it.

"I guess we just haven't really talked about it. There have been so many other things going on. The fake relationship, then that falling apart, then her issues with her parents—we just never really discussed…"

"The future? You never talked about the future with the poor girl you clearly have feelings for?"

Liz dropped her head into her hands and groaned. "*No*," she said, drawing the word out so it had three syllables. "I mean, *I've* thought about it. But I'm in such a weird space right now."

"Sounds to me like she's the one in a weird space. Your issues are just regular, normal people issues, same as everybody else. She's the one whose entire existence has changed." Again, there was no accusation in April's tone, but there was definite disappointment now, and she gave her watch a quick glance. "Damn. I'd better get on the road."

Their good-bye felt off. Stilted. Liz felt the need to apologize to April, who shook it off but grabbed both her hands and squeezed them as she looked Liz in the eye. "I love you, and I want you to be happy. If that means staying here, then do that. You've never talked about anybody the way you've talked to me about that girl." Then she gave Liz a playful shove in the shoulder. "Get your shit together, woman. And let me know what you decide to do about the job." A quick peck on the cheek later, April got into her Lexus, started it up, and waved to Liz as she stood in the snow and watched her go.

"Get your shit together, Liz," she said quietly into the chilly late-January air. Then she dropped her chin to her chest and muttered, "Fuck."

❖

Suzanne had a doctor's appointment at noon, so they'd set it up for Cori to relieve her then behind the register. Now that the holidays were over and they were creeping toward the end of January, business had died down a bit. It was a normal lull—Whimsy had the same one every year—but this one felt somewhat…dangerous. Given that she now had inside information about a possible sale of the building, of a possible need to relocate both her business and her living quarters, any lull in business felt alarming.

Suzanne had scooted, so Cori stood behind the register scanning her shop. God, she loved this place. She'd put her heart and soul into it, and the thought of relocating filled her with worry and dread. But her bank meeting had gone well, and part of her was happy to have something to focus on that wasn't Liz because what the hell had she been thinking? Had she really expected Liz to stay here in Crimson

Valley with her? She'd basically bolted after high school and hadn't looked back, and she'd returned pretty much against her will.

God, I'm an idiot.

She felt that thought deeply. Because there were feelings. Definite feelings. No, she hadn't brought them up, hadn't really addressed them other than in quick passing. But they were there, and she had been a fool to allow that to happen. And now, an opportunity had come up for Liz to leave again, to go back to where she was happy, and who was Cori to deny her that?

She was ringing up a customer, doing her best to put on her happy shopgirl face, making small talk with a tourist, when Liz pushed through the door. Cori felt her eyes on her, knew Liz was looking at her, but she purposely kept her gaze on her customer and made a show of smiling, chatting.

Liz waited quietly until there was only one customer in Whimsy, and they were tucked in a corner by the wool mittens, hats, and scarves woven by a local artist.

"Can we talk?" Liz asked quietly, and goddamn it, she looked pretty, dressed in jeans and a dark blue sweater, her blond hair pulled partially back, her makeup on point. Then Cori remembered that she'd likely dressed nicely for her job-offering friend.

"I'm working."

"Cori. I'm sorry. I should—"

Cori cut her off. "I got good news from the bank this morning."

Liz blinked at her, then cleared her throat. "Yeah?"

Cori nodded and began straightening the displays of sundries on the counter in front of her. "I talked to John Kramer. Remember him? He was a year behind us in school. He's a loan officer there, and he was able to help me. I think I can draw up a fair offer for your dad. If you think he'd be into it. Do you think you could find out?" She could see the wheels turning behind Liz's eyes, and the relief she felt at having steered her in a different direction—at least for the moment—was enormous.

"Yeah. Yeah, I can do that." Liz nodded. She looked down at the glass counter and used her thumbnail to scrape at some invisible spot, just as the front door opened and a laughing group of women came in.

"Hi!" one of them said with great enthusiasm, waving in Cori's direction. "We love your shop. We've been passing it for two days and finally had a chance to come in."

"Oh, it smells amazing in here," another one said.

"Do you have incense?" a third asked.

"I do," Cori said, putting on her helpful shopgirl face once again, as she stepped out from behind the counter. Liz caught her upper arm and Cori stopped.

"Can we talk later?" Liz whispered.

"I'm working late tonight," Cori said as she gently reclaimed her arm so she could help her customers. No, it wasn't the mature way to handle things, but she had zero capacity to deal with Liz right now. She just couldn't.

She forced herself not to look back to where Liz stood and, instead, focused on her customers. Joking with them. Asking them where they were staying, for how long, where they were from. By the time they all had purchases in their hands and were ready to check out, Liz had disappeared. Bear stood at the front window, looking out, his tail down, so she was pretty sure she'd left and hadn't slipped into the workshop in the back to wait her out.

Part of her was disappointed by that.

She rang out the group of women, who smiled and laughed and praised her shop, spending a total of almost six hundred dollars between the five of them. A nice sale, for sure. But then they were gone and the shop was quiet again, and all the thoughts and feelings and emotions she'd shoved aside came sprinting back into the spotlight to sing their solos.

"Nope. Nope. Not doing this," she muttered, grabbing a dust cloth and heading for the shelves, hoping to distract herself. Ernie eyed her warily, then leapt from the shelf he was on and sauntered off to find a new spot, tail in the air and swishing.

It didn't work, the distraction. All it did was have her thinking about Liz while she cleaned. Liz, who she thought about more often than she cared to admit. Liz, who she definitely had feelings for.

Liz, who was leaving.

Her eyes welled up as she dusted.

"Damn it."

CHAPTER TWENTY-ONE

Cori had avoided her last night.

Liz hated that. Not to take anything away from the situation because she understood why she'd been avoided. But still. She wanted to talk to Cori. Cori had clearly not wanted to talk to her. But...she deserved a chance to explain, didn't she?

Didn't she?

"Why are you slamming things?" Lauren asked as Liz roughly put something away behind the front desk.

She sighed. "Sorry. Having a bad day."

Instead of doing what she expected Lauren to do—which was continue on her way to the kitchen, completely uninterested in any details of her sister's bad day—Lauren stopped and studied Liz. "Anything I can do to help?"

The simple kindness in her words, the unexpected gentleness of her tone, was all it took to turn Liz into some kind of waterworks. Her eyes filled and the tears spilled over so quickly, Liz didn't even realize what was happening until her cheeks were wet and Lauren was looking at her with concern. "Oh, Lauren, I fucked up. I fucked up so bad."

A quick glance around, probably to make sure no guests were nearby, and then Lauren went behind the desk into the closet where the cleaning supplies were and came out with a box of tissues. She opened it, pulled one out, and handed it to her sister.

"Wanna talk about it?" Lauren asked after Liz had blown her nose and pulled herself together.

"I don't know." She groaned and gave herself a full body shake. "I just—"

Her words were interrupted by the front door opening.

Cori walked in.

"Hi," she said simply, then kind of stood there on the mat, seemingly unsure what to do or say next.

"Hey," Liz said back, also unsure what to do or say next.

Lauren gave her arm a squeeze, then took her leave, heading off toward the kitchen.

"Cori, I—"

"Listen—" Cori said at the same time, stepping toward the front desk, but only one step, and she held up a hand like a traffic cop, keeping Liz from saying anything more. "I came by to wish you good luck with the job opportunity—I assume you have an interview of some kind?"

Liz gave a slow nod. "Zoom. But—"

"No." Cori cut her off again. "No, you need to do the interview. I came by to tell you that and to wish you luck."

"But—"

"I like you, Liz. I do. A lot. More than I care to admit, really. More than is good for me." A bitter chuckle there. "And because I like you so much, I don't want to be responsible for making you stay someplace you really don't want to be. You know? You left Crimson Valley because you wanted something more than this small town life. I get that. I really do. It's not for everybody. But it's for me. I love it here. I don't want to be anywhere else." She stopped and seemed to gather herself, and then she stepped closer to the desk and reached out for Liz's hands.

Liz put her hands in Cori's, looked her in those beautiful dark eyes, and saw nothing but love and tenderness.

"Do the interview, and knock it out of the park, okay?" Cori pushed up on tiptoe so she could lean over the desk. Then she pressed a quick kiss to Liz's lips, so quick that it was over before Liz knew it was happening. And then she was gone. Her hands let go of Liz's and she hurried out the door, leaving Liz standing there feeling too many things to count.

"And how did that go?" Lauren asked, returning to the front.

Liz just shook her head. "I..." The words eluded her. She searched, grabbed at them, but nothing was tangible. The only thing that kept running through her head on a loop was one simple question.

Had she just lost Cori for good?

❖

Liz had done what Cori asked—she hit her interview out of the park. She wasn't sure how she knew it, exactly, but she did. It lasted much longer than the standard half hour or so. The woman conducting the interview went on to ask her personal questions, and they discovered they had several things in common, including a love of musical theater and that they both played volleyball in college. It couldn't have gone better.

So why did she feel like crap?

She snorted out loud at herself. "Let's be honest," she said as she entered Brennan House through the back door. "You *know* why you feel like crap."

"You talking to me, honey?" Her mother was in the kitchen with the fridge door open and seemed to be staring at the contents.

"No, just my stupid self."

"Your self isn't stupid."

Liz grunted as she reached around her mother for a bottle of water. "What are you doing?"

"Trying to figure out what we need from the store. Your sister keeps the grocery list in her head, which helps no one but her." She stared for another second or two, gave one nod, and shut the door. "How did the interview go?" she asked as she jotted notes down on a pad of paper on the counter.

"It went great," she said, with zero emotion.

"Then why do you look and sound like it went terribly?"

Liz let her head fall back toward her shoulder blades and groaned loudly. "I don't know! *Ugh.*"

"I think you do," her mother said softly, and when Liz lifted her head back up and looked at her, her mother's expression was soft and knowing.

That was really all she needed to say, because Liz *did* know. She knew it without a doubt. Even though they were struggling at the moment, even though things were messy and needed solving, the bottom line was that she didn't want to leave Cori. At all. It really was that simple.

Or was it?

"There are so many factors, Mom. So many." She put her hands to each side of her head as if she had the world's most horrendous headache.

"Are there?" her mother asked, hands on her hips. "Okay. What are they? Let's tackle them one at a time."

Yes. Good. This was good. Somebody else to help her understand. That's what she needed. She ticked off on her fingers as she spoke. "All right. If I don't go back, there's the living arrangements. I have a place in Syracuse with April. I don't want to leave her stuck."

Her mother gave one nod. "Oh yes, that's a good one. Though, isn't April a lawyer? And didn't she live in that apartment alone before you came along?"

Liz blinked at her. "Yeah. She did."

"So she'd be fine then, right? Okay. Next?"

"The living arrangements here. I mean, I love you, Mom, but I don't want to be in my thirties and literally living in my mother's basement." She punctuated that with a laugh to take away any possible insult.

But her mother laughed along with her. "Believe me, honey, I love you, too, but I'd prefer my *grown-ass* children not to still be living with me in their thirties. So you get your own place."

"But I don't have a job to pay for my own place."

"So you get a job to pay for your own place."

Okay, that was an easy one, except…"But in my field?"

"Honey, have you even looked? Have you tried? I mean, I know Crimson Valley is small, but it's not in the Dark Ages. I'm sure there are places that need somebody in marketing or advertising or sales. But you have to actually look. You know? You can't wait for something to just fall into your lap. Life doesn't work like that." Another valid argument from Mom, who was clearly on a roll. "What else is there?"

Liz let out her breath slowly, like a gradually deflating balloon, and leaned back against the counter. "Cori," she said quietly. "There's Cori."

Her mother nodded, because she knew this. Of course she did. "What about her?"

"I don't want to leave her." The words came out immediately, without hesitation. So much so that they even surprised Liz.

"Then don't."

"But I don't know if she feels the same way. I haven't exactly been open about some things, and it feels like she's stepping back. And I can't blame her for that." Her eyes welled up as she put words to her fears, to what she was feeling.

"Sounds to me like maybe you need to sit down with her and have a heart-to-heart." It was exactly something her mother would say, and it was exactly what Liz needed to do. Clearly, she'd needed somebody to point out the obvious, and she mentally rolled her eyes at herself.

The back door opened, interrupting them, and her father came in, stomping snow off his boots.

"It's really coming down out there," he said, then looked up at the two of them, Liz with teary eyes. "What's going on? Everything okay?" he asked with concern.

"I was just chatting with our daughter about the importance of communication in a relationship." Her mother gave him a pointed look, and his cheeks grew just a little bit pink.

"Oh. Yeah, well, listen to your mother. She knows this stuff." He slipped off his coat and hung it on a hook. "This about Cori?" At her mother's nod, her father said, "Well, I just had a long talk with her." At their surprised looks, he clarified. "Business. We talked business. She actually made me an offer on the building."

"What?" Both Liz and her mother asked the question at the same time, which made her father chuckle.

"Yeah. A decent offer. Not nearly as much as Lattimore, but"—he rubbed his hand along the back of his head and smoothed down his hair—"she made some good points. Gave me a lot to think about."

The little bell on the front desk rang, putting an abrupt end to the conversation. Liz's mom headed out of the kitchen but turned in the doorway to look at Liz. "Just talk to her, honey." A warm smile, and she was gone.

"She's not wrong about the communication, you know," her dad said. His expression was soft, and she realized in that moment that there was something about him she'd been trying to figure out in the back of her mind since her return—the difference in him, in his face. It was softer, gentler, more relaxed and content. It was only right then that she realized it. "That was my biggest mistake, and it ended my marriage," he went on, his voice quiet. "I didn't talk. I didn't tell the woman who was the most important person in the world to me what I was going through and what I needed from her to help me." He glanced down at his feet. "I thank God every day that I'm getting a second chance with her, but I'll regret it for the rest of my life, the way I hurt her by shutting her out." He cleared his throat and brought his gaze up to meet Liz's. "If you care about this girl, then tell her. Don't make her guess. Turns out, people don't like that." Then he chuckled. "There it is, advice from your old man. Do with it what you will." Then he winked at her and followed her mother out to the front desk.

Tell her.

Such basic and uncomplicated advice.

Could it really be that simple?

❖

"Do you think he'll go for it?" Suzanne asked as she stood behind the cash register. Her shift was just about up, and Cori was there to relieve her.

Cori shrugged. "I don't know. I feel like I gave a pretty compelling argument. I talked about the tradition of Crimson Valley, how I understood that a big company could offer him more money, but that they'd also likely tear down this building and put up something modern and angle-y that doesn't fit this town's aesthetic—"

"Wait, you said that? The town's aesthetic?"

"Absolutely. He's a real estate guy. Aesthetic is a big thing in real estate."

"It is? How do you know that?"

"I did my research, Suzanne. Who do you think you're dealing with here?"

Suzanne barked out a laugh. "I had no idea. Forgive me. Go on." She made a gesture with her hand for Cori to continue.

"I said they'd likely put up something ugly and wouldn't he rather sell to somebody who grew up here, who knows the town and its people? Etcetera, etcetera." She stopped and took a breath, then held her hands out to her sides, palms up. "I made him a fair offer. That's all I could do. That was yesterday. Now, we wait."

"Well, I will send good thoughts out into the Universe," Suzanne said and gave Cori's arm a squeeze. "Nobody deserves it more than you." She seemed to hesitate for a moment, as if unsure she should say what was on her mind.

"What?" Cori asked.

"I hope it's okay that I say this to you, but…Annabelle would've been really proud of you."

A lump instantly appeared in Cori's throat, limiting her ability to make sound. Or words. She settled for smiling at Suzanne and holding her gaze for a tender moment.

The bell over the door broke the spell with its musical little tinkle, and when Cori glanced up, Liz was walking toward her with a serious expression she couldn't quite read. "Hi. Everything okay?"

"Can we talk?" Liz asked. Her voice was quiet, her eyes were soft, and something about her presence in general was…adamant. That was the only word Cori could come up with. Liz seemed to be brimming with some kind of need, some kind of urgency.

"Sure, um, but I was just about to relieve Suzanne—"

"Go," Suzanne said, waving them toward the back. "I can hang until you're done."

"You're sure?" Cori asked.

"Totally. I got this."

Liz shot Suzanne a look of clear gratitude, and then she and Cori headed back to the workshop, Bear on their heels. Once back there, Cori closed the door and left her palm flat against it for a beat, trying to gather herself. She hadn't expected to see Liz today. Actually, she wasn't sure she'd be back at all.

"Did you have your interview?" she asked, going for small talk, but actually hitting the very subject that had shoved them apart in the first place. *Good job, Cori. Way to keep things light.*

"I did, yeah." Liz was on the couch, Bear pushing against her legs while she dug her fingers into his fur. She unzipped her coat and slid it off, and she looked casually beautiful in jeans and a cream-colored cable-knit sweater.

"How did it go?" Cori stayed by the door as she asked the polite question, though she was sure she probably didn't really want the answer.

"It went great. Fantastic. They emailed me an offer."

Yeah, she didn't really want the answer. "Great. That's great." Injecting any kind of excitement into her voice proved impossible, so she just kind of sounded like a jerk. But she didn't care.

Liz finally met her gaze. "I'm not taking it."

Cori did a lot of blinking then as she tried to absorb the words, which made no sense. "You're not? Why? Isn't it what you've been waiting for since you got here?"

That's when Liz took a long deep breath and let it out very slowly as she gazed off into the middle distance. Like she was gathering her thoughts or looking for words or something, though she seemed to be in no hurry at all to find either. It felt like an hour went by before she finally spoke. "I thought it was, yes. That's true. But something happened in the time I was here that changed things."

"What? What happened?"

"You." Liz looked at her then, and those blue eyes were sparkling. Shining. They were goddamn dancing. Cori didn't know what to make of that. "You happened."

Cori shook her head. "I don't understand." And she didn't. She narrowed her eyes as she stared at Liz. "You have wanted to get out of here since the second you got back. It's been pretty clear, really." She shook her head, irritated with herself as she muttered, "Something I should've paid more attention to, frankly."

And Liz laughed.

Laughed.

Cori gaped at her. "I'm sorry, but what's so fucking funny?"

"You. Me. Us." Liz glanced down at Bear and ruffled his fur playfully. "This guy. All of it. All of this return to Crimson Valley. It's not at all what I expected it to be." Bear made a soft *rowr*ing sound and pushed against her, clearly suggesting she continue petting him. And that just made her laugh some more.

Cori stared. She couldn't comprehend what was going on and she said so. "I don't understand what's happening right now."

"I know." Liz continued to grin like she was the only one who got the joke. "I'm sorry about that. It's because I'm a fool who takes too long to see what's right under her nose."

"Okay." Cori crossed the room and sat on the couch next to her, a little exasperated. "You're gonna have to elaborate a bit here, because I'm lost. The last I knew, you had this great job opportunity—that you neglected to tell me about—and you were doing an interview. You've just told me the interview went"—she made air quotes—"*fantastic, they emailed me an offer*."

"I also told you I'm not taking it."

"But I don't understand, why not?"

And this time when Liz smiled, it was soft. There was no laughter, only a gentle tenderness that Cori would swear she could feel in the air between them. "Because everything I need in life is right here in this room."

More staring, because Cori was sure she'd heard wrong, but Liz went on.

"Remember when you first found out about your biological mother? And then our fake relationship was exposed and everything was a mess?"

"You mean, like, last month?" Cori gave her a look. "Yeah, I remember."

"And you said something like *Nothing in my life is real. Not my parents. Not my family. Not us.* Remember?"

Cori nodded, and when Liz reached for her hands, she let her. Liz's grip was warm and soft.

"What I realized in the past day or two is that I felt more like the real me in our fake relationship than I ever have in my actual life. You bring out a joy in me, a relaxation, a simple happiness in just *being*. And I can't walk away from that. I don't want to. I may be a fool, but I like to think I'm not *that* big a fool."

"I..." Wow. This was a lot. This was so much. And this was completely unexpected. Cori felt a little blindsided, if you could be blindsided by something positive. She didn't let go of Liz's hands. In fact, she tightened her grip.

"It's a lot," Liz said, as if reading her thoughts. "I know. And I'm sorry it took me so long to realize how important this"—she gestured between the two of them—"really is to me."

Cori was quiet because her thoughts were swirling in her head like some kind of whirlpool, and she wasn't sure what to grab on to first.

"And it's okay if this is too much," Liz said, and for the first time since she started talking, she looked a little uncertain. "Maybe I shouldn't have just unloaded like that. But my mom and dad were both adamant that the most important thing in a relationship is communication, so..."

She took a deep breath and blew it out slowly. "I thought I should tell you that I have feelings for you." She cleared her throat. "And they were right. I think it's good that you know, even if you don't feel the same way." She started to pull her hands away, but Cori tightened her grip.

"Where do you think you're going?" she asked, hoping the lightness in her voice came through. She squeezed Liz's hands. "You can't just tell a girl you have feelings for her and leave when she doesn't respond in six seconds. You've got to let her absorb things first." She gave Liz a soft smile. "You've got to give her a chance to find her words, you know? When you hit her with something she never expected, you gotta give a girl some time to gather herself."

Her tone must've been clear because Liz smiled then. "Seriously, how much time does gathering take? I'm out on this limb all by myself here."

Cori lifted Liz's hand to her lips and kissed it. "Then allow me to join you out there. Because I've got feelings, too."

"Yeah?"

"Oh yeah."

Neither of them used the *L* word, and Cori was glad about that. Yes, they'd gone to high school together, but they'd only *really* known each other for a short time. Much too short to let that four-letter word in the door. Not yet.

"I worry about you staying for me, though. I don't want you to resent me later if you wish you'd taken that job. You know what I mean?"

Liz nodded and didn't seem at all fazed by Cori's words. "I figured you'd feel that way. It's valid. All I can say is, I don't think that will happen. But if I feel it start to, I'll talk to you. We have to *talk*. It's vital."

"Says the girl who's terrible at talking."

Liz's grin grew. "Also valid." She squeezed Cori's hands. "It's a lot to ask. I know. But...I really want to give this a shot. Give us a shot. A real one."

"I'd like that." And even then, even after expressing her very real concern, even after feeling relief that neither of them was ready for those three little words, Cori knew. She *knew*. She. Knew.

She lifted her hand and rested it against Liz's cheek, and that gesture alone seemed to settle any tension between them. Liz pushed her face against Cori's hand, then leaned forward, and their lips met in a soft kiss.

This kiss was different, though, filled with promise and joy and a future neither of them had expected, but they were ready to take on together.

They parted slowly, and Cori whispered, "I'm so glad you nearly wrecked your car on my sidewalk that first day."

"Oh my God, the spider!" Liz laughed. "I forgot about him. I can't believe you remembered."

"Remembered? I'm paying him weekly."

"I never in my life expected to be grateful to a creepy, crawly, eight-legged insect."

"But you are?"

"Oh, I so am." Liz took her face in both hands this time. And this kiss was deep and thorough and left them both breathless.

Cori's face felt heated, and every nerve in her body was suddenly turned on and standing at attention. She grinned at Liz and said, "Spiders rule."

And they kissed some more.

EPILOGUE

Three months later…

Spring in the Adirondacks could be fickle. March was a dangerous month, dangerous because people started to look forward to spring. The snow would melt, and if there was a warm day or two, the early flowers would start making appearances. Sunny yellow daffodils and happy purple crocuses would push their way up through the earth as if they were the reconnaissance team for the rest of the flowers, checking ahead to make sure the coast was clear. It was entirely possible for them to get zapped by another frost that night, or worse, be buried in a late snowstorm before they even have a chance to fully bloom.

However, if you made it to April, it was a pretty safe bet that winter was taking its final curtain call and making way for the next act, spring.

That's how it was that year in Crimson Valley. There had been one late accumulation of snow, but that was just about gone and would be fully melted by the end of the day because the temps were headed to the high fifties with blue skies and sunshine, and they couldn't ask for a more gorgeous day for the grand reopening of Whimsy.

Liz had already been up once, at five, and she'd taken Bear out to do his business, and they'd walked for a bit. When she'd come back and turned on the coffee, she'd found Cori still sound asleep, but flat on her back and sprawled completely across the bed, leaving no place for Liz to fit aside from between Cori's outstretched legs.

And so she had.

She'd started at the foot of the bed, lifted the duvet, and nosed her way under until she reached the apex of Cori's thighs, where she gently went to work. She knew the moment Cori had woken up because her hips started to move. Subtly at first. Barely detectable. Until Liz let her tongue slip inside, then replaced it with her fingers, and then there was a definite rhythm to Cori's moving hips. Her orgasm came within minutes, a small cry erupting from her throat.

As Cori's body slowly relaxed and her breathing eased, Liz crawled up until they were face-to-face and placed a gentle kiss on her lips. "I love when your very first words of the day are..." and she began doing an impression of Cori's cries.

Cori gasped in mock horror and playfully slapped at Liz's shoulder. "You stop that."

She laughed and rolled to her side so she could wrap Cori up and hold her close. "It's a big day, baby," she said, then pressed a kiss to Cori's forehead.

"It *is*." She snuggled in more tightly as Ernie hopped up onto the bed and started making biscuits on the duvet.

"Nervous?"

"A little?" A moment passed before she spoke again. "I mean, the shop is mine now. This apartment. This whole building. It's mine." She pushed herself up onto an elbow so she could look Liz in the eye. "I mean, it's not a big deal, but also, it is." And then she slid out of bed and went over to the wall where she slapped her hand against it. "This is my wall. Mine." She grabbed the trim of the doorway. "Also mine." She went behind the door and poked her finger at the wall. "See this little divot from opening the bedroom door too hard and letting the doorknob smack against the wall one too many times? Guess what."

"Also yours?"

"Also mine!" Cori made a *yikes* face that made Liz laugh. It wasn't the first time she'd humorously pretended to be overwhelmed by the responsibility of owning the building now, but Liz knew that there was also an element of truth to the joking. "If anything breaks, I can't just call up the landlord."

"My dad."

"Your dad. I can't just call him up. I have to take care of it myself. You know why?"

"Because you own this building?"

"Because I own this building!"

And Liz burst out laughing because they'd had this exact same conversation at least three times a week since the paperwork had been finalized at the end of February.

Cori jumped back onto the bed, laughing with her, and these were the moments that Liz cherished. These sometimes quiet, sometimes funny, always wonderful moments when it was just the two of them. She brushed some hair back from Cori's face so she could see the sparkle in those brown eyes.

"You're gonna be there?" Cori asked, and Liz knew exactly what she meant.

"Wouldn't miss it. I took the whole afternoon off."

"Oh no, your boss is going to be so annoyed with you. You've only been working there for a month."

Liz snorted in dramatic fashion. "Please. If he gives me any trouble, I'll sic my mother on him." That made Cori laugh. "I do have a showing this morning, though, so I need to get in the shower."

"I can't wait until you're the queen of Crimson Valley real estate."

"That might take a while, baby. I've only been at it for a month. I still need my license."

"Speed it up, then. I want to have sex with royalty." Cori rolled on top of her and sighed. "But I guess you'll do for now."

There was no more talking.

❖

The grand reopening was a smashing success and it was only early afternoon.

Whimsy had been packed all morning and into the afternoon. Packed.

Cori walked around Whimsy and stopped to chat with customers. There were people she knew and people she didn't. Tourists and locals. Friends and strangers. The registers never stopped making noise. The little bell over the door must have been exhausted after so much tinkling.

After buying the building, she'd closed the shop for nearly four weeks, a daring—some would say risky—move, cutting off her income after making a huge purchase. But she had money in savings, and there were things she'd always wanted to do but hadn't wanted to trouble her landlord, Matthew Brennan, about. She painted, first and foremost, and was so happy with the way it had turned out. Different displays boasted different color walls behind them. A deep, toasty brown for behind the candles. A light, lilac shade of purple for the jewelry. A fun azure blue for the tourist corner where the postcards and mugs and magnets with *Crimson Valley* on them lived. She'd pulled up the old, worn gray carpet and replaced it with a surprisingly affordable laminate that looked like hardwood. She'd redesigned the window display to focus on spring, on new growth, on rebirth, because that's what it felt like to her today. A rebirth.

She'd invited everybody, friends and neighbors and fellow business owners. She hung signs everywhere, and Liz had helped her do a couple of blasts, both via email and on social media. She was a pro at such things, and Cori happily turned over the marketing reins to her.

She'd had apple cider warming in two slow cookers by the register. Yes, that was more of a fall thing, but the smell couldn't be beat, so she went with it, and now the third refill was almost gone. She'd ordered a hundred cookies from the bakery down the street, and the owner, Marjorie, had surprised her by frosting them with the same colors as the walls in Whimsy, then topping them with sparkling silver sprinkles. They were gorgeous, and it was possible that Cori had already eaten three of them. Or possibly ten. She'd lost count.

Suzanne had worked behind the register all day, and she looked up now to meet Cori's gaze across the store, her eyes sparkling in happy disbelief. Because of course, Suzanne was as invested in Whimsy's success as she was. After all, it had been Annabelle's pride and joy, and Annabelle had been Suzanne's. It stood to reason.

Her family had been there, too, hanging in the corner by the cookies. Both her parents plus all her siblings had stopped by and hung out for a while throughout the day. Her brother Jeremy—who now insisted she address him as her brother from another mother—was there now, standing with her mother, and he gave her a wink.

"Hey, gorgeous." Liz's voice was close to Cori's ear as she came up behind her and wrapped her arms around Cori's middle. "I'd call this a rousing success, wouldn't you?"

The feeling of Liz's body pressed up against hers was no longer new, but it still did things to her. And she couldn't let herself dwell on that for too long or fantasies would take over her brain, and she'd get a hit of whatever it was that made you feel like you were in love—because she was. She knew it. They still hadn't used the word yet, but they were together almost every day. Liz still lived in her mother's house and spent several nights a week at Cori's, but now that she was working for her father in his real estate office—and loving it, which was a surprise to both of them—she was actively looking for her own place. One big enough for both of them.

Okay. Enough about that. Focus. She gave her head a subtle shake, but couldn't stop smiling.

"How'd the showing go?" Cori asked, craning her neck so she could see Liz's face. And also, the business suit she wore. Was her wardrobe the best part of her new job? Cori would have to argue with a vehement yes, thank you very much. Today's suit was black pants and a black blazer with subtle silver pinstripes, the collar of the white shirt underneath the jacket out and open, revealing a sexy peek of collarbone and just enough cleavage to tease. And don't get her started on the heels, because good God Almighty...

"Got an offer already. Two, actually."

"Seriously?" Cori turned in her arms. "That's fantastic. Congratulations."

"Maybe you'll be sleeping with royalty sooner than you think." Cori laughed, and Liz gave her a quick peck, then slid a hand down her arm and linked their fingers. "I can't get over how amazing this place looks."

Cori nodded her agreement. She'd done so much work, but the new display on the far wall was the one she was most proud of. Yes, her candles made her happy, and she'd been making them like crazy so she'd have a stockpile, and there were two little stands filled with business cards that contained all the info for placing custom candle orders. Liz had gotten on that almost immediately. But the display that made her happiest was the one filled with products made by local artists. The wall behind the display was a mural she'd hired a local painter to do, and it said *Celebrating the Art of Our Mountains*. It was gorgeous and brought a whole new sense of pride and elegance to Whimsy. The items on display were from all different mediums—paintings, sculptures, jewelry, knitting, woodcraft. It filled her with such a sense of pride for her hometown.

"This is exactly the vision I've always had for this shop," she said quietly to Liz. "Even when I first started working here in high school. I would talk about it with Annabelle, tell her how I thought it could be such a great way to showcase Crimson Valley. And the mountains themselves."

"Yeah?"

She nodded. "And then when Annabelle died, I guess I let that vision die with her, because what was Whimsy without her? Does that make sense?" At Liz's nod, she continued. "Maybe it's age. Maybe it's being a grownup instead of a teenager, but now? I think she'd be really proud of this place."

"I think she'd be really proud of *you*," Liz said.

"Do you?" Cori asked. It was something she wished she had some way of knowing. Was her mother proud of the person she'd become?

"There's not a doubt in my mind. You're smart and kind and funny. You're empathetic. You're creative. You're gentle. And you love fiercely. What's not to be proud of?"

Cori held her gaze. "I do love fiercely."

Liz nodded. "I know it."

"I love you fiercely."

As if she'd known it was coming, Liz didn't miss a beat. "And I love you fiercely right back."

Cori's eyes welled and she wrapped her arms around Liz, squeezed. When they parted, Liz's eyes were also wet, and they laughed at each other through tears. "This is way better than my high school fantasies were, FYI."

Liz barked a laugh. "What? Oh, I expect to hear all about these fantasies…"

"Hey, what's going on over here?" It was Suzanne, who'd stepped out from behind the register during a quick lull to grab a cookie.

"Cori was just asking me if Annabelle would be proud of her, and I was explaining *of course* she would be and then she said she loves me." Liz snatched the cookie from Suzanne's hand and took a bite. "So, there's that."

"And she said she loves me, too," Cori added. "So, there's that."

"And Cori used to have fantasies about me in high school. So, there's *that*."

Suzanne's smile grew until she was laughing with them. Once they calmed, she grinned at them both as she said, "I've told you before, but I will tell you as many times as you need to hear it. Annabelle would be so proud of the woman you've become, honey. So incredibly proud."

She took a bite of cookie and chewed, looking from Cori to Liz and back. "As for the two of you?" She took another bite. "She'd be proud of that, too." Then she kissed each of them on the cheek and headed back to the register.

"I think I would be like her," Liz said thoughtfully, as she watched Suzanne go.

"What do you mean?" Cori helped herself to another cookie because why not? She bought them.

"I mean, if I ever lost you? I don't think I'd be with somebody else. I'd just hang out until it was time for us to meet again." She looked at Cori and gave a half shrug, as if she'd just said something as simple as *It's snowing today*.

As for Cori, well, she couldn't even think about what it would feel like to lose Liz. She was far too invested, and her feelings were far too big and ran far too deep. They'd talk about that soon, she knew, but for now, she simply leaned into Liz and whispered, "I love you, you know."

Liz smiled and said, "I know. I love you, too." Then she kissed her head and they stood and ate cookies and sipped warm cider and watched people wander around Cori's store.

And it was so much more than enough.

About the Author

Georgia Beers lives in Upstate New York and has written more than thirty-five novels of sapphic romance. In her off-hours, she can usually be found searching for a scary movie, sipping a good Pinot, or trying to keep up with little big man Archie, her mix of many little dogs. Find out more at georgiabeers.com.

Books Available From Bold Strokes Books

Coasting and Crashing by Ana Hartnett. Life comes easy to Emma Wilson until Lake Palmer shows up at Alder University and derails her every plan. (978-1-63679-511-9)

Every Beat of Her Heart by KC Richardson. Piper and Gillian have their own fears about falling in love, but will they be able to overcome those feelings once they learn each other's secrets? (978-1-63679-515-7)

Fire in the Sky by Radclyffe and Julie Cannon. Two women from different worlds have nothing in common and every reason to wish they'd never met—except for the attraction neither can deny. (978-1-63679-561-4)

Grave Consequences by Sandra Barret. A decade after necromancy became licensed and legalized, can Tamar and Maddy overcome the lingering prejudice against their kind and their growing attraction to each other to uncover a plot that threatens both their lives? (978-1-63679-467-9)

Haunted by Myth by Barbara Ann Wright. When ghost-hunter Chloe seeks an answer to the current spectral epidemic, all clues point to one very famous face: Helen of Troy, whose motives are more complicated than history suggests and whose charms few can resist. (978-1-63679-461-7)

Invisible by Anna Larner. When medical school dropout Phoebe Frink falls for the shy costume shop assistant Violet Unwin, everything about their love feels certain, but can the same be said about their future? (978-1-63679-469-3)

Like They Do in the Movies by Nan Campbell. Celebrity gossip writer Fran Underhill becomes Chelsea Cartwright's personal assistant with the aim of taking the popular actress down, but neither of them anticipates the clash of their attraction. (978-1-63679-525-6)

Limelight by Gun Brooke. Liberty Bell and Palmer Elliston loathe each other. They clash every week on the hottest new TV show, until Liberty starts to sing and the impossible happens. (978-1-63679-192-0)

Playing with Matches by Georgia Beers. To help save Cori's store and help Liz survive her ex's wedding, they strike a deal: a fake relationship, but just for one week. There's no way this will turn into the real deal. (978-1-63679-507-2)

The Memories of Marlie Rose by Morgan Lee Miller. Broadway legend Marlie Rose undergoes a procedure to erase all of her unwanted memories, but as she starts regretting her decision, she discovers that the only person who could help is the love she's trying to forget. (978-1-63679-347-4)

The Murders at Sugar Mill Farm by Ronica Black. A serial killer is on the loose in southern Louisiana, and it's up to three women to solve the case while carefully dancing around feelings for each other. (978-1-63679-455-6)

A Talent Ignited by Suzanne Lenoir. When Evelyne is abducted and Annika believes she has been abandoned, they must risk everything to find each other again. (978-1-63679-483-9)

All Things Beautiful by Alaina Erdell. Casey Norford only planned to learn to paint like her mentor, Leighton Vaughn, not sleep with her. (978-1-63679-479-2)

An Atlas to Forever by Krystina Rivers. Can Atlas, a difficult dog Ellie inherits after the death of her best friend, help the busy hopeless romantic find forever love with commitment-phobic animal behaviorist Hayden Brandt? (978-1-63679-451-8)

Bait and Witch by Clifford Mae Henderson. When Zeddi gets an unexpected inheritance from her client Mags, she discovers that Mags served as high priestess to a dwindling coven of old witches—who are positive that Mags was murdered. Zeddi owes it to her to uncover the truth. (978-1-63679-535-5)

Buried Secrets by Sheri Lewis Wohl. Tuesday and Addie, along with Tuesday's dog, Tripper, struggle to solve a twenty-five-year-old mystery while searching for love and redemption along the way. (978-1-63679-396-2)

Come Find Me in the Midnight Sun by Bailey Bridgewater. In Alaska, disappearing is the easy part. When two men go missing, state trooper Louisa Linebach must solve the case, and when she thinks she's coming close, she's wrong. (978-1-63679-566-9)

Death on the Water by CJ Birch. The Ocean Summit's authorities have ruled a death on board its inaugural cruise as a suicide, but Claire suspects murder, and with the help of Assistant Cruise Director Moira, Claire conducts her own investigation. (978-1-63679-497-6)

Living For You by Jenny Frame. Can Sera Debrek face real and personal demons to help save the world from darkness and open her heart to love? (978-1-63679-491-4)

Ride with Me by Jenna Jarvis. When Lucy's vacation to find herself becomes Emma's chance to remember herself, they realize that everything they're looking for might already be sitting right next to them—if they're willing to reach for it. (978-1-63679-499-0)

Rivals for Love by Ali Vali. Brooks Boseman's brother Curtis is getting married, and Brooks needs to be at the engagement party. Only she can't possibly go, not with Curtis set to marry the secret love of her youth, Fallon Goodwin. (978-1-63679-384-9)

Whiskey and Wine by Kelly and Tana Fireside. Winemaker Tessa Williams and sex toy shop owner Lace Reynolds are both used to taking risks, but will they be willing to put their friendship on the line if it gives them a shot at finding forever love? (978-1-63679-531-7)

Hands of the Morri by Heather K O'Malley. Discovering she is a Lost Sister and growing acquainted with her new body, Asche learns how to be a warrior and commune with the Goddess the Hands serve, the Morri. (978-1-63679-465-5)

I Know About You by Erin Kaste. With her stalker inching closer to the truth, Cary Smith is forced to face the past she's tried desperately to forget. (978-1-63679-513-3)

Mate of Her Own by Elena Abbott. When Heather McKenna finally confronts the family who cursed her, her werewolf is shocked to discover her one true mate, and that's only the beginning. (978-1-63679-481-5)

Pumpkin Spice by Tagan Shepard. For Nicki, new love is making this pumpkin spice season sweeter than expected. (978-1-63679-388-7)

Sweat Equity by Aurora Rey. When cheesemaker Sy Travino takes a job in rural Vermont and hires contractor Maddie Barrow to rehab a house she buys sight unseen, they both wind up with a lot more than they bargained for. (978-1-63679-487-7)

Taking the Plunge by Amanda Radley. When Regina Avery meets model Grace Holland—the most beautiful woman she's ever seen—she doesn't have a clue how to flirt, date, or hold on to a relationship. But Regina must take the plunge with Grace and hope she manages to swim. (978-1-63679-400-6)

We Met in a Bar by Claire Forsythe. Wealthy nightclub owner Erica turns undercover bartender on a mission to catch a thief where she meets no-strings, no-commitments Charlie, who couldn't be further from Erica's type. Right? (978-1-63679-521-8)

Western Blue by Suzie Clarke. Step back in time to this historic western filled with heroism, loyalty, friendship, and love. The odds are against this unlikely group—but never underestimate women who have nothing to lose. (978-1-63679-095-4)

Windswept by Patricia Evans. The windswept shores of the Scottish Highlands weave magic for two people convinced they'd never fall in love again. (978-1-63679-382-5)

A Calculated Risk by Cari Hunter. Detective Jo Shaw doesn't need complications, but the stabbing of a young woman brings plenty of those, and Jo will have to risk everything if she's going to make it through the case alive. (978-1-63679-477-8)

An Independent Woman by Kit Meredith. Alex and Rebecca's attraction won't stop smoldering, despite their reluctance to act on it and incompatible poly relationship styles. (978-1-63679-553-9)

Cherish by Kris Bryant. Josie and Olivia cherish the time spent together, but when the summer ends and their temporary romance melts into the real deal, reality gets complicated. (978-1-63679-567-6)

Cold Case Heat by Mary P. Burns. Sydney Hansen receives a threat in a very cold murder case that sends her to the police for help, where she finds more than justice with Detective Gale Sterling. (978-1-63679-374-0)